I0695170

A novel by Daryl Leonardo

For Richard,
without whom, this story would
probably never have been written.

silver boy

prologue

When I was younger, my brother, Artie, and I gathered up all the blankets and pillows we could find around the house, and we built a fort in my bedroom. We filled it with all of our favorite things. Artie brought his football, a bag of Oreos, and a whole box of Capri Suns — a meal made for champions, he called it. And I brought my little rag doll, Daisy. We sat inside that fort and played cards and told scary stories, our faces up lit by a flashlight Artie swiped from our dad. It was the best of times.

But it was also, kind of, the worst of times. Because even as kids, we had stuff to worry about.

"I overheard Mom and Dad talking about how you're gonna get held back in kindergarten," I remember Artie saying. "They said you cry too much when you're at school. How come?"

"The other kids don't like me," I told him. "They're always making fun of me."

"Why?"

"They say, 'Playing with dolls is for girls,' but I like my doll. She's my best friend." I remember Daisy well. She had a soft felt body, brown yarn for hair, two tiny dots for eyes, and no nose. But she smiled, nonetheless.

"Well, if she's your best friend, you should keep playing with her," Artie said. He then picked up an Oreo and held it up to me. "Does Daisy want a cookie?" I took the Oreo on Daisy's behalf. Artie then pulled out a Capri Sun and proceeded to stab the pouch with its straw before sucking it dry. "So, Andrew, what do you want to be when you grow up?" I just shrugged, too busy twisting apart my Oreo to have an answer. "Do you wanna know what *I* wanna be when I grow up? The greatest person ever!" He answered before I could even respond.

I can't recall if I had any idea of what I wanted to be when I grew up before then. But as I sat there, hugging Daisy and licking the cream filling from my Oreo, an answer came to me. And suddenly, I knew just what I wanted to be when I grew up.

"I know what I want to be," I said.

"Oh, yeah? What's that?" Artie asked, eagerly leaning in.

"I want to be just like my big brother."

chapter one

Birthdays are complicated. People give you gifts that you have to pretend to like so you don't look like an asshole. They make plans, and it's always this big production. Now, don't get me wrong, I do like and appreciate the celebration and excitement of it all, but my birthday always fills me with this sense of... failure, I guess is the word. It reminds me that I'm older than everyone else in my class. That I was held back in kindergarten for being "emotionally underdeveloped," whatever that means. And that I'm officially an "adult" now... in high school... as a junior. Because of this, I try not to make a big fuss about my birthday. Unfortunately, not everybody knows this about me.

It's morning — before the start of first period — and I'm standing at my locker trying to figure out if I'll actually need my textbooks for my first set of classes.

"Happy birthday," a girl's voice says happily, punctuated with an upward inflection. I turn around to see who it is and… it's Becca. I should've known by the tone. She's one of those girls who is *always* made up. Like, so much so that she's really pretty, but I actually don't know that for sure, because I've never seen her face. Which is cool, I mean, what she does to her face is her business. It's just… she's holding a cake. And she's flanked by her two friends, Jen and Angela — they're basically discount versions of her — and they're holding balloons. Well, Jen's holding balloons. Angela's just there. Either she got lucky with not having to hold anything, or she's being punished. I never know with girls.

"Uh… what's all this?" I say, trying to keep my face looking happy, despite the fact that I hate everything right now.

"For your birthday, silly. Duh!" Becca explains. "How come you never told me?"

"I don't like to make it a big deal."

"Well, thank God for your friend, Jacob. Your birthday would've passed by, and nobody would've known." She hands me the cake, which she's kept in a disposable cake tin, and takes the balloons from Jen to hand them to me. "I hope you like chocolate. I made the cake myself. From scratch."

"Scratch out of a box," Angela chimes in, rolling her eyes. Funny, she looks about as over this as I am.

"Shut up, Angela!" Becca snaps. I think it's safe to say that Angela was, in fact, being punished. I elbow my locker shut and Becca links her arm onto mine. Before I can say anything, she's dragging me along with her down the hall and away from her friends. "So, Andrew, I wanted to ask you something."

"What's that?" I say, trying to keep pace without dropping the cake while pulling along the balloons.

"So, you're, like, six foot tall, blond, and blue eyed. I mean, you do have a little butt chin dimple — it's actually, like, really cute on you though — and I'm, like, gorgeous, right?" I'm not really sure if she's expecting me to respond, so I don't at first. But when she doesn't immediately go on, I take the hint.

"Sure," I say.

"Exactly. And a gorgeous girl, like me, should be with a gorgeous guy, not unlike yourself. You have abs, right?"

"Uh… yeah?"

"I rest my case." I have no idea what's going on. Just trying to follow along with what she's saying is tricky enough with how fast she's talking. Is she… Wait…

"Are you trying to ask me out?" I ask.

"No, why would *I* ask a guy out?" she replies. I breathe a momentary sigh of relief. "*You're* supposed to ask *me* out. This is me giving you permission. So…"

"So…?"

"Ask me out." Is she for real right now? She's really asking me to ask *her* out. Wow. I gotta hand it to her, she's got some balls, figuratively. Unfortunately, I want whoever I go out with to have literal ones.

I didn't have a big *ah-ha!* moment when I realized I was gay. It wasn't like a switch flipped on. It was something I recognized slowly over time. Growing up with my brother, I always found a lot of comfort in resting my head against him, so the idea of being on a guy's shoulder felt right to me. And then when puberty hit and dating became a thing, all I was ever interested in were guys. I'd get breathless in the locker room, having to change next to them. And whenever I'd end up at a department store, I'd linger in the men's underwear section just so I could ogle the headless models on the packaging. On top of that, when I started watching porn, it was uncomfortable for me because I found girl parts a little jarring to look at. That's how gay I am. So, imagine the joy I felt discovering they made porn with only men.

Unfortunately — or fortunately, depending on how you look at it — my sexuality isn't something that I talk about. I'm not the kind of guy to be gay. My dad's into sports, my brother's into sports, so I'm into sports. Not that I don't like it. Football's made my life in high school pretty sweet. It's how I met my best friends, Riles and Jake. It's how I got into this situation with Becca, who by the way is still staring at me, waiting for me to ask her out. On second thought, maybe I should quit football...

"Um, you kinda put me on the spot here, Becca," I finally answer. "Can I think about it?"

"What is there to think about?" she replies. "You and me, we could be, like, a total power couple." What can I say to get out of this situation without looking like a complete dick? She just *had* to make me a cake. See, this is why I don't tell people stuff.

"Well, summer's right around the corner. We'd hardly see each other if we made this a thing." Good job, Andrew, just make it seem like a bad idea.

"But I have a car," she says, as if that solves everything, which it kinda does so... Shit.

"Yeah, but I don't. I have to borrow my parents' and they're always working. So, you know, it wouldn't be fair. Can't make the girl do all the driving, right?" She seems to ponder the thought for a moment. Suddenly, the bell rings. Thank God. "I'll think about it. I promise." And with that, I dip out of the conversation and head toward my first class.

The way our school is set up is kinda dumb. There are three separate buildings on campus, two on one side and the third — we call it the annex — on the other, with a regular neighborhood street separating the two sides. None of the buildings are connected and all of them look like they were built in different time periods.

I make my way out of the main campus building — everyone refers to it as main campus since it's the building with the cafeteria, auditorium, and all the lockers — and cross the street towards the annex. It takes a little while to get to my first class because everything is so spread out, but I'm not in a rush. My first class is Piano. It's not like I'm gonna miss much. We always spend the period just sitting at our keyboards, headphones plugged in, practicing scales. Not the most exciting thing, but I can't complain. It's one of those classes you take just to fulfill your elective requirements. Easy A.

When I get to my Piano class, it's super awkward. Having to carry a cake and a bunch of balloons around doesn't exactly scream "it's a normal day" for me. Plus, the balloons don't seem to want to cooperate when it comes to going through doors, so it feels like I'm making a big scene of myself just trying to get into class. Luckily, the stupid things are tied down by a cheap, plastic ornament, so I'm able to shove them off into the corner by the trash can when I get through the door. I can tell everyone's staring at me. Ugh, it's gonna be a long day.

I walk over to my keyboard — they're not assigned or anything, everyone just kinda sits in the same spot out of habit — and I steal an extra chair for the cake. I can feel myself scowling at it as I set it down. I'm sure it's a nice cake. Becca even took the time to cover it with chocolate frosting. It's just… I know that I'm gonna have to carry this thing and those balloons around all day, which means I'm gonna be making a show of myself at least five more times today. Did I mention my birthday isn't my favorite thing?

C, D, E, F, G, A, B, C.
C, B, A, G, F, E, D, C.
C, D, E, D, C.
C, D, E, F, E, D, C.
…

God, this period is going on forever. Within the hour, I've practiced the C Major scale, the G Major scale, the F Major scale, the A Minor scale, Melodic Intervals, Harmonic Intervals, you know, all the basics. I've played the exercises in my piano book so many times that the notes are starting to sound like a plea for death to escape the boredom. There's gotta be more to this that makes playing piano as a beginner fun, right? Like, it can't just be all mindless repetition. I wonder what else they've got in this book.

I start flipping through the pages and find a couple songs that are just one or two lines long. Nothing that warrants me taking a shot at it. I know right now I'm supposed to be practicing *Jingle Bells* but the bit they've got in here only covers, like, four notes and it's not even

Christmas, so… I skip ahead toward the very back of the book and land on a piece of sheet music titled *Moonlight Sonata — 1st Movement.* The part that they've got in here is just about a page long and it looks complicated, but not *overly* complicated. Like, I recognize half the notes just at a glance, and it looks like it repeats itself a lot. This shouldn't be too hard to figure out.

I set the piano book onto the keyboard and examine the first measure. But before I can pluck out the starting note, I feel my phone vibrate in my pocket. After suffering through this class for what feels like forever, I don't even try to resist the urge to check it. I pull out my phone, discreetly hold it under my keyboard, and find a text from my brother. Actually, it's not even a text. It's just a gif. Or is it pronounced jif? Whatever. It says "Happy Birthday" with animated confetti floating down around it. I don't know why but getting a text like this from my brother feels… a little hollow.

My brother and I, we aren't close. We used to be, up until I got to third grade. He had graduated on to junior high. We weren't at the same school anymore. Suddenly, he had new friends that he wanted to hang out with, while I became his weird little brother who hugged on him like a girlfriend. Naturally, we drifted apart until we barely talked. We still don't talk, really. So, getting a birthday greeting from him feels more like it's out of obligation than him actually giving a shit.

I'm staring at the gif, debating whether or not I should even bother sending a thanks, when I feel a presence hovering over me.

"Mr. Logan," the voice of my teacher, Mrs. Dolittle, rattles in my ear. In a reflex, I quickly clasp both of my hands around my phone, shoving it between my thighs, and look up at her as innocently as possible. Not the least bit — but totally — suspicious. "You wanna play me what you've got there?" I look down at my piano book opened to *Moonlight Sonata*. Yeah… I'm not gonna be able to play this.

"Uh, I need more practice," I say.

"Yeah? Well, maybe you should put the phone away." So, I do. Thankfully, that seems to satisfy her, and she slowly starts to walk away. "You know the rest of the class is working on *Jingle Bells*."

Yeah, I know. But it's not even Christmas.

At lunch, I head over to the cafeteria on main campus with my buddy, Riles — we have fourth period together — and we meet up with our other friend, Jake. Riles is a big dude — about my height but built like a giant teddy bear. And Jake is this short stocky dude — like, five foot seven or something — with beady eyes. Between the two of them, Jake is probably more attractive, but Riles seems like he'd be a better time in bed… Not that I'm constantly thinking about sleeping with my friends, or anything. And even if I *was* constantly thinking about sleeping with my friends, I would not be hopping into bed with Jake any time soon. He's on my shit list.

"Hey, it's the birthday boy!" Jake greets me as we approach the table he's sitting at.

"Hey," I reply, setting down the balloons and cake I'd been carrying around all day. I take a seat so that I'm level with Jake and lean forward. "So, Jake, why'd you tell Becca it was my birthday?" His face drops.

"Oh… Well, I didn't mean to. It just sorta came up."

"Came up how?"

"Well, she came up to me in fourth period yesterday, wanting to make plans with us this weekend. Like, a group date or whatever, and I told her you were busy with a birthday thing."

"So you told her when my actual birthday was?" I ask demandingly.

"Well, yeah. What else was I gonna say?" Jake replies. "And so what if people know it's your birthday? What's the big deal?"

"Dude, you know how he feels about his birthday," Riles cuts in, taking a seat next to me. Jake shoots him a look. "You feel like a failure, right, Drewster?" Riles adds, so then I shoot him a look. "What?"

"Okay, fine. Whatever. I'm sorry," Jake says almost mockingly. I swear, I want to punch him in his stupid face. "It's not like you didn't get anything. Look, you got balloons and a cake."

"Yeah, that I had to carry around school all day," I scold him.

"Unappreciative, man," he shakes his head.

"You're giving me a ride home, by the way," I demand. "I'm not taking all this on the bus. It's your fault I have them."

"Can I break into that cake?" Riles asks, cutting the tension. I push the cake toward him. "Ah, sweet. I'm gonna go grab a fork." With that, Riles gets up, leaving me alone with this ass hat.

"Hey, grab me a milk box, would you?" Jake yells after him. He then turns to me and gives me an awkward smile. You know, the kind where you press your lips together so they're really small, because you don't know what to say, so what else are you gonna do? "So…"

"So…"

"Oh, come on, dude. Lighten up. You can't be *that* mad."

"Just let me feel what I feel, bro."

"I'm just saying, it could be worse," he then says. "You could be like those faggots over there. Fuckin' queers." He nods towards something behind me. I turn to look over my shoulder and see two guys, Erik and

Nick, standing in the lunch line with their friend, Molly, or Miranda, or whatever. I forget her name. I just know it starts with an M. Anyway, Erik is this short, kinda pudgy, potato-looking Asian dude with glasses, and Nick is… Well, Nick's fuckin' hot. I think he's some sort of Hispanic. He's got a light natural tan, dark brown hair, thoughtful squinty eyes, and the most perfectly placed beauty mark on the outside of his right eye. And then there's that ass… Fuck… I have to hold my legs together to keep myself at bay.

Unfortunately for me, Nick is dating Erik. How? I have no idea. Now, I'm not gonna say that Erik isn't attractive. He's perfectly passable. In fact, I made a pass at him last year. It wasn't so much that I was attracted to him, but rather, he was the only other gay guy that I knew at the time. Sometimes, you just *need* things, you know what I mean? Anyway, that didn't exactly work out, and somehow, he and Nick ended up together. Meanwhile, I'm sitting here, in the closet, pretending I'm okay with my friend calling them faggots. But what am I gonna say about it? You either go with the flow or the flow goes against you. I'm just glad they mostly keep to themselves. I don't think they ever told anyone about me. And even if they did, it would've been their word against mine.

Suddenly, all the feelings I have about my birthday and people finding out about it seem… stupid.

Because Jacob's right. It could be worse. People could find out about something else.

chapter two

I'm sitting in sixth period Bio, staring at the back of Erik's head. Yes, *the* Erik. The potato boy with the hot boyfriend. He's seated a couple rows in front of me, wearing a gray cardigan that's clearly meant for a taller frame. He's also got this cowlick sticking up from the back of his head that's just begging to be gelled down. Is this what's considered desirable these days? Because I can't make heads or tails of it. What would a guy like Nick see in this little spud? I'm racking my brain about it when I hear our teacher, Mr. Reed, call my name.

"Mr. Logan," he says, breaking my train of thought. I'd zoned out while he was about to start passing back the quiz we took last Friday. I get up to go collect mine, and as I'm approaching his desk he calls out, "Mr. Park." Mr. Erik Park, in fact. The potato himself. I grab my quiz off Mr. Reed's desk and look it over. B minus. Not bad. A pretty good grade, if you ask me. But before I can give myself a pat on the back, I look over and see Erik standing next to me. Mr. Reed hands him his quiz directly. "Good job, Mr. Park," he says, and suddenly, any sense of self-satisfaction I had is pushed aside with their exchange.

"Good job, Mr. Park," I repeat the words in my head in the most mocking tone I can imagine. What did he do to warrant a "good job?" Did he get an A or something? A perfect score? As if he needed any more praise. He already got the guy… *Good job, Mr. Park*. God, what a fucking nerd.

After sixth period lets out, I find myself walking behind Erik. I'm not following him or anything, it's just that my locker and his locker happen to be in the same hallway. That being said, I can't help but stare at him the entire walk over. The guy, as stubby and as nerdy as he is, confuses the hell out of me.

"Good job, Mr. Park," our teacher's praise for him echoes in my mind. And even though I know Mr. Reed was talking about the Bio quiz, I can't help but think that maybe, just maybe, Erik Park has something figured out that I don't.

I get to my locker and open it, trying to put everything out of my mind. But no matter how hard I try to mind my own business, I keep finding myself stealing glances at Erik, trying to figure him out. It's like walking into a movie at the half-way point, and you don't know what's going on, but you can't stop watching it.

I'm about to shut my locker and head over to meet Jake so I can get that ride home, when I see Nick coming down the hallway towards Erik. He sneaks up on the potato and pokes him on his sides, making him jump. It's annoyingly adorable. But mostly annoying.

"Good job, Mr. Park," the words repeat in my head once more. What is his secret? Is he packin'? Does he have, like, a magic butthole or something? I mean, I've kissed Erik before, back when I made a pass at him. It's not like his tongue tastes like bubble gum. What is it? If I only knew…

The house is quiet when I get home. Mom's already off to work for the night at the nursing home. She works as a nursing assistant and, apparently, spends her shifts wiping old men's asses, and arguing with women named Ethel about how many Jell-o cups they're allowed to have. It sounds like a terrible way to make a living, especially for someone as glamorous as a former prom queen, but she seems content with it. At least it's sorta in the realm of what she was going to college for. She was studying to be a doctor, but then she got pregnant and had to drop out, so she could work and save for the baby. My brother's the worst.

Dad should be home in about an hour, so I've got the place to myself until then. I take my balloons and head into the kitchen to put up whatever's left of the cake Becca gave me, and hopefully find some booze. Today's one of those days I could use a buzz. I pull open the refrigerator door, shove the cake tin onto an empty shelf, and poke around to see if Dad's got any beer. I find a handful of bottles tucked away in the back, behind a giant premade store-bought sandwich and a jug of orange juice. Score! I help myself to a bottle and shut the door. Then I stop, noticing an old report card belonging to Arthur Logan, my brother. It reads as if someone's screaming his praises. AAAAAA... All As. At the bottom, it displays a 4.2 GPA. I didn't even realize it was possible to get anything above a 4.0, but him and his stupid advanced placement classes. Ugh. My dad got real excited when he saw it.

"An athlete *and* a genius!" he declared, posting the report card onto the fridge. I think about how I did on the Bio quiz I got back today. Suddenly, my B minus doesn't seem like a "pretty good grade." It's just as well. I only felt that satisfaction for a moment.

"Good job, Mr. Logan," I mutter sarcastically under my breath.

I find the bottle opener in the utensil drawer, pop open my beer, and grab my balloons, dragging them lazily out of the kitchen as I make my way towards my room. In order to get to my room, I have to cross the living room, which houses a mantelpiece that serves as an altar to my brother. His graduation photo sits in the center between a series of trophies, prizes he won for winning spelling bees, debate competitions, and other athletics, like track and field, because being quarterback of the football team wasn't enough. He couldn't just be normal and do nothing during the off season like the rest of us. There are other things on the mantelpiece, like my parents' wedding photo, but nothing that demands as much attention as Art. He's such a butt.

When I get to my room, I shove the balloons into a corner, slip off my backpack, and plop myself onto my bed. I flip on my TV — it's one of those old non-HD TVs that's super bulky because old tech always is — and pull out my phone. The TV's only on for white noise. It keeps me company while I search for something more interesting on social media.

I'm scrolling endlessly through my Instagram feed, swiping up on a bunch of familiar faces from school, videos from amateur musicians, and even a few hot Instagram models. My favorites are always the ones in the gray sweatpants. They show everything. Eventually, I find my way to Nick's page. Am I following him? No. Do I check his profile on a near daily basis? I plead the fifth. He does have a new picture up though. And he's not alone. Erik Park is smiling at me, half his face scrunched up as Nick plants a fat kiss on his cheek. I stare at the picture for way too long. I can feel myself scowling. It's kinda pathetic. I really shouldn't be so fixated on this, but I just don't get it.

I continue to scroll through Instagram and jump back and forth between social media platforms for a little while longer when a knock comes on my door.

"Come in," I say, and in comes my dad, having just arrived from work.

My dad works as a cable installer in San Francisco. Are cable installers even necessary anymore, what with cellphones and Wi-Fi being a thing? Whatever, he has a job that he commutes to every morning from the suburbs, and it pays the bills. Though, I'm not sure working as a cable guy was how my dad imagined his career would end up. Like my mom, my dad used to be hot shit growing up.

In college, my dad was a football star. He and everyone around him expected him to get drafted into the NFL, but then he met my mom. They started dating and things between them moved quickly. Too quickly, in fact. Before the end of their sophomore year, my mom was pregnant with Art. She didn't go back to school after that summer. My dad held on a little longer, but the stress of having a baby on the way took a toll on him. It started affecting his playing. Then one day, he got tackled real bad and sustained a major knee injury, and that was pretty much it for that.

My parents are the kind of people that life gave a sip of lemonade to before shoving them aside to have them squeeze lemons all day. Still, they don't seem unhappy. And if they are, they don't mention it. They just get really excited when one of their kids does something great. I mean, just look at the mantelpiece.

"So, you're the one drinking all my beer," my dad says, wearing an unconcerned smile. I raise my bottle as if to toast. "You know, *I* don't care. Just don't let your mom catch you."

"What, Mom never drank underage?" I reply, taking a sip.

"You take pride in being a smartass?" I shrug. "Anyway, here. It's not much, but happy birthday." Dad hands me an envelope then proceeds to stand there, watching me all awkward with anticipation. I take the hint and open the envelope. Inside is a card with a cartoon of an old decrepit looking man. Next to him is a phrase drawn out in a way that looks like a child had written it: *"You're young, pretty, and excited about life…"* it reads. I open the card and, sure enough, the rest of the phrase is there. *"…that'll change. Happy Birthday!"* My dad's beaming. "Picked it out myself. It's funny, right?"

"Hilarious," I say, just to humor him. He nods wearing a self-satisfied smile. He's practically patting himself on the back with it. Hey, at least the card came with a Benjamin. "Thanks, Dad."

"Sure. Now you can pay for lunch on Saturday. We'll be livin' it up like Gatsby."

"You know he dies at the end of that, right?" My dad looks at me as if I just said the most offensive thing.

"You really like to suck the fun out of everything, don't you? You know, your brother never gave me this much shit," he laughs, making it clear to me he meant it as a joke, but…

"Speaking of Art," I begin. "Is he coming on Saturday?"

"Yeah, of course. Why?"

"No reason. Just curious. I thought he might be busy since he works a job and all that."

"No, he'll be here," Dad answers casually. "It's your birthday. Why wouldn't he be?"

"He didn't come for Mothers' Day."

"He couldn't get it off." Dad narrows his eyes at me, as if trying to read whatever might be written on my face. "Why? Do you not want him to come?" he asks. Apparently, I don't hide my feelings well, but I don't want to talk about them. Men don't talk about their feelings, you know — not with their dads anyway — so I let out a nervous laugh.

"Nah, I'm just curious," I insist, shaking my head way too hard to avoid looking suspicious. My dad probably thinks I'm crazy. He's staring at me like I am.

"Uh, okay, then," he says, giving me one more puzzled look before exiting the room. I let out a sigh, though I'm not sure if it's one of relief, for avoiding an awkward conversation, or frustration, over the fact that my brother's coming home. Either way…

"Great," I mumble quietly to myself. "Just great…"

chapter three

G, C, E, G, C, E...
G, C, E, G, C, E...

Hmm... I don't think this is right. It doesn't sound like anything. *Moonlight Sonata* is one of those songs where you'd immediately recognize it just by the sound and, uh, this ain't it. I wonder what I'm doing wrong. What are these hashtags. Are these sharps? Is this whole measure supposed to be sharp? I'm tempted to pull out my phone, but Mrs. Dolittle's walking around, and I'd rather not get my phone taken away. I should just ask. What could it hurt?

"Mrs. Dolittle," I say, raising my hand. She turns and starts walking over.

"What do you need?" she asks as she approaches me at my keyboard.

"Am I getting these notes right?"

"*Moonlight Sonata?* Again, Andrew? Don't you think that's a little advanced? Have you even practiced the rest of the book?"

"I like a challenge," I shrug. She looks at me all narrow eyed, as if I'm just saying this to get out of practicing whatever we're supposed to be practicing, which, I guess, she's right. But, like, I'm still practicing piano. Plus, the stuff we're supposed to be practicing is boring and not at all appropriate for the time of year. I mean, come on. *Jingle Bells* in May? Ugh.

"Fine. What's your question?" Mrs. Dolittle sighs after a moment.

"Am I getting these notes right?" I ask, showing her the notes I've got written out on the piano book.

"No. This piece is written in C-sharp minor, meaning —"

"— everything's shifted one."

"Well, not everything. The E's the same." Mrs. Dolittle leans over me to demonstrate. I watch her fingers as she plucks out each note. Seems easy enough.

"Ah, Cool. Got it. Power to the hashtags," I say. Mrs. Dolittle rolls her eyes.

"Anything else?" she asks.

"Nope. I think I can figure it out from here. Thanks."

"Alright then. Don't write in these books. They belong to the school." I nod and playfully salute her. She rolls her eyes again, and then walks off, continuing to make her rounds. I spend the rest of the class period marking up my piano book.

. . .

What? It's for educational purposes. It's not like I'm doodling dicks in them. I'm not a heathen. If I could just figure out all the notes and chords to this page of *Moonlight Sonata,* maybe Piano won't be such a drag. I might even kick off the summer with a cool new party trick. Can't say as much for the rest of my classes though.

My second period is Algebra II. We're simplifying radicals. Radical… Third period is English. We're reading Edgar Allen Poe. That guy's depressing. And what is the deal with English? We have to take English every single year, as if we don't already speak it. Do people really have that much trouble differentiating there, their, and they're? There's autocorrect for that. It's ducking awesome.

Anyway, fourth period is US History with Mr. Milano. His class is the worst, I swear. The man assigns a chapter to read and then sits behind his desk, fiddling with a Rubik's Cube the entire time, like he might actually solve it before the period's end. Spoiler alert: he won't.

He never does. This would be fine — a free period always is — if it wasn't for the fact that the man smells like cheese. What kind of cheese? I don't know… Foot cheese? Like I said, "the worst."

Luckily, I don't have to sit through Milano's class alone. Riles is in this class, which at least makes the period bearable, but, man, is it going slow. I'm staring at the clock, literally counting down the seconds, every single tick and tock of that little clock hand, as it circles round to the moment of freedom. The lunch period cannot get here fast enough.

"Five bucks says I'll make off with that damn cube," Riles whispers from the seat behind me. I look over at Milano. He's so caught up in that Rubik's cube, the whole class could probably walk out of here without him noticing. Come to think of it, why haven't we tried that?

"No way, man," I reply. "He's on that thing like a fat kid on cake. Or like you, the other day."

"Shut up. That birthday cake was good."

"Um, Mr. Milano," I hear a whimpering voice say from the desk beside me. It's Tim Martinelli. He's a scrawny, pimple faced little brown noser who thrives on browning his nose, all for the sake of collecting a few extra grade points. It's usually at the expense of everyone else, which is why my ears perk up.

"Yes, Tim?" Milano says, his focus staying entirely on his Rubik's cube.

"Did you wanna collect the homework from last night?" Half the class lets out a synchronized groan. I don't even remember there being homework from last night. Like, really, Tim?

"Why are you like this?" I ask. Tim looks at me all wide eyed and scared. Poor bastard should've kept his mouth shut.

"Fuck you, Tim!" Riles says, not even trying to be quiet about it.

"Now, none of that, Mr. Mueller," Milano chimes in, without an ounce of genuine concern. "You can all drop off the assignment at the end of class."

"Oh, shit, dude," Riles whispers, his voice dripping with a sudden excitement. "That cube's as good as mine." It takes me a moment to connect the dots. This fucker's gonna try to swipe the thing when everyone's turning in their homework. I think I might be out of a five. Damn it, Tim!

"I can't believe you actually got it," I say, laughing to Riles as we make our way out of the annex.

"There's a trick to this thing. There's gotta be," he replies, fiddling with the Rubik's cube he managed to swipe from Mr. Milano. "Anyway, pay up."

"No way, man."

"Dude, you bet. You owe me five."

"Nah, you had an unfair advantage with Martinelli's sucking up."

"Still counts. Come on, at least pay for my nuggets," Riles whines.

"Fine. I'll pay for your nuggets, but that's it. I'm not paying for your whole damn lunch," I say.

"Cheapskate."

Riles and I cross the street and head into main campus to the cafeteria. When we get to the cafeteria, I don't see Jake anywhere, which is a little weird since he's usually the first one of us here, but whatever. Riles and I make a beeline for the lunch line, where I have to fight him off from grabbing more than one tray of chicken nuggets. I end up paying for two. Honestly, I don't know why I hang out with these people.

"You're the best, Drewster," Riles says as we exit the lunch line to look for a table.

"You're a menace," I reply. He just cackles in response, and I can't help but roll my eyes.

We find an empty table near the entrance of the cafeteria and spread ourselves out. I unwrap the foil from my cafeteria burger as Riles pops a nugget into his mouth.

"So, what are you up to this weekend?" he manages, mouthful of chewed up nugget. "Wanna catch a movie, go theater hopping?"

"Can't," I say, taking a bite of my burger. "My brother's coming home this weekend."

"Oh, for real? I love Artie." I shoot Riles a look. Like, really, dude?

"You and everyone else." I realize I'm probably being a little bitch right now, but the idea that my brother is cool to my friends is annoying. Riles is *my* friend. He's supposed to be on *my* side. I bought him not one, but two trays of chicken nuggets. Where is the loyalty, bro? Ugh, I can't.

"Someone's bitter," Riles says, chewing on his nugget, which again, *I* bought.

"I'm not bitter."

"You're so bitter."

"I'm not —" I catch myself raising my voice and have to stop for a second, so I don't freak out on him. "Look, I just don't want to hear about him, okay? I don't need to hear about how great he is." I take another bite of my burger and chew it aggressively. Riles shrugs, letting out a sigh.

"Well, at least you have a brother," he offers, sounding more bored than sympathetic.

"You have a sister," I reply.

"Dude, she's eight. That doesn't count." He pops another nugget into his mouth. "I'm just saying, I think it'd be cool to have someone that's, like, my age who I can just chill and hang out with, you know?"

"And what am I? Just hot garbage to you?" I say all straight faced and sarcastic.

"Well, you *are* the hot one of the group," Riles laughs. I just stare at him, continuing to chew. "Oh, come on, lighten up, Drewster. Stop being so sensitive. You know you're my boy. You're my number one." Eh, he's right. I am being too sensitive. I crack a smile, hoping to shake myself from this mood. I hate that I'm so bothered right now. Luckily, I can't really dwell on it too much because Riles continues. "Whatever you do though," he says, "don't tell Jake I said that. I swear, if you do, I'll lie my ass off."

"No problem there," I chuckle. "I'm not planning on telling that guy anything anymore."

"Huh, speaking of the devil, here he comes. And he's brought your girlfriend." Riles nods toward something behind me. I turn to look over and see Jake coming toward us, followed by Becca, Jen, and Angela. What is going on?

"Hey, Andrew," Becca says cheerfully, taking a seat at our table. Jen and Angela do the same, while Jake heads straight for Riles to try to steal a nugget.

"What's up?" I reply, setting down my burger. After how Becca approached me on my birthday the other day, I'm a little bit suspicious of her, to say the least.

"Oh, nothing much, I just wanted to talk to you. I figured we could all have lunch together. Spend some quality time, you know?" She leans her head to the side flirtatiously, whilst twirling her hair around her finger. I stare at her for moment.

"Okay." I don't think she likes that this is how I answer, because her eyes narrow like I said something offensive. I get the sense that everyone at the table is staring at us now, not knowing what to make of this exchange. Honestly, *I* don't really know what to make of it. Did she think I was gonna ask her out? Did she bring her friends to put a little added pressure on me? I said it before, the girl has balls, but…

"This is uncomfortable," Jake says.

"What's uncomfortable is you leaning on me and stealing my nuggets, bro!" Riles says, practically yelling and pushing Jake off of him. Meanwhile, Becca's staring at me, looking like she's waiting for me to say more. I offer her an awkward tight-lipped smile and take a big bite out of my burger. If I eat slow enough, maybe I won't have to talk to her. You know, you shouldn't talk with your mouth full.

Fifth period is P.E. Since there are only a few weeks left until the end of school, my P.E. class is essentially a free period on the football field. As long as you change into your uniform and do something other than sit around, the teachers don't care what you do. Riles and Jake also have P.E. this period, so we're spending it on the field, tossing around a football.

"I don't get it. Why don't you wanna go out with Becca?" Jake says, throwing me the ball. "She's hot."

"She's desperate," I reply, passing the ball back to him.

"So? That makes her prime real estate. You can park a car in an open garage."

"Too bad you can't park for shit!" Riles yells.

"Shut up!" Jake yells back.

"You shut up!" Jake then throws the ball at Riles, who manages to catch it despite him.

"Both of you, shut up!" I shout, gesturing for the ball. Riles tosses it over.

"For real, dude, why don't you wanna go out with her?" Jake asks again. "She's hot. She's into you. She baked you cake."

"It was a good cake," Riles adds.

"So what's the deal?" Jake continues.

"I dunno," I shrug, then throw the ball to him. "Not my type, I guess."

"So, then what is your type?" Riles asks. I pause. The question catches me off guard. What *is* my type? If I were to describe it, I guess I would say it's someone roughly my height, give or take a few inches. I like dark features. Dark hair. Dark eyes. Maybe a nice little distinctive thing, like a beauty mark somewhere. Maybe even a little exotic looking… Wait, am I describing Nick? Erik Park's Nick? Fuck!

"Yeah, dude, for as long as we've known you, you've never had a girlfriend," Jake adds, passing the ball to Riles. "Despite having all these gorgeous girls practically throwing themselves at you." Well, there's a reason for that…

I want to tell Riles and Jake. I do. But if I were to tell them, how would they react? Would things be normal, or would everything suddenly become super awkward between us? Could I still be one of the boys without them looking at me differently? Considering how they refer to Erik and Nick as faggots, I doubt it. There are just too many questions when it comes to that, and too many of those questions don't have happy answers. I don't know if I'm ready to entertain the idea. So, I don't.

"Maybe that's the problem," I say. "Maybe I don't want girls throwing themselves at me."

"I don't know, man. That sounds like a great problem to have," Jake replies, catching a pass from Riles. He then tosses the ball to me. "At least you'll never have to resort to online dating."

"Huh, yeah," I agree. Holding the ball in my hands, I let what Jake just said sink in. Online dating… Now there's an idea I haven't thought about before.

Honestly, me hopping onto an app or dating site has never crossed my mind. I always assumed you had to be eighteen to get on one — legitimately, at least. I know a few kids at school who've been on them since they were, like, twelve, but that was always such a sketchy idea to me. I am a young, attractive, mostly innocent gay dude. I wasn't about to make myself accessible to perverts. But you know, now that I'm eighteen… maybe I should. I mean, the only two gay guys I know are dating each other. And given the fact that I'm practically pining for one of them — is that the word, pining? — maybe it is time I start dating. Or, at the very least, finding a garage to park my car in, as Jake would put it. And I don't even have a car.

Like, an actual car.

Not a penis. I have one of those.

. . .

Yeah, I should definitely start dating.

chapter four

Online dating, huh?

I don't really hear very many good things about online dating. Most of what I've heard have been horror stories, sad catfishing tales, or just pathetic, weirdo tryhards trying too hard. But then again, most of my information comes from sensationalist true crime vlog channels and whatnot, so I don't really know. What I do know is that sixth period just let out, and I'm standing at my locker, watching Erik Park canoodle with his superhot boyfriend. Well, they're not actually canoodling. They're more just standing next to each other and giggling by Erik's locker, but that's more action than I'm seeing at the moment. I want that. I want someone to not-canoodle and giggle with. I want someone to have genuine romantic affections for.

Come to think of it, I've never actually seen Erik and Nick be affectionate with each other at school. Not more than what I'm seeing now, anyway. The only reason I found out about them is because I overheard Erik and his friend, Molly/Miranda What's-her-face, talking about it. I'm pretty sure that's how most people found out about Erik and Nick dating. Through conversations that got eavesdropped on and people being suspicious of them always being together. And then, of course, the rumor mill. I think if they were a little more careful, they probably could've kept it a secret, you know, if they wanted to. They pretty much just keep to themselves. No one would've found out.

Huh…

I'm sitting on the bus, staring out the window, watching the world pass by. I keep thinking about the idea. Me, online dating, really? I don't know. Maybe. There's just so much to think about. Like, am I really gonna put myself out there like that? And if I do put myself out there, wouldn't that be risking putting *myself* out there? Online dating is pretty commonplace these days, so there's always that chance that someone I know could find me, right? I can't say I'm not tempted, but… I don't know.

. . .

What if I just look? What could it hurt, right? I pull out my phone, open the browser, and search the words: online dating apps. The first few results are links to lists of the "Best Dating Apps of the Year." Whoop-de-do. I'm not even gonna click on them. I'd be an idiot to consider anything so mainstream that it would land itself on any "best of" lists, so I keep scrolling.

And scrolling.

And scrolling.

Next page.

And scrolling.

Most of what I'm finding are just lists. I'm ready to give up, when about four pages into the results, I come across a link that reads: "AphroDATEme — Find Love, Pleasure, Passion & More." Umm… sure? Why not? I've never heard of this app, and considering it's buried pretty deep in the results, it should be safe. Besides, I'm just looking.

I click the link and am taken to the welcome page, where I'm greeted by a cartoon woman in a toga saying, "Let Aphrodite be your guide and bless you with a date tonight." Aside from an icon at the bottom of the page prompting visitors to download the app, there's really nothing else here. What the heck? I go ahead, click the icon, and… straight to the sign up. Fuck.

So, you're telling me that I can't even look around before I commit to this? I'm just gonna have to dive right in? That's stupid! That's like buying pants without trying them on. What if they don't look good? What if they don't feel right? I'm gonna have to take my pants off and go all the way back to the store, hoping they give me a refund. And even if they do give me a refund, I'll have no pants! I'm not doing it. I'm not. I refuse. I'm not doing it.

    . . .

    . . .

    . . .

I did it. I signed up. My username is GoldenBoy513 — GoldenBoy was already taken. And now, the app's prompting me to fill out my bio and upload a profile pic. Ugh, what am I doing? I guess I might as well go through with it. We've come this far. I've already made a profile. But what am I gonna put in my bio? I don't have time to give it much thought before my bus gets to my stop. I shove my phone into my pocket and decide to deal with it later. Except, I can't get it off of my mind.

The whole walk home from the bus stop, I'm thinking about what I'm supposed to say about myself. Describing yourself is such an awkward thing to do. Usually, when I fill out bios on social media, I just write something like, "Hey, I'm Andrew. I be straight chillin'.

[Sunglasses emoji]" Would that fly on a dating site, or would I just look like a total douche? What if I added, like, an eggplant emoji? Ugh, that's even worse! What do guys say about themselves to attract other guys?

God, I hate this.

Hi, I'm Andrew.
I enjoy football.
I'm a high school junior — don't ask.

No, I shouldn't write that. The guys that are gonna be on a dating site are supposed to be adults. The fact that I'm in high school would probably scare them off. I have been working on this bio since I got home and that was, like, an hour ago. And all I have written so far is "Hi, I'm Andrew. I enjoy football." I don't even know if I'm gonna keep the football part, but what am I supposed to say? I have no other hobbies. I have no other interests that I care about mentioning. I'm lying here on my bed, staring at an empty text box, and realizing now that I'm not a very fascinating person.

Hi, I'm Andrew.
I enjoy football.
I don't know what else to right here.

I guess that'll have to do. It's the truth.

Now, all that's left to do is to post a picture. My stomach is in knots at the idea of it. I don't know who's gonna be on this app. I don't know who's gonna see my face next to the words "male-seeking-male." I don't really know what I'm in for, or what I'm exposing myself to. What I do know is that I spent the last hour freaking out over this dating app profile, and I just want to be done with it so I can finally check out guys. I open up my camera app and take a quick selfie. Then, I upload the picture onto AphroDATEme, take a deep breath, and hit save.

I'm in your hands now, Aphrodite. Let's find someone to date me.

chapter five

There are, like, no guys on this app.

I was scrolling through the selection of guys on AphroDATEme the rest of Thursday and pretty much the whole day Friday. No luck. I did get a couple messages right off the bat, but they were all duds:

"Wanna hook up?"

"You lookin for a sugar daddy?"

"Dick pics?"

The most promising message came from this older guy — late twenties — with a white square as his profile picture. We got to talking for a bit and I asked to

44

see what he looked like. When he sent me a pic, I noped the fuck out of that one real fast. Now, I'm willing to date older — up to thirty or so — but if you look like you could be my *dad's* dad, I can't.

After Mr. White Square, most of everyone else I encountered were headless torsos, uggos, and old people. As far as the uggos go, I have standards. And all those torsos, as tempting as they may be, put me at a disadvantage. I learned my lesson from Mr. White Square: always make sure to see their face. I mean, the heads attached to those torsos could be ugly *and* old. Just like Mr. White Square.

Maybe I did something wrong. Maybe, when I signed up for my profile, I didn't make my dating radius, or whatever, big enough. Then again, I don't have a car, so it wouldn't make a difference. Looks like I put too much faith in Aphrodite. That ho.

I'm sitting in the backseat of my dad's SUV, scrolling through Aphrodite's catalogue of guys, just hoping I might stumble onto someone new. We're on our way to the Amtrak station in one of the neighboring cities to pick up Art. He's coming home for the weekend to join us for my belated birthday lunch. I can't say I'm excited to see him though because I don't really miss him. I see him every day on the altar that is the mantelpiece in our living room.

Dad drives us along a winding road going through wooded hills, while he and Mom sing along to that old Nelly song, "Dilemma." Mom sings the girl parts and Dad does the rap. It's probably the whitest thing you could imagine. Why do they know all the words?

Eventually, the trees start to clear, and the road takes us into the downtown area of the city. Despite it being Saturday, it's not very busy at all. The area's quiet and gives off this sort of cute, small town America vibe. It's easy to forget a big city, like San Francisco, is less than an hour's drive away.

"Here we are," Dad announces as we pull into the parking lot of the Amtrak station. He parks the SUV in a spot facing the platform, which is accessible right from the parking lot, where we can watch for any approaching trains. It's not long before one pulls in. "This might be him." Dad unbuckles his seatbelt and climbs out of the car. Mom does the same but stops short of shutting her door when she notices me still sitting here.

"You're not coming?" she asks.

"I'll just wait here," I say.

"You don't want to come greet your brother?"

"I'll greet him when he gets here."

"Okay," Mom says, sounding almost disappointed. She shuts the door and heads off. I take these last few moments alone in the backseat to continue scrolling through the guys on AphroDATEme:

Uggo.

Old.

Headless torso.

Another headless torso.

Uggo *and* old.

Random picture of a guy's feet. Seriously? Is there really no one else on here? I'm starting to feel like this online dating thing is just a big waste of time.

Suddenly, I hear the car door open beside me. In a panic, I hit the power button on my phone and quickly shove it into my pocket.

"What's up, little brother?" Art says, now standing next to me, backpack hanging from his shoulder. I nod, casually acknowledging him without giving much care, the way you would when passing some rando in the hallway. "What, you too cool for me now? Come here." He throws his arms around me and gives me a big firm hug. "Here, I brought you something." He then slips off his backpack, reaches into it, and offers me a stuffed cow in a college tee. "I saw it in the school store and thought of you."

"You thought of me as a cow?" I ask, totally unimpressed.

"No, I just mean I remembered how you used to have this stuffed toy as a kid. I hadn't seen that thing in a while, so I thought I'd get you a new one."

"Oh, that's cute!" Mom says, peering over Art's shoulder. "Get me one too."

"Sure. Next time, Mom," Art replies, and then they all pile into the car. It's a wonder we could all fit though since, apparently, I'm such a cow. Definitely tossing this thing under my bed when we get home.

Art's the worst.

"So, how's everything going, Artie?" Dad asks as he pulls onto the freeway heading towards home. "How's the smoothie shop treatin' you?"

"It's good. I can't complain," Art says.

"It's not too much for you?" Mom questions. "Working and being a full-time student?" Art shakes his head.

"Nope. Besides, I can always request time off if I need it."

"Okay, well, just make sure you're taking care of yourself."

"Listen to your mother," Dad jumps back in. "Don't stress yourself out like I did. It cost me my football career."

My parents and Art banter for a little bit, while I stare out the window, just zoning out. I'm not really thinking about anything. I just don't care to listen to all the great things that Art's doing. I'd rather be scrolling through uggos and oldies, but I can't exactly do that without outing myself. Not with my brother sitting right next to me.

I'm losing myself in the passing scenery of the California State Route 4 — or Highway 4, same thing — when I feel Art nudge me.

"What?" I ask. He nods towards the front seat.

"I asked where we're going," Dad says. Did he ask that? I hadn't heard. Either way, I haven't given it much thought. But I don't really have to. I feel like for every occasion we end up at the same spot, so that's what I go with.

"How about Antonini's?" I suggest.

"That's what you want?" Dad asks.

"Yeah." I shrug.

"Antonini's it is then."

Antonini's is this faux European restaurant in town that really leans into the idea of affordable fancy. You know, the kind of fancy that bougie people claim isn't fancy but is still pricey enough to feel like a real *treat yourself* kind of place. It's something to look forward to. I can feel my mood start to brighten at the thought of chugging down bottomless Italian sodas that my dad will freak out about when he sees the bill, because they're not actually bottomless. Consider it revenge for his attempt at rapping, if you can even call it that.

When my family and I walk into Antonini's, we're greeted by the familiar face of Erik Park's friend, Molly/Miranda What's-her-face. I'd say we were welcomed, but she's not very welcoming. She's a really pretty girl with dark hair and fair skin, but she wears this look on her face that just makes you feel like she's constantly plotting your death. I swear, all of Erik Park's relationships make no sense to me. For all the shit I talk about him, at least Erik's pleasant. Can't say the same about *this* girl.

"Hi, welcome to Antonini's," she says, smiling in a way where I can tell she's biting her back teeth. The fact that she's working here fills me with comfort, because it means that she can't be as mean as her face. Not if she wants to keep her job anyway.

"Hey, I didn't know you work here," I reply.

"Well, now you do."

"It's, uh, Molly, right?" She narrows her eyes. "Miranda?"

"Mackenzie."

"Oh, do you kids know each other?" Mom says excitedly butting in.

"Sort of," Mackenzie replies, not taking her narrowed eyes off me. "We go to school together." There's a brief moment of almost tense silence between us. Then, as if a switch was flipped, her demeanor changes to something a little more peppy. "So, table for four?"

We follow Mackenzie into the dining room, which is made up to be as cheaply elegant as possible. Like, everything is clean, the walls are painted all rustic like the walls of some European villa, the decorative plants are real, the servers are all in long-sleeve button ups, but there are no tablecloths. Honestly, tablecloths in restaurants seem like such a waste, but that's one of the reasons I've heard people claim that this place isn't fancy. I'm sorry, when a place charges more than ten dollars for a sandwich, they're fancy.

Mackenzie shows us to a table in the middle of the dining room. It's pretty quiet at the moment with only a few other tables filled and everything is pristine. It's looking like we might've beat the lunch crowd.

"Here are your menus and your server will be right with you," Mackenzie says, wearing the phoniest of smiles. She takes one more piercing glance at me, before turning to leave.

"Well, she seems nice," Mom offers, taking a seat.

"Yeah, I don't think she likes me very much," I reply, sitting down next to her.

"Why? What'd you do to the poor girl?" Dad asks as he and Art take the remaining two seats.

"Nothing," I say. Though that's not entirely true. Last year, when I made the pass at Erik, it didn't go well, and Mackenzie got involved. We ended up getting into a bit of a spat over it in the hallway and she slapped me, right there in front of everyone. The girl hits hard too. That's probably why I couldn't remember her name. I had hoped it'd be water under the bridge by now, but that's high school for you. Whatever. She doesn't matter. I'm not gonna let it bother me. I'm just gonna sit here, order a bottomless Italian soda, and stress myself out over whether I want a seafood pasta dish or steak.

"Mom, Dad, I wanted to talk to you guys about something," Art says, while we're busy looking over our menus.

"What's up, kiddo?" Dad asks, his eyes glued to the pasta section.

"Well, you know how I've been working at the smoothie shop? I've actually been saving up, and I was hoping that maybe you could help me buy a car?" I stare at Art from over the top of my menu. Is he serious right now? A car? I might be being weird about it but is this really appropriate conversation for this occasion? I mean, I feel like asking your parents to help you buy a car at your brother's birthday lunch is, like, I dunno, poor form. Still, I don't want to seem like an ass, so I just stick my nose into my menu and continue to debate between pasta and steak.

"How much money do you have put away?" I overhear Dad ask. Pasta or steak? What do I want?

"Couple thousand," I hear Art say. "I figure if I find a car cheap enough, I could keep the payments low." Pasta or steak?

"Are you hearing this, Liz? My boy's already got this all thought out. Look at him talking about buying a car." Pasta or steak?

"Is that a yes?" Art says. I think I'm leaning more towards pasta.

"Of course, kiddo. I'm proud of you," Dad replies. Actually, I think I want steak.

"Do you know what you're getting, Andrew?" I hear Mom ask, but I don't respond. I just keep debating pasta or steak, pasta or steak, trying to block out the conversation between Art and my dad. Seriously, Art's been back with us for, like, an hour, and already he's making stuff about him. Like, oh, Dad, I want a car. Will you help me buy one? Blah-blah-blah-blah-blah. Look at all the money I saved. "Andrew?"

"Huh?" I snap out of myself and see Mom staring at me like she's waiting for me to answer something. What was her question?

"Do you know what you want?" she asks again. I take a quick glance around the table and realize that Mom's the only one paying any attention to me. Art and Dad are talking about whatever the fuck they're talking about. I don't even know what they're talking about anymore, but it's irritating, nonetheless.

"Um, it's between the seafood pasta or a steak. I can't decide," I reply, just to give my mom an answer. I start to get this feeling in my stomach. Like, an emptiness of some sort. And it's not because I haven't eaten yet. Or maybe it is. I don't know. Pasta or steak?

Suddenly, I hear my phone chime. Without thinking, I reach into my pocket, pull it out, and stop when I see the notification on my lock screen. It's from AphroDATEme. And it says I've got a message. My heart skips a beat. For what, I don't know yet.

"Everything okay?" I hear Mom ask.

"Uh, yeah. Jake's just having some girl trouble," I lie, saying the first thing I can come up with. "Actually, I have to use the bathroom. I'll be back." I set my menu down and excuse myself from the table. Then, I head directly to the bathroom, which is located at the front entrance, passing Mackenzie at the host stand along the way.

Once inside the bathroom, I unlock my phone and click the notification. I don't really know what I'm expecting. Given the wack selection of guys on AphroDATEme, this message could very well be another dud from an old uggo, or a pair of feet, or some shit. Still, this online dating thing is brand new to me, so just getting a message is exciting. Even if it does turn out to be a dud.

The message is from a user named RudeFern69. I click on the profile picture attached to it and my jaw drops. The guy is actually cute. He looks to be Hispanic of some sort, I think. He's got a nice natural tan, blue hair with black roots, a cross hanging from his left ear, and a piercing on the right side of his bottom lip. He's staring back at me with deep brown eyes and a smirk, dripping with so much confidence it almost reads as arrogant. But I'm no stranger to a little bit of cockiness. I can hang. What's he gotta say? I navigate back to my inbox and open his message.

"*write," it says. What? I have no idea what this is about. I send a question mark as a response and wait. A few seconds later, his reply comes in. "Your bio. Wasn't sure if that was a typo or a bad attempt at being clever." I'm still lost. My bio? What about my bio? I don't recall writing anything worthwhile. Curious, I navigate to my profile and scroll down.

Hi, I'm Andrew.
I enjoy football.
I don't know what else to right here.
Oh…

"Well, this is embarrassing," I message him, feeling kinda stupid. How'd I miss that? I literally wrote three sentences. He replies with a laughing crying emoji. Great…

"It's okay. You're cute. You don't need to be smart [Winky face emoji]," he says in his follow up message. I'm insulted but intrigued. "So, Andrew, tell me about yourself. I'm sure there's more to you than typos and football." Is there? I don't really know. I couldn't come up with anything else to put in my bio, and I had all the time in the world to fill that out. He messages again, "I'm Rude by the way."

"Rude? As in you're mean?" I write.

"As in short for Rudy," he replies.

"Short? It's four letters."

"Yes, but fewer syllables." I chuckle. He seems like a smartass, but I'm not *not* interested. I'm hoping he's who he is and not some catfish. Anyway, as much as I hate to cut this short, I should probably get back to my family. They're probably waiting to order.

"Hey, I'm actually at a family thing. Can we talk later?" I write to him.

"I'd be offended if we didn't," he writes back. I smile to myself. Finally, something to look forward to that isn't food.

Speaking of… Pasta or steak?

chapter six

RudeFern69. Otherwise known as Rudy Luis Fernandez. Over the past few days, he and I have talked almost non-stop outside of school hours and it's actually really fun, which is surprising because none of it is about sex. Not explicitly, anyway. Almost all the messages I got before him were *only* about sex. There's something about the banter with him that keeps me coming back for more. Maybe I'm just excited. I don't know.

On Saturday, when the family and I got home from Antonini's, I messaged Rudy. I was super excited about it, and we went on to have a nice long conversation:

GoldenBoy513: Hey.

RudeFern69: Hey. How was the family thing?

GoldenBoy513: It was okay. Just my belated birthday lunch.

RudeFern69: Happy belated birthday.

GoldenBoy513: Thanks.

RudeFern69: What'd you have?

GoldenBoy513: Antonini's.

RudeFern69: Sounds fancy.

GoldenBoy513: Depends who you ask.

RudeFern69: Do they have tablecloths there?

GoldenBoy513: Well, I think it's fancy.

RudeFern69: So they don't have tablecloths?

GoldenBoy513: They do not.

RudeFern69: Good. Tablecloths at restaurants seem like such a waste.

GoldenBoy513: THAT'S HOW I FEEL!

RudeFern69: All caps and exclamation. You must be really passionate about tablecloths.

GoldenBoy513: I just don't like bougie things. Bougie people are the worst.

RudeFern69: That's fair. For the record, I prefer my restaurants without tablecloths [Winky face emoji]

GoldenBoy513: Are you flirting with me, sir?

RudeFern69: Well, this is a dating site, so I was… until you called me sir.

GoldenBoy513: I'm in high school. Everyone's a sir to me.

RudeFern69: Are you really?

GoldenBoy513: Yup. Finishing up my jr. year.

RudeFern69: How old are you?

GoldenBoy513: Just turned 18.

RudeFern69: You get held back or something?

GoldenBoy513: Actually, I did. In kindergarten.

RudeFern69: Oh, thank god. For a minute I thought I was flirting with a child.

GoldenBoy513: Until a few days ago, technically I was.

RudeFern69: Are you trying to turn me off?

GoldenBoy513: Am I turning you on?

RudeFern69: Let's just say I'm intrigued.

GoldenBoy513: Same.

We talked like this, pretty much the whole day. I learned that Rudy lives well across the county but goes to the junior college near the good mall in the neighboring city. He's studying to be a pharmacist because, and I quote, he "likes drugs." He's kinda stupid, but I like it. We talked and talked, swapping favorite colors, preferred movie and music genres, hated vegetables, and so on, stopping only to break for dinner. Mom and Dad don't typically bother me when I'm shut in my room, and Art was doing whatever Art does when he's home. He was probably talking to Dad about car stuff, and finances, and all the things that make our parents "so proud." I would've been annoyed about it, but my mind was focused on someone else.

On Sunday, Art asked me out to lunch, but I lied and said I had a whole bunch of homework to catch up on. I mean, I probably do, but I don't really care. My main concern was making sure I was free to chat with Rudy. He works as a barista, and mentioned he had an opening shift that morning. I had to be free around the time he got off.

RudeFern69: I hate everything.
GoldenBoy513: Bad day at work?
RudeFern69: Busy af. Why do people need coffee in the morning on the weekends? Better yet. Why are people even awake in the morning on the weekends?
GoldenBoy513: Idk. maybe they have plans.
RudeFern69: To ruin my plans?
GoldenBoy513: What were your plans?
RudeFern69: To sleep in. duh.
GoldenBoy513: Lol. So angry.
RudeFern69: You would be too if you had to be up at 4am for no reason.

GoldenBoy513: Ouch.

RudeFern69: Wbu? What are your plans?

GoldenBoy513: Avoid my bro until he leaves tonight.

RudeFern69: Don't like him?

GoldenBoy513: He's alright, I guess. More that I hate the vibe when he's home. Parents are up his butt.

RudeFern69: Gross. Lol.

GoldenBoy513: Your stupid [Winky face with tongue emoji]

RudeFern69: You're*

RudeFern69: Stupid.

RudeFern69: [Winky kiss emoji]

GoldenBoy513: I hate you.

RudeFern69: [Winky kiss emoji]

Monday and Tuesday were Monday and Tuesday. Nothing all that special. With the school year slowly crawling to its end, all my classes seem to be lasting forever and a day. The only thing that's been keeping me going are my conversations with Rudy in between classes. It's tough though. Him having work and me having entire class periods in between chats is a bit of a mixed bag. It can be good when we leave off on something cute, and I can nurse the butterflies in my stomach during class. But when the chats are paused mid-conversation, it makes the period feel *that* much longer. Instead of forever and a day, it's more like forever and a year. Which is how this morning started off.

"Morning sunshine," he wrote to me. The timestamp on the message read 4:14am. "You're probably not awake yet, but I'll be pouring shots for you."

"Hope you're having a good day at work," I wrote back. "I'd love to see you in your uniform. Hoping you're not a catfish."

"On break. Want proof?" he replied as I was getting dressed for school. "Give me something to write down. I'll send you a selfie on my next break."

"Write down my full name." I've told him. If he's been paying attention, he'll know it.

"I'll do you one better." That was the last message I got from him this morning. Now, I'm sitting in Piano, unable to concentrate on *Moonlight Sonata* because I'm eagerly awaiting to find out if the guy I've been talking to all week is who he says he is. I probably should've asked for proof before I let myself get so invested. God, I'm such an idiot.

You know what? I just need to focus on what I should be doing right now. Keep myself distracted. Concentrate on learning to play this repetitive and depressing song instead of counting every single second within every single minute before I get Rudy's reply. *Moonlight Sonata,* now.

G hashtag, C hashtag, E normal.

G hashtag, C hashtag, E normal.

Add some chords in the key of C-sharp minor because of the hashtags.

The hashtags.

The hashtags.

I swear, either this song goes nowhere or I'm completely zoning out. Honestly, what am I even worried about? If Rudy does turn out to be a catfish, we've only been talking for, like, four days. It's not like it's gonna kill me or anything. Still, I gotta know. It'd be such a waste to have four days' worth of messages with a guy and the guy turn out to be *not* the guy, you know what I mean? Ugh, this is the worst.

I wonder when his next break's gonna be. I wonder how long before he messages me back. That's when I feel it, my phone vibrating in my pocket. Suddenly, the world stops. This is it. He's messaged me back. Is it safe to check though? I look up to see what Mrs. Dolittle's up to. She's currently making her rounds around the room, going from keyboard to keyboard, checking in with every one of my classmates along the way. I feel my leg start to bounce. Do I have enough time to check my phone without getting caught?

. . .

You know what? Fuck it. I gotta see this message. I pull out my phone and quickly open the

AphroDATEme app under my keyboard. Just as expected, there's a message from Rudy — along with a handful of others I couldn't give two shits about. I open his message and am greeted by a selfie. It's a picture of a Hispanic looking dude with a lip ring, dressed in a gray tee and brown apron. His hair is silver with black roots, but otherwise he's the guy in the profile picture that got me so interested by calling out my typo. He's *real.* And how do I know he's real? Well, he's holding a piece of receipt tape with words scribbled out in red Sharpie. The words read:

Andrew Bryan Logan.

Would you kindly go out with me this Friday?

I stare at the picture for a moment, smiling to myself. Then, my eyes go straight to the word "Friday" and… holy fucking shit. Friday? As in, like, two days from now? I don't know why, since the whole point of me signing up for a dating app was to meet guys, but the idea of meeting a guy, especially one that I seem to get along with freaks me out. I don't know what to say. Should I say yes? I mean, why wouldn't I? I'm just about to type in my response when the sound of Mrs. Dolittle's voice sends me in to a panic and I nearly drop my phone.

"I see this becoming a recurring problem for you," she says. "Hand it over." She holds out her hand and stares at me impatiently.

"I'm sorry. What?" I reply, playing dumb.

"Your phone."

"What phone?"

"Andrew." She stares at me, and I stare back, trying my best to look innocent. We're at a standoff, one that I know I'm not winning. I sigh and reluctantly hand my phone over. "Now, you want to show me what you've been working on?" Is she for real? First, she takes my phone and now she wants to embarrass me by having me play *Moonlight Sonata,* knowing full well I'm likely not gonna get it right. What a bitch. But it's her class, so I unplug my headphones from the keyboard and proceed to play. Or try to, anyway.

G hashtag, C hashtag, E normal.

G hashtag, C hashtag, E normal.

Add this chord. Add that chord.

Blah, Blah, Blah.

Blah, Blah, Blah.

My piano playing's not great, but I make it to, like, the sixth measure before it completely falls to shit, and Mrs. Dolittle has to stop me, putting me out of my misery. Thank God. She stares at me for a moment through narrowed eyes. I don't know what else to do but sit here all awkward and uncomfortable.

"Come see me after class," she finally says. "You can have your phone back then." Great… Guess I might as well keep practicing.

When class finally lets out, I grab my things, throw my backpack onto my shoulder, and make my way over to Mrs. Dolittle at her desk. I'm bracing myself for a stern talking to and a lecturous finger wag. That's a word, right? Lecturous? Well, it should be. I'm just hoping I don't end up sighing or rolling my eyes too much at her. A "you're only hurting yourself by having your phone out in class" talk's coming, I know.

"Mr. Logan," Mrs. Dolittle says all condescendingly when I get to her desk. She pauses for a moment before saying any more. I offer an awkward tight-lipped smile in response. I mean, what am I supposed to say? "You know you're only hurting yourself by having your phone out in class, right?" See? Just like I said.

"Yeah, sorry," I say. She picks up my phone, which was left lying on the desk, but doesn't hand it to me.

"Have you ever taken piano lessons?"

"No, never. Why?"

"Have you ever thought about taking piano lessons?"

"Not really." Where is she going with this? I just want my phone back. What's with the third degree?

"Well, I think you should. I was pleasantly surprised," she says. "You practice *Moonlight Sonata* at home?"

"We don't have a piano," I explain. She cocks her head to the side and narrows her eyes, like what I'm saying is totally unbelievable.

"You *don't* have a piano?" I shrug. "So, you mean to tell me, what you played for me you just… picked up?" I shrug again.

"I mean, it tells you how to play stuff in the book," I say, still not really sure what the point of this conversation is.

"Wow," Mrs. Dolittle laughs. "Well, I am impressed." She then hands me my phone, finally. "Here, and don't let me catch you with it again." I nod and quickly turn to leave. That conversation did not go the way I was expecting it to, but whatever. I got my phone back. I open the AphroDATEme app and navigate to my messages with Rudy.

"I'd love to," I write to him. And just like that, I've got a date on Friday.

chapter seven

Riles and I are heading over to the cafeteria at lunch. Aside from all that business in Piano, it's been a pretty uneventful day so far. Rudy's been MIA for the most part. He sent a few emojis here and there, and the one "I can't wait to meet you" message after I sent him my response, but otherwise he's been quiet. Between his barista gig and school, I figure he must be caught up with one or the other. Unfortunately, that means he hasn't been much of a distraction for me since this morning, so I've had nothing to do but dwell on that exchange with Mrs. Dolittle. Why did she wanna know if I've had piano lessons? Was what I played really all that impressive? I never thought about piano as more than just a party trick for myself. Could I actually be good at it? Like, could I be a musician and I just don't know it? Huh…

"Hey, Riles," I begin, as we cross the big street that runs through the middle of campus. "What do you think about me playing piano?"

"You play piano?" he asks.

"No, but, like, what do you think about me learning to play piano?"

"I don't know. Should I think anything of it?" That's actually a really good question. Why am I asking Riles about this? It's not like I need his approval or anything.

"I mean, I guess not."

"If you wanna learn piano, learn piano. Makes no difference to me," he says. "As long as *I* don't have to learn piano."

"Why don't you want to learn piano?"

"Dude, have you seen my fingers? They're like fat sausages." He holds up his hands to show me and I can't help but laugh. His fingers *are* pretty fat. "It's the worst. Like bratwurst!" he complains.

"Well, you *are* German," I add.

"Scheiße!"

"Wow, impressive."

"That's about the extent of my German. That and 'schadenfreude.'"

"Yeah, that explains a lot."

When Riles and I get to the cafeteria, we find Jake posted at a table in the corner. We're about to head over to meet him and drop our bags off before getting in the lunch line, but I stop when I see that he's not the only one at the table. Becca's with him. And without the other two members of her girl squad trio. What's she doing there? I'm really hoping she's not hanging around to badger me about going out with her, but really, what else could it be?

"You okay, man?" I hear Riles ask from beside me.

"Yeah, sorry. I'm just spacing out. It's been a long day," I explain. Riles pats me on the shoulder, nudging me forward, and we approach the table. I'm gritting my teeth. I'm not looking forward to having a conversation with Becca. Not about dating, anyway. I'm not interested. Why can't she just drop it? It's been over a week since she's asked. I don't know, maybe I'm an asshole for thinking this way. I mean, she could very well just be hanging around us to eat lunch. Maybe she got in a fight with her friends or something, and she needed someone else to spend the lunch period with. Yeah, let's go with that. Benefit of doubt.

"Becca, hi," Riles greets her.

"Hey," she replies, before immediately setting her sights on me. "Hi, Andrew."

"Hi," I smile uncomfortably. Benefit of doubt, Andrew. Benefit of doubt.

"So, Andrew, I was hoping we could talk." Fuck.

"What about?"

"I was actually hoping we could talk alone, if you don't mind." I look to both Riles and Jake, hoping one of them is catching on to how uncomfortable I am. One of them has gotta sense it, right? One of them is gonna bail me out… Oh, who am I kidding? They're both staring at me as expectantly as she is. I guess there's no getting out of this one. I let out a sigh and nod. She gathers her things — which consists of a large purse but a tiny backpack — and the two of us make our way out the cafeteria and into the hallway.

"Alright, so what do you wanna talk about?" I ask. Admittedly, the hallway's not the most private place to talk, but this is high school. The important part is being out of earshot of people you hang out with. Everyone else minds their own business or pretends to. Then again, if you really wanted privacy, there's always behind the bleachers of the football field, which is why people only go there to have sex or get high, and I'm doing neither, so…

"What was that?" Becca begins, already sounding annoyed.

"What was what?"

"That sigh in there."

"What do you mean?"

"You sighed when you agreed to talk to me. Like, do you not want to talk to me, Andrew?" I mean… no. But of course, I don't say that. I'm not a dick.

"Becca, I don't even know what this is about. Why would I not want to talk to you?" I say, playing innocent. Yes, I'm lying through my teeth, but I feel like if I play dumb, maybe she'll go easy. She narrows her eyes as if trying to read me. I just smile awkwardly. What else can I do?

"Can you just be honest with me for a second without, like, playing dumb?" Becca says after a moment. "Have you thought about what I asked you on your birthday?"

"What? About going out with you?"

"Yeah." I get the urge to let out another sigh, but I fight against it. How do I reject someone without, like, straight up just shooting them down? I don't typically have to reject girls. Usually, they make it known they're interested by waving and giggling or whatever. Sometimes they'll send a note, but I just ghost them, and that's that. Becca's of a different breed. She shoots her shots when she sees them. The girl's fearless. I'm not trying to hurt her feelings. She's just not my type, obviously. Wait… Duh!

"Becca, it's nothing against you. It's just… you're not really my type."

"Then what is your type?" Fuck. I probably should've expected her to ask that. People always ask that. God, I'm an idiot. I'm panicking. What do I do to get out of this line of questioning? Pivot. Pivot!

"Look, I'm not… I'm not… really in a place to be dating or getting into a relationship right now," I say. I'm grasping at straws here. But you know, it's actually not a terrible answer, so let's go with it. "You know, the school year's almost over, we got finals coming up, and then I don't even know what's happening in the summer. It just… it just wouldn't be fair to you, you know?" She's staring at me silently. I feel like I just triggered a landmine and I'm waiting for it to explode. The moment seems to last forever.

"Well," she says finally. I brace myself for the worst. "I wish I'd known that before I baked you that cake." She glares at me, clearly annoyed. I notice she's slightly teary-eyed. She's probably *that* pissed off.

"It was really thoughtful though," I say, hoping to lighten the mood.

"It was boxed."

"Still."

"Ugh, whatever," Becca replies, rolling her eyes. She quickly turns and walks off. I feel bad, but what was I gonna do? I wasn't gonna go out with her. I let out a sigh I've been holding in and head back into the cafeteria to rejoin Riles and Jake. I swear, if Riles got chicken

nuggets and has more than one tray, I'm stealing one. He
owes me.

chapter eight

I'm sitting in my bedroom after school, scrolling through the app store on my phone. The whole piano thing with Mrs. Dolittle has been living in my mind all day. With Rudy busy doing whatever he's doing, I've got nothing else to focus on. Well, I could do homework, but who wants to do that? Instead, I'm looking for a free piano app that isn't bogged down by too many ads. While I'm scrolling through apps, I get a notification. Speaking of the devil:

RudeFern69: Hey beautiful.
GoldenBoy513: Hey.
RudeFern69: Wyd?

GoldenBoy513: Looking for a piano app.

RudeFern69: You play piano?

GoldenBoy513: Not really. I have a piano class. My teacher seemed impressed. Said I should think about lessons.

RudeFern69: You going to?

GoldenBoy513: Idk if I'd be any good.

RudeFern69: You said your teacher was impressed.

GoldenBoy513: Idk why. I don't think what I played was all that impressive. Besides, I'm not really a music guy.

RudeFern69: And what kind of guy are you?

GoldenBoy513: A sports guy.

RudeFern69: Why can't you be both? You'd be the lead of a feel good teen comedy.

GoldenBoy513: Ew you watch those?

RudeFern69: You don't?

GoldenBoy513: Its not really my thing.

RudeFern69: You know a lot of things that aren't your "thing." You don't ever do anything just for the hell of it?

GoldenBoy513: I do, but its not really my thing [Winky face emoji]

RudeFern69: Neither is punctuation. It's* [Winky kiss emoji]

GoldenBoy513: Your annoying.

RudeFern69: You're*

GoldenBoy513: Lol. I hate you.

RudeFern69: Lies. Anyway, how was your day?

GoldenBoy513: I actually had to let a girl down today. She asked me out.

RudeFern69: Don't like her?

GoldenBoy513: I'm into guys.

RudeFern69: Does she know that?

GoldenBoy513: No one does.

RudeFern69: So you think. Were you at least gentle with her?

GoldenBoy513: More gentle than I plan to be with you [Winky kiss emoji]

RudeFern69: Someone's optimistic.

GoldenBoy513: Aren't you?

RudeFern69: Yeah. In a different way.

RudeFern69: Btw, I'm about to fall asleep so if I stop responding...

GoldenBoy513: Gotcha. Sweet dreams.

RudeFern69: Are made of this.

GoldenBoy513: What?

RudeFern69: You're right. You're not a music guy.

GoldenBoy513: ?

Huh. He probably fell asleep. God, I can't wait to meet him on Friday. The thought of it has me feeling all sorts of nervous, but, like, an excited nervous, you know? Speaking of which, I should probably talk to him about what our plan is: Where are we meeting? At what time? Stuff like that. But that can wait until tomorrow.

Thursday. May 22nd.

Another day at school. Summer break cannot get here fast enough. Thankfully, no other drama. After my talk with Mrs. Dolittle yesterday, I actually tried to "apply myself" and focus on practicing *Moonlight Sonata*. I did it long enough to make it through the period without pulling out my phone. Win. Also, playing piano is starting to be… I dunno, kinda fun. Or maybe I just like getting better at things. Either way, another win.

Becca didn't show up at our table at lunch today, so that's one less thing to worry about. Unfortunately, my rejection of her prompted a lot of questions from Jake: "Why don't you want to go out with her?" I'm gay. "What kind of girls do you like?" I'm gay. "Do you mind if I take a shot at her?" Go right ahead, buddy. At least he had the decency to wait till the day after to pummel me with these questions.

I feel bad, I mean, it's not like Becca was a shit person. Because of her, I had a date to Junior prom a few weeks ago. I wasn't even planning to go, but she told me to. So I did. With her. I probably should've said no then. I could've nipped it in the bud. But honestly, I don't want to think about her anymore. Especially not when I could be thinking about happier things, like making plans for tomorrow with Rudy.

I'm sitting on the bus, staring out the window as you do, when Rudy messages me. We've been trying to message each other throughout the day, but he had class, and I had class, and it seemed like none of our breaks between classes lined up. So, we haven't been able to figure it out.

RudeFern69: 'ello darling.
GoldenBoy513: Why do I picture you wearing a dress and smoking a cigar while saying that?
RudeFern69: Is that your kink?
GoldenBoy513: Lol.
RudeFern69: I would never smoke a cigar. Now, a joint…
GoldenBoy513: You get high a lot?
RudeFern69: I'm high right now. It's how I function.
GoldenBoy513: Forreal?
RudeFern69: No.
RudeFern69: Yes.
RudeFern69: Tbh, you wouldn't be able to tell the difference.
GoldenBoy513: Says you.

GoldenBoy513: So what's the plan for tomorrow?

RudeFern69: When do you get off school?

GoldenBoy513: Around 3.

RudeFern69: Let's meet at 4. We'll get dinner or something.

GoldenBoy513: Can it be later? I wanna see if I can borrow the car from my dad when he gets home.

RudeFern69: I open Saturday. Unless you wanna meet for like ten minutes. If you want, I can pick you up.

GoldenBoy513: No. Let's meet at 4. I'll figure it out.

RudeFern69: You don't want me to pick you up?

GoldenBoy513: I don't want the first time we meet to be you picking me up from school. That's a little weird. And I don't want people asking questions.

RudeFern69: Oh, right…

RudeFern69: Yeah, me at a high school does seem kinda pedo, doesn't it? [Grinning face with sweat emoji]

I'm smiling so hard to myself I almost don't realize the bus is getting close to where I get off. I reach up to pull the cord, requesting a stop, and send Rudy a quick laughing crying emoji. Time to make the walk home. It's only a mile, but it always seems way longer after a boring ass school day. At least, I have the thought of Rudy and all his messages to keep me company.

Dad's not due to get home for, like, another couple hours, so when I get home, I toss my backpack into my room and spread myself out on the living room couch. I turn on the family TV — a giant 55-inch HDTV — to one of those trashy afternoon talk shows. You know, the kind where a pregnant teen brings on five guys who could all be her baby's daddy. Spoiler alert: it's none of them. But fuck, how'd she get five guys to sleep with her? I haven't even gotten one yet. Speaking of…

I open AphroDATEme and scroll through my chat log with Rudy until I get to the selfie he sent me, the one where he's holding the receipt asking me out. I stare at it for a bit. To think, by this time tomorrow, I could be looking at him, like, not just in picture form. But, like, him for real. I wonder what he's like. I wonder if he's just like he is in his messages. I wonder what he sounds like. Suddenly, I get the urge to play piano, of all things.

I exit out of AphroDATEme and open the free piano app I ended up downloading yesterday. I try to imagine Rudy as a song. What kind of song would he be? What genre? What mood? I imagine he'd use a lot of sharp notes — power to the hashtags — so he'd probably be in the key of C-sharp minor. Just like *Moonlight Sonata*… On second thought, I don't think he'd be anywhere near as depressing. But that's the only key I've been practicing, so that's what we'll go with. He'd definitely be as romantic though.

The time passes so quickly while I'm playing around with this piano app. I don't even realize how long I've been fiddling with the thing until I hear my dad come in through the garage.

"Hey, I'm home," he announces. I get up and head to the kitchen to meet him.

"Hey, Dad," I say. He's at the sink, emptying the Tupperware from his lunch bag. "Is there any possibility you could come home early tomorrow? I need to borrow the car."

"My SUV? For what?" He stops what he's doing and turns to me.

"I, uh, have a date."

"A date? With who?" He's looking at me all suspicious.

"Some girl."

"Some girl?"

"Yeah, some girl."

"And where did you meet this girl?" What is up with him? It's a simple yes or no about him getting home early. What's with all the questions? Why is he so concerned?

"At a barista shop," I blurt out. It's called a coffee shop! What the hell is a barista shop, Andrew? Get yourself together, bro! "I mean, coffee shop. You know what I mean."

"What time's your date?" he asks.

"We're planning to meet up right after school. So, do you think you can get home early?"

"I don't know, kiddo. I'm not the boss. I don't want to make you any promises. Why can't you just move the date to later?"

"She works the opening shift on Saturday. She goes to school and works. This is the only time that works for her," I explain. I'd say I'm starting to lose hope, but to be honest, I kinda already knew this whole car thing was a long shot. You can't blame a guy for trying though.

"Tell you what," Dad says suddenly. "Why don't you take the bus to meet your date and then I'll come get you after?" Huh… Do I really want my dad coming to pick me up after a date? That sounds like such a square move. And risky, considering the date I told him I have isn't with a *she*. I suppose it could work if I just wait until after Rudy leaves to have him pick me up…

"Okay, yeah, that'll work," I say. Dad goes back to the sink to wash his Tupperware, and I go back to fiddling with the piano app on my phone. I'm turning to leave when another question pops into my head. "Oh, hey, I'm curious, Dad. How come you never put me into piano lessons growing up?"

"Piano? Since when did you want to learn piano?" he asks.

"You never thought to just put me into it? Some parents do just because. You know, like karate, or dance, or something?"

"We did. We put you into sports," he explains. "Artie got into Little League, so you got into Little League. Artie got into football, so you got into football."

"Okay, but those are all things that Art wanted to do," I say. "What about the things that *I* wanted to do?"

"That *was* what you wanted to do. You said you wanted to do everything that Artie wanted to do. You always said, 'I want to be just like my big brother.' Said it all the way up until he started junior high. And even after that, you still wanted to do everything he did. You never matched his grades, but you took up all his activities. I'm actually surprised you didn't sign up for track and field, but I was kinda relieved. Frankly, if you boys would stop picking up these hobbies, I could probably afford to go on vacation once in a while."

Huh…

I always knew that the sports thing trickled down. It started with my dad, so naturally Art got into it, and then I did. I knew that. I just figured that that was the natural progression of things. But hearing it reiterated like that — Art did this, so I did that. Art did this, so I did that… I dunno. It just feels different. Like, it's not mine. Like, everything I have, everything I do was decided on by someone else. A part of me wants to be mad at Art for deciding to follow in Dad's footsteps and having such a strong influence on me growing up. But the other more rational part of me is thinking, damn…

And what the fuck was that comment about my grades? Thanks for rubbing it in, Dad. As if displaying Art's old 4.2 GPA report card on the fridge and the whole mantlepiece shrine weren't enough of a reminder that someone else got here first. Someone else did it better. Someone else did *me* better.

Or, by the sound of it, maybe I just did them worse…

chapter nine

I'm sitting on a bench just outside a local 24-hour diner. I've got a big knot in my stomach, overwhelmed with a mixture of excitement, worry, joy, and anticipation. I'm dressed in a pale blue short-sleeve button up, faded blue jeans, and white sneakers. I tried to dress nice but casual enough to not spark questions from Riles and Jake at school. Maybe I should've worn something fancier. But, like, how fancy is too fancy for a first date? Much less a first meeting. I'm thinking too much about this. I guess I'm just a little nervous.

From the bench, I've got a pretty good view of the freeway off-ramp. I watch as all sorts of cars exit the freeway and drive past me on the street just beyond the narrow parking lot. Maybe I can catch a glimpse of him as he pulls in, as if seeing him would put me any more at ease. God, what am I doing? Am I really freaking out over meeting a guy I met online in person? What is wrong with me? This is no big deal. People meet people they meet online in person all the time. This really shouldn't be so scary. I just need to chill. Just chill, Andrew.

"Well, what do we have here?" I hear someone say. Their voice is light with a slightly feminine quality. They speak with an upward inflection that's less excitable and more sarcastic. Though I've never heard this voice before, I know immediately who it belongs to. I look over to my left and there he is, RudeFern69. Rudy, in the flesh. He's smaller than I imagined but every bit as cute. Cuter even. His silver hair is pushed back in a relaxed fashion, and he's dressed in a gray oversized sweatshirt, the front of which is tucked into a pair of form fitting black jeans. He flashes me a slight smirk and I feel my heart skip a beat.

"Hi," I say, getting up. As I do, I realize just how much smaller he is than me. It might make going in for a hug a little awkward. Should I go in for a hug? Would that be too much? I don't really know. I just shove my hands into my pockets and smile awkwardly. Ugh, why am I so nervous?

"Look at you, looking all cute with your backpack," he replies. I forgot I had my backpack on. Why didn't I just leave it in my locker? It's not like I'd need it over the weekend. Great, now I'm suddenly super self-conscious.

"Yeah, I came directly from school," I explain.

"Been here long?"

"Like ten minutes or so."

"Sorry, the drive over was a little longer than I planned for. Then I hit traffic."

"It's okay." We go silent for a moment. I don't really know what else to say here, which is weird since we've been messaging all week without a hitch. I don't know. This whole meeting in person thing feels so awkward. Or maybe I'm just smoother over messages.

"So…" he begins.

"So…" I begin.

"Should we go in?" he suggests.

"Oh, yeah."

"You know, you're a lot taller than I was expecting."

"Is that a good or bad thing?" I ask. Rudy shrugs, eyeing me up and down and offering another smirk. We make our way to the front entrance, where I promptly grab the door and hold it open for him.

"Wow, a real gentleman," he says, though from his tone, I can't tell if he means it or if he's just teasing me. "And they say chivalry is dead."

The host seats us in a booth near the back corner of the diner. It's pretty quiet here at the moment. If this place does get a dinner rush, I don't imagine it'd be very big. It's not, like, the best place in town. It's one of those diners that you end up at when nowhere else is open. Which is what I'm counting on. Less of a likelihood that someone I know will walk in. I pick up the menu and begin to look over it, then stop when I notice Rudy sitting there, staring at me.

"Can I... help you?" I ask, rather uncomfortably. He puts on a slight smile and shakes his head.

"No. I'm just admiring God's handiwork," he explains, eyeing me down as he did when he commented on my height.

"How'd he do?"

"Are you fishing for compliments now? Have you no shame?" He says this through squinted eyes, and I can't help but smile nervously in response. I'm not sure if he's flirting with me or making fun of me. Either way, I must look like an idiot. Relax, Andrew. Just chill. But God, he's so hard to read.

"Sorry, I'm really nervous," I explain. "It's weird. I feel like I know you, but I don't really know you, so I don't know how to act."

"Well, just be yourself." He says it like it's easy. I mean, that's the obvious thing to do, but how do I do that when I'm so nervous? "If it makes you feel better, I'm already attracted to you." That *does* actually make me feel better. "And, if I thought less of you, I'd take you right here on this table," he adds casually. I can't tell if he's being serious or if he's just trying to lighten the mood, but I suddenly burst out laughing.

"You know, I'm not totally opposed to that idea," I say, my nerves starting to ease.

"So you *don't* have shame." I shrug and he laughs. Just then our waiter, an angry and tired looking middle-aged man, approaches, interrupting the moment.

"Can I get you anything to drink?" he asks unenthusiastically. Rudy and I both just order water, and our waiter goes on his way.

"So, uh, tell me about yourself," I say.

"What more do you want to know?" Rudy replies. He's looking at me with piercing eyes, like he's curious about me and where this conversation might go. His gaze is disarming. When I open my mouth to speak, I find that I'm stumbling over my words.

"Uh… what's… your… favorite scary movie?" He cocks his head to the side.

"Is that really what you want to know?" he asks, looking all confused. I shrug. "You could literally ask me anything. Come on, don't be so afraid of me. We've been talking all week. I don't bite… unless you want me to." The thought of him biting me… You know, I hadn't considered the idea of pain for pleasure, but when I picture Rudy biting me…

"Here are your waters," our waiter returns, interrupting the moment once again. At least this time, he's brought more than just his angry tired face. "You guys ready to order or you need more time?"

"More time, please," Rudy answers quickly, his eyes never breaking from mine. Our waiter leaves, then Rudy leans in. "So, Andrew, what do you want to know? Like, *really*. Ask me anything." I stare at him for a moment, not sure what to say or do. I can't for the life of me think of anything to ask him. I feel like if there's something that I want to know, it'll just come up. Why are conversations on dates infinitely harder than regular everyday conversations? And if he wants me to ask him something, maybe he should ask *me* something, you know?

"You first," I say. He narrows his eyes and leans back. I think I might've caught him off guard.

"Okay," he replies. He then takes a second. "What are you looking for?"

"What do you mean?"

"Like, with this whole online dating thing. What are you looking for?" What am I looking for? I signed up for AphroDATEme to meet guys and find someone to be cute with. I guess that means I want a relationship. I *think* I want a relationship…

"A relationship, I guess," I answer. "I mean, what else do you sign up for a dating app for?"

"A lot of things," he replies. I laugh, because duh! God, I'm such an idiot, but Rudy doesn't seem to mind. He's smiling, so that's something.

"What about you? What are you looking for?" I ask.

"A lot of things."

"Like, what specifically?"

"I'm not sure, but I think I might've found it," he answers. Wait. What? Is he... Is this going way better than I thought it was?

"Wait. Are you talking about me?"

"We'll see. Anyway, we should figure out our order. Our waiter doesn't look too happy about having us." Rudy nods and I look over my shoulder to see our waiter staring at us from behind the diner counter. He really doesn't look happy. I don't think much about it though. In all honesty, that could just be his face.

"Eh, we'll tip him good," I say.

"Oh, big spender," Rudy replies.

"Only if I'm interested."

"And are you interested, Mr. Logan?"

"Only if you are." That's a fuckin' lie. I'm very interested. But considering how goofy and nervous I came into this date, I gotta at least *try* to be alluring. And I think it might be working too. Hopefully.

Rudy and I both get a burger and fries. As dinner goes on, the conversation picks up and things flow easily, just as they did when we talked over messaging. We talk about little things:

"Why don't you just pick up your burger?" I ask when he starts to cut his into little pieces.

"I don't like shoving big things in my mouth at the dinner table," he explains. "I do that after." And I just about choke on my burger.

We talk about big things:

"So, when did you realize you were gay?" he asks.

"Um, I don't know. It was something I realized slowly over time," I answer. "I never really thought about it until dating became a thing. But even then, I already knew I liked guys. Something about the idea just felt right. What about you?"

"Uh, I think I was around six or seven. I remember watching my parents change my baby sister and just being so confused. Like, why did her butt go all the way to the front, you know? I was horrified."

We talk and talk, laughing between thoughtful moments, sharing conversations both big and small. I don't think I've talked to anyone like this before. I can't recall ever feeling so open to letting someone get to know me. At least, not without needing to put up a front or deny anything. I hadn't realized how unfamiliar I was with the concept of simply telling the truth. The *whole* truth. It's weird. It's exciting.

After we finish eating, we sit and talk some more, maybe another hour or so — long enough to see the dinner rush come and go, as well as watch the sky fade into the early evening. Time is going by so fast. The conversation is too much fun. I could probably sit in this booth for forever talking to him and never get bored. Sadly, there comes a time when I see him check his phone. He lets out a sigh. I know what that means. Time to come down from the high.

"I should probably get going," he says with a bit of a frown. "I've got a long drive home. It's been fun though." Is it bad that I'm happy he seems as bummed to end the night as I am?

"Right, you got an early morning," I reply. "Let me pay for the tab. It's the least I could do for making you drive out here."

"Please. No. I asked you out. This one's on me."

"No, it's totally fine. I've got it. Besides, the man should always pay, and I'm taller." He scoffs at this.

"How very sexist of you. Just for that, you should pay." He then smiles. It's a genuine happy smile that I can't misinterpret for sass. God, he's so pretty. And to think he could be mine. A part of me almost feels like he already is.

We're outside now. I'm walking Rudy to his car. I check my phone and see it's nearing eight o'clock. It's a shame that it's so early, but, for him, it's getting late. I want to spend more time with him. I want to talk about more serious stuff and have him ruin the moment with his sexually charged way of conversating.

Conversationing? Huh, maybe I do need to be taking English every year. Whatever, if I can say it, it's a word.

"So, GoldenBoy513," he begins, as we slowly cross the parking lot. "I don't think I ever asked you, why that username?"

"Well, 513 is my birthday," I explain. "And, um… I don't know. I guess I was tired of never coming first."

"Insert sex joke here."

"What?"

"Nothing," he chuckles to himself. "I take it that it has something to do with your brother. You mentioned your parents being up his butt."

"Yeah, our mantlepiece is basically a shrine to him."

"So, you wanted to be the golden boy for once?"

"Pretty much," I say, as casually as I can manage. Rudy looks at me curiously for a moment.

"Now, why would you want someone else's title?" he then asks.

"What do you mean?"

"I mean, if your brother is the golden boy, you should have a title of your own. You could be like… the Silver Boy."

"Silver Boy?" I ask, raising an eyebrow. "I like the sentiment, but silver's not gold."

"Doesn't mean it's not valuable," he defends. He says it like it's an obvious thing. And maybe it is. It does have a certain ring to it. *Silver Boy.* Huh…

"So…" I say when we get to his car.

"So…" he replies, turning to me. He smiles. I take a moment to look at him, taking in his features: his dark eyes, his pronounced cheek bones, his bubblegum lips decorated with a black metal ring. I wonder what that ring tastes like. I wonder what *he* tastes like. I take a quick glance to check that no one's around. Seeing that the coast is clear, I step towards him and begin to lean in, letting my eyes shut as I enter the moment. However, the moment is stopped when I feel something resting on my face. I open my eyes and realize it's his hand. I can just catch sight of him between his fingers. He's literally got his hand all up on my face, holding me back.

"Uh, did I read the moment wrong?" I ask, my voice muffled against his palm. At least his hand's soft.

"No, you read it right," he answers, removing his hand from my face. I take a step back to look at him.

"So, what was that?"

"Sorry. I… Look, Andrew, you're a really great guy. And I really like you. I just… I don't know if I'm ready for you yet."

"What does that mean?"

"It means exactly what I said." He offers me a weak smile. There's a hint of something in his expression that I can't quite make out. Is it nervousness? Fear? What would he have to be afraid of? Between the two of us, he's the more experienced one. If anything, I'm the one who should be afraid. "You're a really great guy and I would love to see you again."

"But?" There's a but, I'm sure of it. There's always a but. Otherwise, why not accept my advances if I'm such a great guy?

"But nothing. You're a really great guy and I want to see you again," he repeats, but this time the words seem hollow. Like, as much as I want to believe him, there's a part of me that doesn't. But I'm not about to make a scene in the middle of a parking lot, especially when there's still a bit of light out.

"Okay, yeah, we'll do this again sometime," I say, trying hard not to sound all defeated.

"Okay." There's an awkward sort of tension in the air now. It's as if the whole dinner date didn't happen. Like, we got rewound to the beginning of it, when it was still so weird and uncomfortable talking to each other in real life. "Do you need a ride? I can drive you," he offers.

"I'm good. My dad's coming to get me," I reply. "Besides, the freeway's right there."

"If you want, I can wait with you."

"Nah, it's cool. He thinks I'm with a girl. You should get going. You got an early morning."

"Okay," he says. He reaches for his car door but seems to hesitate before opening it. "It was really great meeting you. We'll talk soon, okay?" I nod and give him the phoniest of smiles. It's all I can manage, but he accepts it, opens his car door, and climbs inside. Minutes later, I wave to him as he pulls out of the parking lot.

I plop myself down on the curb and text my dad. It'll be a good twenty minutes or so before he gets here.

While I wait, I replay the moment of the failed kiss attempt in my head, trying to make sense of it. The night went great. At least, I thought it did. He talked like it did. So why didn't he want to kiss me? Does my breath stink or something? We did have onions in our burgers, which means both of our breaths probably would've stunk. What difference would it have made? I don't get it.

"Hey, how'd the date go?" Dad asks when I hop into the passenger seat of his SUV. He's way more chipper than I'm prepared to handle. Great… "You two get along?" I shrug. I just spent half an hour sulking in the florescent glow of a 24-hour diner after getting rejected. Excuse me if I'm not in the mood to talk. "I'm guessing it didn't work out for you?" I shrug again. "I'm sorry, kiddo. But don't let it get you too down. Not everyone's gonna be a good fit for your team. Maybe this one just wasn't for you."

"Yeah, maybe," I say. The response seems to satisfy Dad because he doesn't say any more, thank God. But thinking about what he did say, maybe he's right. Maybe I got a little ahead of myself. As much hope as I had when it came to Rudy, I don't know…

Maybe Dad's right.

Maybe Rudy's just not for me.

chapter ten

G hashtag, C hashtag, E normal.

G hashtag, C hashtag, E normal.

I'm lying on my bed, tapping on the keys of my piano app, mindlessly practicing *Moonlight Sonata*. The vibe of its moody and depressing melody seems fitting, considering how disappointing last night ended up being.

G hashtag, C hashtag, E normal.

Why didn't Rudy want to kiss me?

G hashtag, C hashtag, E normal.

He said he didn't know if he was ready for me yet. What does that mean?

G hashtag, C hashtag, E normal.

Could he be seeing someone else already? Could it be that he's not available and he's playing the field behind some other dude's back? Is that it? If only he wasn't so vague about everything.

G hashtag, C hashtag, E normal.

G hashtag, C hashtag, E normal.

Fuck! Fuck this stupid ass song. I don't even want to be playing it right now, but I've gotta be doing something, otherwise I'll literally just be sitting here, thinking about Rudy. I'd play something else, but this is the one song that my fingers have memorized. I'm not about to go out of my way to look for something else. Not right now. I should've just focused on learning to play *Jingle Bells.*

G hashtag, C hashtag, E normal.

You know what? Never mind. I can't just lay here anymore. It's almost lunch time. I'm gonna get something to eat. I roll myself out of bed and head over to the kitchen, where I find Mom standing at the counter chopping vegetables.

"Morning," I say, grabbing a bag of potato chips from the cabinet where we keep all the snacks and what not. "What's for lunch?"

"Baked chicken and vegetables," Mom replies. "Are you just getting up?"

"No, I was practicing piano."

"Piano?"

"Yeah, I downloaded a piano app." I pull up a seat at the table and help myself to some chips. It's a lot brighter out here than it is in my room. Maybe the Vitamin D will help with my mood. Plus, with my mom making conversation, I might actually be able to get you-know-who out of my mind.

"Since when are you interested in playing piano?" Mom asks, coming over to the table. I shrug.

"I mean, I have a piano class. It's not a big deal or anything."

"Well, are you actually interested in playing piano?" I shrug again. Where is Mom going with this? She takes a moment and I watch as she seems to consider something. "Come here. I want to show you something." She then turns and heads toward the door that leads out into our garage. I get up and follow her, wondering what this could be about.

Our garage is a mess, filled with stuff my parents collected throughout the years that they never got around to getting rid of. One wall serves as a closet expansion lined with shelves, which houses purses and shoes from when Mom worked at a discount department store, prior to getting her job at the home. Another wall is reserved for Dad's tools. Back when they were really strapped for cash, he'd take on handyman jobs here and there on his days off. He doesn't do them much anymore, so his tools sit around gathering dust. The last wall is hidden by boxes and crates piled up from floor to ceiling. I follow Mom to the last wall, squeezing past the front of her car in order to do so. It's a wonder how my parents can fit a car in here, given how much stuff we've got.

"Mom, why do we have so much stuff?" I ask, looking over the pile. Like, seriously, what is all this? "We're not hoarders. Why not just get rid of it?"

"Some things are hard to get rid of," she replies, picking up a box which is sitting atop something wrapped in an old raggedy blanket.

"We could have a garage sale."

"You know what I mean, hon. Some things are just worth holding on to. I mean, look at this." She places the box on the cement floor and opens it, revealing a whole mess of old stuff toys, their color fading from age. She proceeds to sift around them a bit, before pulling out a felt rag doll, with brown yarn for hair and no nose. "If I remember right, this one was your favorite."

"Oh, my God, it's Daisy! I haven't seen her in forever. Has she been here all this time?" Mom nods. I take a second to look the doll over and then toss her back into the box with the rest of the old toys.

"You don't want to hold on to her?" Mom asks, now wearing a slight look of concern.

"I'm a little old to be playing with dolls, don't you think? Besides, it's meant for girls." Mom gives me a look.

I can't really tell, but she seems… I don't know, disappointed. "Is this what you wanted to show me?"

"No, actually, what I wanted to show you is this." She places her hands on the thing wrapped in the old blanket and then proceeds to unwrap it, revealing a worn and dusty electronic keyboard. It's covered in scratches, probably from being shoved away with all the boxes.

"Whose keyboard is this?" I ask. How is it that I didn't know it was here? How is it that I've never seen it before?

"Well, it used to be mine," Mom answers, her eyes lingering lovingly on the old thing.

"What? I didn't know you play piano."

"I *used* to play piano."

"How come you stopped?"

Mom shakes her head and sighs.

"Life," she says. "I was gonna sell it, but I didn't have the heart to. Then Artie spilt juice on it and that was that."

"Fuckin' Art."

"Hey!" Mom smacks my arm. She likes to pretend the language still offends her, but she's smiling so I know the smack is playful. She then turns back to the keyboard and goes quiet for a moment. "It's sad, you know, the reality that sometimes we put parts of ourselves away to become what we think we're supposed to be." Mom turns to me and gives me a curious look I can't quite make out. "This will be good for you to learn on, don't you think? If you're interested. I mean, the keys aren't weighted and, if I remember right, some of them screech when you press them, but it's something."

"Yeah, for sure," I say.

"I don't remember what happened to the stand, but the plug and pedal should be in one of these boxes. You just have to look around. I'm gonna go inside. It's hot in here." And with that, Mom hurries out of the garage and back into the house. It's funny, I always thought I knew my parents pretty well, but this whole surprise piano in the garage thing has me all mind blown. Like, how did I not know that my mom used to play piano? Like, what? But then again, there are some things my parents don't know about *me*, so I guess it's not too crazy.

It took a bit of digging after lunch to find the plug and pedal, but I managed to get the keyboard set up in my room. I had to clear off my desk just to give it a space. It's a bit smaller than the keyboard at school and the keys give little to no resistance, but I think I can work with it. It's basically the same thing, right? I grab my backpack and pull out my Piano book. I don't think I'm supposed to take it. I remember Mrs. Dolittle, at the beginning of the semester, saying that the books live in the room. But,

I mean, I took it to learn. What good are educational materials if you can't take them to study? I'll bring it back.

I press down on the keys, starting from the lowest note on the keyboard, and slowly work my way up. Note by note, the sound climbs the scales as my fingers travel the journey from left to right. It's surprisingly smooth, considering how old this thing must be. But then, as I get towards the middle, I strike a sour note. It's a sudden *blaaang* sound that comes out way louder than the rest of the notes. It's as if the keyboard is screaming in pain. I push the key again.

Blaaang!

Blaaang!

BLAAANG!!!

Yikes. It's the fucking Middle G. Are you kidding? Aside from Middle C, that's, like, the most important key. Well, shit. I continue along the course and find only one or two more sour notes. I guess that's not too bad. The notes repeat themselves, so I could always learn to play a song either higher or lower. Still, there's something about not having that Middle G that's just so disappointing. If I could just hit that spot without it screaming.

Just then, I get a notification on my phone, which I left sitting atop the keyboard. Without having to grab it, I see it's a notification from AphroDATEme. It must be Rudy. If I'm being honest, I'm not sure I want to talk to him. I'm still feeling a little raw about the whole him not kissing me thing and I don't know if I want to open myself up to him again. Not yet at least. But then, my phone chimes again. What does he want? I grab my phone, open AphroDATEme to check and, to my surprise, it's not from Rudy. No, it's from someone else. Someone with the username Lovely_RedBottoms.

I tap on the attached profile picture to get a better look at this Lovely_RedBottoms. He's a plump dude, and his picture is of him making duckface kissy lips with a sassy glint in his eye. I take a quick scroll through his photo album. His hair is cut short, and he seems to love a vest and t-shirt combo. In fact, he looks like he could be a former member of a boy band who went and got fat. That being said, he's not unattractive. Except for when he makes that stupid duckface, but let's be honest, no one's attractive making that stupid duckface.

I go back to my messages. Right below the message from Lovely_RedBottoms is my chat log with RudeFern69. Rudy. Seeing his username again, makes me hesitate. Should I respond to this new guy when things between Rudy and me went so well? But if it went so well, why do I feel so down about it? Why didn't he just kiss me? I stare at the two usernames, debating whether or not I should respond to the new one, when I get a text from Jake.

"Hey man! Wanna catch the Sunday manatee with me and Riles tomorrow?" the text reads. Umm… What? Immediately after, another text from him comes in. "We could go theater hopping. Make a day of it." Oh. That dumbass. Manatee, really, dude?

"Bro, it's matinee," I text back.

"Your mom's a matinee."

"Fuck off."

"So you coming or what?"

"Sure. Sounds good." I fuckin' hate Jake, but he's my buddy, so what can I say? I close the text box with him and head right back over to AphroDATEme. What could it hurt to just message the Lovely_RedBottoms back? I open his message. He's actually sent two.

"Hey," the first one reads.

"What's a guy like you doing on an app like this?" the second one says. I take a second. How do I want to respond to this? I start to think of Rudy, and I begin to replay all of last night in my mind. God, he was something else. I really thought that maybe, just maybe, we had something. Maybe there was something special between us, you know? Then I get to the end of the night, and suddenly I hear my dad's voice.

"Not everyone's gonna be a good fit for your team. Maybe this one just wasn't for you," his words repeat in my mind. Maybe…

I take a breath and start to type.

"Looking for guys like you," I write.
Hit send.

chapter eleven

I'm sitting at a table outside of a coffee shop in the early afternoon, nursing an iced americano and basking in the midday sun. I'm dressed in a baggy Hawaiian shirt I swiped from my dad, a pair of khaki shorts, and I've got on some aviator sunglasses that I grabbed from Art's room. It's already starting to feel like summer, so I figured I'd dress accordingly. I'm just trying to stretch out my legs after the half hour drive it took to get here.

See, the coffee shop I'm at is clear across town from where I live. It's situated on the outer edge of a shopping center, facing inward toward a series of local storefronts trying desperately to stay afloat next to a couple of big department stores. And where I'm seated actually gives me the perfect view to people watch. I'll be able to see my date approaching, which is why I'm here.

Somehow, yesterday I managed to talk Lovely_RedBottoms into going out with me. It was a quick conversation, cut and dry. Nothing too juicy:

> **Lovely_RedBottoms:** Hey.
>
> **Lovely_RedBottoms:** What's a guy like you doing on an app like this?
>
> **GoldenBoy513:** Looking for guys like you.
>
> **Lovely_RedBottoms:** Really?
>
> **Lovely_RedBottoms:** To be honest, I was kinda scared to message you.
>
> **GoldenBoy513:** Why?
>
> **Lovely_RedBottoms:** I haven't had a lot of great experiences on here with guys like you.
>
> **GoldenBoy513:** Guys like me?
>
> **Lovely_RedBottoms:** You know, gorgeous. [Grinning face with sweat emoji]
>
> **GoldenBoy513:** Lol. Well, thanks.
>
> **GoldenBoy513:** Hey, I know this is super short notice but what are you doing tomorrow?
>
> **Lovely_RedBottoms:** Nothing. Why?
>
> **GoldenBoy513:** Would you wanna hang out?

Lovely_RedBottoms: Like on a date?

GoldenBoy513: If you want it to be. No pressure tho.

Lovely_RedBottoms: Wow. Um… sure.

And just like that, I had a date. It happened really fast. I don't know what came over me. Maybe it was just the fact that I wasn't sitting on the idea of meeting him for however many days. There was no sense of worry or anticipation. And maybe that's how these things should happen. Like, why bother building something up that you're not sure is gonna work? Why not just jump in and see what happens? So, that's what I'm doing. I borrowed my mom's car to get here and I'm just gonna see how it goes.

While I'm waiting, I've got my piano app open and I'm absentmindedly plucking away at the keys to pass the time. It's kinda tough to get anywhere with it though since I've got the volume on low, being in public and all. Then, I get a text from Jake.

"Hey man you ready?" he writes. Ready? Ready for what? Another message comes in. "Riles and I are gonna swing by to get you." Shit. I totally forgot that I'd made plans to go to the movies with him and Riles. I guess I had my mind caught up on other things. What do I say that won't piss him off? And more importantly, what do I say that will get them to not go to my house? I told my mom I'd be hanging out with them today to get the car; I can't exactly have them show up at my door.

"GoldenBoy513?" I hear a voice say while I've got my nose buried deep in my phone. I look up and see a plump guy dressed in skinny jeans and a t-shirt and vest combo standing in front of me. I take a quick glance at him and notice the high tops he's wearing are covered in sequins and glitter, so much so it looks like an arts and crafts store exploded on his feet. That's not to say his shoes are ugly. They're just… loud. And here I thought my dad's Hawaiian shirt was a bold choice.

"Lovely_RedBottoms?" I ask, silencing my phone and slipping it into my pocket.

"Dan. Or Danny. Short for Daniel, but whichever is fine." He smiles, offering me a hand to shake. Poor guy seems nervous. Funny enough, I'm not. But I feel for him, considering I was him just the other night with Rudy. I stand up, take off my brother's aviators, and shake his hand.

"Andrew," I say. "Or Andrew. Short for Andrew, I guess." He laughs to himself, looking a little embarrassed. I slip my brother's aviators into the breast pocket of my dad's shirt, grab my drink from the table and casually take a sip. "Do you want anything? My treat." He nods and the two of us head inside the coffee shop where he orders one of those fancy blended ice coffee drinks with tons of caramel. At that point, it's not even coffee anymore, but I'm not judging. "So, uh, what do you want to do? I got the whole day free." I tell him as we're stepping out of the coffee shop.

"I don't know," he replies, sipping on his drink.

"Oh, come on. You don't have anything you want to do today? I'm down for about anything."

"Anything? Really?" He asks with a slight look of disbelief. I shrug.

"Why not?"

So we're currently standing in the shoe section of one of the department stores in the shopping center. Daniel is looking to see if they have any nice white canvas sneakers that he can draw on. Apparently, customizing shoes is a thing that he does, which explains the sequins and glitter on his high tops. Don't get me wrong, it's a cool enough hobby, but when I said I'd be down for about anything, I didn't expect shoe shopping to be on the list of things he might suggest. I don't know, I thought he'd suggest something like mini-golf, or laser tag, or getting some frozen yogurt. Hell, I'd even be chill with just chillin' at the coffee shop. But shoe shopping, really?

While Daniel's busy comparing two shoes that I swear are exactly the same, I feel my phone start to vibrate. I pull it out and check the screen. It's Riles. Shoot. Do I answer it? I don't want to be rude to Daniel by answering my phone, but at the same time, he's lost in his own little world of footwear, and I'm just… here. What do I do? And what do I say to Riles if I do answer it? He's probably calling about the movie we were supposed to catch, and I don't have an excuse not to go. At least not one that I can give him.

"So, Andrew, what's your favorite kind of shoe?" Daniel asks. I almost don't catch it; I'm too preoccupied debating about whether or not to answer Riles' call. The choice is made for me though when my phone stops ringing.

"What?" I reply, shoving my phone back into my pocket.

"Your favorite kind of shoe?" What the hell kind of question is that? Is this really what we're doing and talking about on our first date? I don't know how to answer that. Thankfully, I don't have to because he just goes on talking. At this point, I'm not sure if he's talking to me or to himself. "I personally love a good high top, but on the weekends when I'm feelin' myself, I pull out the red bottoms."

"Wait a minute, your username is a shoe reference?"

"Yeah, what'd you think it was?"

"Uh… Something else," I laugh, then he laughs, and suddenly we're laughing together.

"Does your mind always go to such naughty places?" he asks. There's a slight twinkle in his eye. It's the first time he's focused on me this entire date. Until now, the whole time he's been focused on shoes. I wonder if he's got a foot thing. Why anyone would be into feet is beyond me, but to each their own, I guess.

"Only on the weekends," I reply. Trying to look cool, I lean against the nearest shoe rack, placing my arm on a shoe box which then comes tumbling down. I do my best to catch it, but fumble so hard my football coach would never let me off the bench if he saw this. Daniel bursts out laughing again. Great, at least someone's enjoying themselves.

"You're too cute," he says, bending down to help me.

"Yeah? You like clumsy guys?"

"Depends on the guy." He shrugs then offers me a shy smile. Whatever it is I'm doing, I think it might be working. We put the fallen shoes back into their box, and I get up to put them back onto the rack.

"So, uh, you said you make shoes?" I ask, hoping to move the conversation along.

"I customize them."

"What made you wanna do that?"

"I don't know. I've always been into fashion. One day, I was bored so I just started drawing on my shoes.

Then, I started gluing stuff to them. People seemed to like them, and it made me feel good so…"

"Do you, like, sell them or anything?"

"Eh, I've made some for friends. I don't know if what I make is good enough for people to want to pay money for it. There's just a lot of competition out there."

"Yeah, I know the feeling." Daniel and I make eye contact, and something starts to click for me. Almost like we've found ourselves riding on the same wavelength. I see the twinkle in his eye again and it's got me excited. Maybe this date isn't a complete wash.

"So, you never answered my question," he then says. "What's your favorite kind of shoe?" Never mind. Just when I thought this date might actually be salvageable…

Anyway, we're making out in the backseat of his car. After Daniel decided none of the shoes he was looking at were worth buying, we found ourselves walking around the parking lot of the shopping center just talking. It was decent enough conversation. Better than the shoe talk, but nothing too exciting. That is until he mentioned he was glad I asked him out and that he finds me super attractive. That's when I asked him if he wanted to do stuff, and now here we are.

Kissing Daniel is… interesting, to say the least. When he kisses, he's all tongue and no lips, which would normally be bad, but his tongue's pierced, so his technique sorta works for him. It's like taking a spoonful of peanut butter that you think is the creamy kind, but it's actually the chunky kind. Like, it's not bad at all. It's just surprising. And with his mouth wide open, I can taste the hint of coffee on his breath from the blended drink he had earlier. It's kinda gross, but I can't stop myself. I want more.

Unlike a certain someone who I won't name at the moment, Daniel doesn't hesitate to kiss me. He doesn't put his hand on my face and push me away. He welcomes me with excitement that escapes on his shallow breath. I've got him on my lap, and I can feel his body pressing against mine in a way I've so longed for. There's a feeling growing deep within and below. It grows and grows until there's a throbbing sensation, and I can't control myself. I can't contain myself anymore. While our tongues continue to tangle themselves in one another, I reach down and attempt to undo the button on his jeans. Though I stop when I feel his hands suddenly grab onto mine.

"What are you doing?" Daniel asks breathlessly.

"Isn't this what you wanted?" I reply, making another attempt at his button. He stops me again, this time pushing my hands away.

"Stop it. I don't want that." Daniel then climbs off of me and scoots away so that there's a bit of space between us. I don't understand what's happening. I thought things were going so well. What gives? "I think this is moving really fast. I don't want to do anymore unless it's with someone I'm in a relationship with."

"So let's start a relationship," I suggest. It comes out casually. I don't know why I say it. It just feels like the thing to say, you know? I know I don't want this to stop. Not here. Not when it's throbbing.

"You don't mean that," Daniel says.

"Yeah, I do," I insist, as confident as if it were the truth.

"Look, Andrew, you're a nice guy and you're really cute. But we barely know each other."

"We could get to know each other."

"Maybe." He seems sad, unconvinced. Whatever excitement I had building quickly starts to shrink until it's as small as I feel. It's crazy how quickly things can turn. Just when I thought everything was going so well. The silence in the car is heavy with the afternoon heat mixed with our sweat. That would sound way sexier if anything more had happened.

As we sit in the quiet with only the steady hum of the car's AC, I decide there's nothing here for me after all. I grab my brother's aviators from my dad's shirt pocket, slip them on, then push the car door open.

"I should probably get going," I say. He nods, showing little, if any, emotion. That cold shoulder kinda hurts. I step out of the car and turn to say one more thing. "I'll be in touch. We'll talk soon." Maybe we will, maybe we won't. Who knows? Either way, so much for Daniel.

When I get home, I find Mom and Dad cuddled up on the couch watching an episode of some home buying show. You know, those shows where people who work as freelance candle makers, or some shit, are looking to buy a house and their budget is, like, five million dollars. They're always looking for a small house with room to grow, so they'll be needing twenty-two bedrooms, thirty-seven bathrooms, fifteen acres of backyard, and a space to "entertain." I just imagine these people holding visitors hostage while they attempt to perform some sort of fire juggling act on a unicycle. Ah, aspirational television. You gotta love it. Anyway, I hand my mom her car keys and try to leave towards my bedroom before this show can suck me in too.

"How was the movie?" I hear Dad ask, and I stop before I can get very far.

"What?" I reply.

"Riley and Jacob stopped by," Mom says, jumping in. "They said you guys were supposed to go to a movie." Fuck. I totally forgot to text them not to come over. Gotta think. Gotta think fast.

"We did," I lie, surprising even myself with how quickly it came out. "I don't know why they came over here. I told them I was gonna meet them there. Had to sit on the curb like a loner 'cause they showed up late."

"Uh huh…" Mom eyes me all suspicious, while Dad keeps his eyes focused on the TV, pretending he's not hearing this, as if he's not the one who started it. I swear he likes to throw me under the bus. Dad might be the man of the house, but really Mom's the one in charge. She's the one I gotta worry about getting in trouble with, so it comes as a relief when she lets me off the hook. "Okay," she says, her eyes still narrowed with suspicion.

"Okay then. I will be in my room," I reply, backing away slowly and then turning to head down the hall to my bedroom. It's been enough of a day. All I want to do is lay down and forget about Daniel, and his shiny shoes, and his coffee breath. Maybe I'll even try to find that home buying show my parents are watching on my TV. It'd help keep my mind off things. I mean, having one rejection was bad enough, but having two over the same weekend — nah, bro. I'm good off that.

I'm good…

chapter twelve

Monday. May 26th.

I'm sitting in third period English, tapping my fingers on my desk as if it were keys to a piano. My teacher, Ms. Maple, is reading *The Raven* by Edgar Allen Poe aloud to us because I guess that's her idea of a fun time, considering there's less than three weeks of school left. She's a sad and depressing woman who looks like she could snap at any moment. Now that I'm thinking about it, *The Raven* seems pretty appropriate.

I'm starting to space out. It's not that I find the poem boring, it's just that Ms. Maple is taking her sweet time, stopping at the end of every other sentence to ask us what we all think the narrator is saying. At this point, I don't fuckin' know because we keep stopping. That's when I feel my phone vibrate in my pocket. I pull it out to check it underneath my desk, and to my surprise, it's from Rudy.

"Hey, you. Hope you're having a great day at school. My first final kicked my ass," his message reads. Huh, I don't know how I feel about this. Hearing from him after not hearing from him all weekend, especially after the kiss thing is… confusing. And considering I had time to go out with and make out with someone else since, a part of me wants to just go, "Nevermore." It is what it is, you know? And what it is, is nothing at all. So, I fight off the urge to reply and shove my phone back into my pocket.

"'On the morrow he will leave me, as my hopes have flown before,'" Ms. Maple reads. You said it, Edgar. You said it.

Just as Ms. Maple takes another break to question the class on what she'd just read, the bell rings. Thank God. This period was going on way longer than it ever should. I gather my things together, shove it all in my backpack, then exit the room, lazily making my way over to fourth period History. Ugh, Milano. Honestly, knowing that I've got an hour of suffering through the smell of foot cheese makes Ms. Maple reading and discussing poetry with herself sound like a fun time. At least this is past the half-way point of my day. And Milano pays less attention in class than half the class does, so it shouldn't be too bad.

"Yo, Drewster!" I hear a familiar voice call from behind as I'm crossing the street towards the annex. I turn around and see Riles jogging towards me, looking jolly as ever. I give him a second to catch up, thinking nothing of it. "Hey, man," he says, slowing to match my pace.

"Hey, what up?" I reply.

"Nothing much. So, what happened to you yesterday?" Shit. The day's been dragging on so long, I didn't bother to come up with an excuse as to why I bailed on the movies yesterday. I had half-hoped he'd forgotten about that. I mean, *I* pretty much did.

"Yesterday, uh… Yeah, yesterday was a… Yesterday was a day. I'd really rather not talk about it."

Riles nods.

"Fair enough," he says, and I breathe a sigh of relief. I just bought myself some time to come up with an actual story. I know Jake's gonna ask about yesterday too. And unlike Riles, Jake's a little more *enthusiastic* about things. Once his mind's fixed on something, he doesn't let it go. I doubt he'd let me off the hook as easily. Looks like the next hour is gonna be spent thinking up some kind of excuse. Story time. Fun…

Mr. Milano has randomly decided to start teaching. I don't know why. It's basically the end of the year. He must be making up for lost time or something. I had planned to spend the period plotting out what I was gonna say to Jake about yesterday, but no. Instead, I had to listen to Mr. Milano give a lecture about *The Articles of Confederation,* which then turned into something about owning an alligator in Florida because states have different laws and stuff. I don't even know. I just heard the word alligator and was like, "That's cool." But as informative as that was, it really just distracted me from getting my story straight — not that my story is straight to begin with. If only Riles had given back his damn Rubik's cube.

Anyway, we're walking over to the cafeteria — me and Riles — and my brain is doing some serious mental gymnastics, trying to think of an explanation that would satisfy Jake. What do I tell him? Oh, I didn't go to the movies with you, and I wasn't home yesterday because, uh, I died. Ugh, kill me now.

I know it might seem like I'm overreacting, but I've known Jake since freshman year. He's never been one to let things go. One time, he went through a drive thru to pick up some food and they forgot to give him a straw for his drink. He complained about it for literal days and still refuses to go to said drive thru. It's been, like, a year. And that's not even the most extreme case.

Back in freshman year, my dad took me to this sports center with all these trampolines for my birthday. With my mom and brother coming, we couldn't fit more than one extra person in the car. I decided to invite Riles — he's always been more chill — and didn't mention it to Jake. Why would I? Well, Riles' dumbass let it slip and Jake got pissed because he didn't even know it was my birthday, which I guess is something he expected me to tell him. But Riles didn't know either until I invited him. Anyway, Jake started avoiding me for a while, acting like me excluding him meant I didn't want to be his friend. And when I confronted him about him being a brat, he swung on me. The dude might be small, but he's scrappy. I kicked his ass though, and we didn't talk for a while. Eventually we made up, but he's been butthurt about it ever since. Which actually, now that I think about it, might be why he was so quick to tell Becca about my birthday. He said he didn't mean to, but I wouldn't put it past him.

"Hey, look who decided to show up," Jake says when me and Riles find him in the cafeteria at lunch. He's staring at me with his little beady eyes, looking all expectant, when we approach the table he's sitting at. I feel my stomach tighten and start to sink. I still don't have a well thought out excuse for him. "What happened to you yesterday?" he asks, and I sigh. I can't help myself.

"I'd rather not talk about it," I reply.

"Dude, what do you mean you'd rather not talk about it? I texted you, we went to your house, your parents said you already left to meet us, and then you ghosted us. What happened to you?" I sigh again.

"Look, yesterday was… a day, okay? And I really don't wanna think about it anymore."

"Think about what anymore?"

"Dude, Jake, just drop it," Riles says, jumping in. "He says he doesn't wanna talk about it, so he doesn't wanna talk about it." He then drops his backpack onto the table and walks off toward the lunch line. Part of me wants to do the same, but I see Jake staring at me, and against my better judgement, I have to make sure we're okay.

"You look annoyed," I say, taking a seat at the table across from him.

"I am annoyed," he replies. "Drew, I don't understand why you're not telling me what happened yesterday. You're supposed to be my best friend." Ugh, why is he pulling out the best friend card? It's so petty. Like, ew.

"Well, if you were my best friend, you'd accept that I don't want to talk about it." I'm starting to get really frustrated with him. Why does he have to make this so difficult?

"And if you were *my* best friend, you'd just be willing to tell me." We're staring at each other, both our eyes narrowed like a pair of poker players trying to read each other. Which one of us is gonna fold first?

. . .

Me. It's gonna be me. Jacob Levi Bowen is too stubborn. We'll be having this staring contest all day if I don't let him win.

"Fine, you really wanna know what happened yesterday?" I say suddenly, folding my hand. "I popped a tire on the way to meet you." What? I wasn't gonna tell him the truth. That was the first thing I came up with. I'm bullshitting. Kinda like how I write my papers in English when I don't bother to do the assigned reading. "My mom's car didn't have a spare and when I called my parents, they didn't pick up, so I sat there for, like, an hour just hitting redial until they finally answered." Jacob's looking at me with this bewildered look, which makes me nervous because I'm not sure he believes me.

"That's what you didn't want to talk about? A popped tire?" Yeah, that excuse didn't land as well as I would've hoped. It kinda just makes me seem overdramatic. I guess I could lean into that.

"Look, the whole thing was super annoying, and I was already having a rough morning as it was. Okay?"

"So, then why didn't you just answer your phone? Me and Riles could've came and got you. We could've helped."

"Bro, I was trying to reach my parents after blowing out their tire. I'm sorry that you weren't at the top of my priority list!" My voice comes out way louder than it should. I was getting so frustrated with him. Jacob looks pissed, and I realize now just what I said and how bad it must've sounded to him.

"Wow, tell me how you really feel," he says.

"Dude, come on. You know I don't mean it like that."

"Do I?" he replies, and the question hits me like a sucker punch to the gut. I care about my friends. I hate to think that they think I don't. And I hate that he's making me feel like that right now.

"Sorry," I offer. "Can we not talk about it anymore?"

"Yeah, sure," he says. Thank God, this conversation could not have ended soon enough. I pull off my backpack, thinking I'm gonna head over to the lunch line, but then stop when Jacob says something else. "You know, Drew, sometimes I get the feeling that you're hiding stuff from me. Especially lately." Don't do it, Andrew. Don't take the bait. We're almost out of the woods. Don't turn back now. But I can't help myself.

"What do you mean?" I ask.

"I dunno," Jacob shrugs. "You've just been really vague. *Are* you hiding something from me?"

"What would I have to hide?"

"You tell me." Why can't he just let things go? Why can't he just accept whatever I'm willing to give? I scoff and shake my head. Then, I get up and head over to the lunch line. I'm a mix of emotions right now. I want to tell Jacob. I want to come clean and tell him everything, but I'm just so pissed that he's prying and that I'm being made to feel guilty for not sharing everything. Like, let me be, you know? I don't want to come out because someone wants to know everything. I don't want to come out for someone else, I'm not dating anyone. This is about me. And if I want to keep it a secret, why can't people just let me? Where's the harm in that?

chapter thirteen

Tonight, I'm standing outside of the local 24-hour diner — the same diner where I had my date with Rudy. He's been messaging me a few times every day since Monday, and on Thursday I finally decided to message him back. I didn't want to, but he's been incessant, "tapping on my chamber door." Like *The Raven*… I think Ms. Maple got to me.

RudeFern69: Hey. How you been?
GoldenBoy513: Hi.
RudeFern69: !!!!!

RudeFern69: He speaks! And here I thought the dead don't talk.

GoldenBoy513: ?

RudeFern69: Were you ghosting me?

GoldenBoy513: Sorry. Been busy. Finals coming up. You know how it is.

RudeFern69: That I do.

GoldenBoy513: So what's new?

RudeFern69: Not much. Been busy. Finals. You know how it is.

RudeFern69: Anyway, I been thinking about you a lot. Hoping I could see you again.

GoldenBoy513: Yeah. Sure.

GoldenBoy513: Now's not really a good time tho. Maybe in like a week?

RudeFern69: Yeah. Why don't you just message me when you're free.

GoldenBoy513: Will do.

Awkward, right? And to be honest, I still haven't figured out how I feel about the whole situation. At this point, I'm kinda convinced that Rudy's not the one, but he keeps coming back, so I don't know. Right now, I don't really want to think about him because I'm here waiting for my date.

Yesterday, after Rudy and I talked, I noticed I had an unread message from a GlitterBabeXOXO. When I clicked on the profile picture to check him out, he was not at all what I was expecting. With a username like his,

I was expecting to see someone who looked like a sassy beauty vlogger or something. Maybe even a full on drag queen. I mean, I could get down with it. I think. I'd be willing to try. But no, instead what I found was a slightly hefty, slightly older, well put together, normal looking dude. And when I say "normal," I mean it in the sense that vanilla ice cream is normal. So, why not?

Just like with Lovely_RedBottoms, I approached GlitterBabe with the same straight forwardness — or in this case, *gay* forwardness — that got me the date with the shoe man. So, to Daniel's credit, at least I got something from that experience. You know, aside from blue balls and the sorry slap of rejection.

GlitterBabeXOXO: Hi.

GlitterBabeXOXO: I just wanted to say you're very attractive.

GoldenBoy513: Thanks.

GlitterBabeXOXO: I also like football.

GoldenBoy513: You read my bio.

GlitterBabeXOXO: Yeah, it was a pretty hefty read.

GoldenBoy513: Lol.

GoldenBoy513: You like that typo I left in there?

GlitterBabeXOXO: So that was intentional?

GoldenBoy513: Not at all.

GlitterBabeXOXO: Hahaha!

GoldenBoy513: So what are you doing tomorrow? You wanna meet up?

GlitterBabeXOXO: Wow. How very forward.

GoldenBoy513: Eh, I know what I'm looking for.

GlitterBabeXOXO: And what's that?

GoldenBoy513: Probably the same thing you are. [Winky face emoji]

GlitterBabeXOXO: Hehe why not?

GoldenBoy513: It's a date then.

And here we are. I never would've thought it'd be this easy to find guys to go out with. For the longest time, the only two gay guys I knew were dating each other, and here I am about to go out with my third guy in, like, two weeks. It's crazy how the world opens up for you when you just put yourself out there. I feel like I've been blessed by Aphrodite. Don't tell Jesus though, because my family's Catholic. Non-practicing, but still.

GlitterBabe should be here pretty soon. We agreed on a dinner date. I'm dressed in some khaki pants and the nicest button up I could find in my dad's closet. I've even got on one of his ties. I figured I should dress appropriately, you know? And with the date starting later, I was able to borrow Dad's SUV, so I won't have to wait around afterwards. This guy's older; I want to come off as impressive and mature as possible. I mean, how lame does "I'm waiting for my dad to pick me up" sound on a first date? Been there, done that, look how that turned out.

I'm tapping the keys of my piano app on my phone when I notice a slightly hefty, slightly older guy in a bomber jacket and glasses approaching. I shut my phone off, slip it into my back pocket, and go to meet him.

"GlitterBabe?" I ask.

"Uh, yeah," he replies with a sort of embarrassed smile. "It's Paul."

"Andrew."

"Yeah, I got that from your profile. I gotta say, you're very good looking." I crack a smile at the compliment. This is off to a good start.

"You don't think I'm overdressed? I could always take something off."

Paul furrows his brow, and he gives me this look like he doesn't know what to say, but then he bursts out laughing.

"You're funny," he says. "Should we go in?" I nod and we walk over to the entrance, where I promptly hold the door open for him. I notice he doesn't comment on it, and I'm struck with a sudden flashback of Rudy. I picked this diner again because I know it's cheap and not the most popular place to be at on a Friday night. But maybe next time I should pick somewhere else. Anyway, we get seated at a table and our waitress, an older lady who looks like she'd be named Doris or whatever, hands us a couple of menus. I try to put Rudy out of my mind. Right now, it's about me and Paul.

"So, why GlitterBabe?" I ask while flipping through a menu, as if I'm not just gonna default to ordering a burger and fries.

"Embarrassing, isn't it?" Paul says, smiling. "It was my girlfriend's idea. You know, a friend who's a girl. When I told her I was gonna try online dating, she insisted in being the one to set up my account, and she had to pick the worst name imaginable. She threw in the XOXO for 'stylistic effect.'" He laughs. "And you, GoldenBoy513? I assume the number's your birthday, but Golden Boy? Is that just what people call you?"

"I mean, I try," I say. I'm trying to seem impressive. I'm not about to get into the ins and outs of why I picked my username right now. It's not the right vibe for that. We're smiling, we're laughing. We're keeping it chill.

"So, Andrew, what do you do?" he then asks.

"I'm just in school right now," I reply.

"What's your major? What are you studying?" My stomach twists a little. I hadn't mentioned to him that I'm still in high school, but now that we're sitting here talking about what we do, it feels a little late for that. And remember, I'm trying to seem impressive.

"Uh, you know, general ed stuff. Nothing all that exciting." That's when Doris shows up at our table to check in with us. Thank God and/or Aphrodite. Whoever's up there. Paul orders a soda and I get a water.

"You boys ready to order some food, or do you need a minute?" Doris asks.

"A minute," I say, sending Doris on her way. I look at Paul, who's now flipping through his menu. I'm analyzing his face. He's got a piggish little nose and some chubby cheeks. I can't decide if I think he's cute or not. Does that make me an asshole? I then catch myself wondering if he should've ordered that soda. *That* makes me an asshole.

"Why are you looking at me like that?" Paul asks. I've been so caught up in my own head, I didn't even realize he was looking back at me. "Do I have something on my face?"

"No, I'm just admiring God's handiwork," I say, repeating the line Rudy used so effectively on me. Paul furrows his brow, looking at me like I'm being stupid. I probably am, but I think it's working on him because he starts smiling. "So, Paul, what do you do?"

"I work at Mobile Mart," he explains.

"The cell phone place?"

"Yup. I spend my days selling unlimited texting plans to old people who can't text. Half the job is helping them set up their social media accounts." He laughs. I don't know why, what he said wasn't funny, but I laugh along to humor him.

"Was that, like, the dream; to sell cell phones?" I ask.

"No, I'm actually working on getting a Psychology degree. I want to be a child social worker."

"Wouldn't you have to be a child to be a child social worker?" He bursts out laughing at this, and I'm starting to find it a little infectious. I could get with this. "So, you like kids?"

"Yeah, I love kids," he replies. "That's one thing that I really want; to start a family. It's just tough though because I feel like a lot of gay guys don't want to have kids."

"Well, at least you can have fun trying," I joke. Paul furrows his brow again, then lets out a small chuckle.

"Yeah, I guess so."

Doris returns to drop off our drinks and to take our food order. I default to ordering a burger and fries, while Paul orders a meat lover's breakfast for dinner, complete with a side of pancakes. I can't help but wonder if that was a good decision on his part...

Fuck! I am an asshole! Stop it, Andrew! Stop it! It's none of your business. And honestly, I don't know why I'm so focused on it. Daniel had a similar frame. But then again, Daniel had the foot fetish to keep me distracted. Get it together, Andrew. If you're gonna get anywhere with this dude, keep the conversation going and focus on the positives! What are the positives though? Well, for one, he's been laughing a lot, so I take it that means he's interested. That's something.

When our food arrives, I notice the arrangement of ham, eggs, and sausage that make up the meat lover's breakfast. Paul rubs his hands together, all excited to dig in. It's kind of amusing.

"Someone's excited," I comment.

"I'm so hungry. I love meat," he replies, wasting no time unwrapping the rolled napkin from his silverware.

"I'm sure you do."

"What?" He stops, his fork hovering over the sausage. He's staring blankly at me, like a deer in headlights. I return his gaze with a smile and a wink. His eyes shift around momentarily before he drives his fork into the sausage. I casually pop a fry into my mouth.

About half my burger into dinner, Paul and I find ourselves talking into a nice groove. It's become a little more than small talk, but not quite intimate conversation. But that'll change if I have anything to do with it.

"If you were a farmer, and you were stuck on a deserted island, and could only grow one type of crop, what would it be?" Paul asks.

"Is being stuck on a deserted island something you think about a lot?" I reply. "Because I can tell you one thing. Growing crops would not be at the top of my priority list." It would be sex, but I'm trying to be impressive so I'm practicing my noo-aunce. Noo-ants? You know, subtlety.

"Well, then you'd probably die," Paul says casually.

"So, what would you pick?" I ask.

"Probably corn. It's really versatile."

"You sure it wouldn't be eggplant?" Paul furrows his brow again at this and gives me the slightest of slight smiles.

"Eggplants aren't very versatile," he explains.

"Oh, but they're so much more fun that way." I raise my eyebrows, suggestively. Paul laughs, but he seems a little stiff now. If that's how he wants to play it, I've got a stiff one ready to go.

After we're done eating, Doris comes by to clear our plates and offer us dessert. I decline and she hands us the bill before disappearing behind the diner counter.

"This was fun," Paul says.

"Yeah," I agree. "Hey, where do you live, if you don't mind my asking?"

"Actually, not too far from here. I live with my grandma."

"That's cool. I was thinking we could hang out," I explain. "I live with my parents, so it'd have to be at your place."

"Uh, sure, maybe. I guess."

"Cool. So, I'll meet you there?"

"What?" Paul furrows his brow yet again. The guy really likes to furrow his brow. This time though, he doesn't laugh or smile. "You meant, like, tonight?" Is he playing hard to get? Am I really gonna have to explain myself? Isn't it obvious?

"Well, I was thinking we'd meet up at your place after this and, I don't know, fool around? I'm down for anything." Paul stares at me, his brow still furrowed. There's a weird moment of silence between us before he says anything.

"I'm sorry, Andrew, but I'm... I'm really uncomfortable right now," he says. Uncomfortable? Why? Why would he be uncomfortable? I don't understand. "What exactly did you think this was?" he then asks. What does he mean? What is he asking me? I thought it was a date. Isn't this what people do on dates? They hang out for a bit, decide if they're into each other, and then, you know, get *into* each other? Isn't that what this is?

"I don't know," I shrug, not wanting to sound stupid, though I think it might be too late for that.

"Were you just trying to get me into bed?" Paul asks, and I don't know how to respond to that. Yes? No, that seems like a dick move. But why? I thought we were having a nice time, so of course I'm gonna try to get him into bed. Is that so wrong? I... I honestly don't know what to say, so I don't say anything. I just sit here, waiting for him to say whatever he needs to. "Well, I feel like an idiot. Thank you for hanging out, but I think I'm gonna get going." Paul reaches into his pocket, pulls out his wallet, and drops a twenty on the table. "It was nice talking to you," he says, scooting his chair back.

"Hang on," I say. "You're just gonna leave? Just like that? I thought we were having a good time. What gives?" Paul pauses, then takes a breath.

"Andrew, look. I haven't had a lot of good luck with this online dating thing. You seem like a nice enough guy, but if you're only looking for one thing, I don't think anything's gonna work out between us. So, uh, I'm gonna go. It was nice meeting you." And just like that, he gets up and leaves. Wow. Way to make a guy feel bad.

I decide I'd rather not sit around looking like a loner, so I drop a ten on the table and quietly exit the diner. Doris can keep the change. No sense in everyone having a bad night over this. I'm so fucking annoyed. Who the hell does Paul think he is? He doesn't know the first thing about me, and here he is implying — painting me as some sort of man slut. I haven't even had sex! And believe me, it's not for lack of trying. Ugh, I'm over this. I'm over this whole night. I just want to go home.

When I get in my dad's SUV, I pull out my wallet and my phone out of habit. I keep those things in my back pockets because I hate the way they feel in my front pockets, but I also hate sitting on them. The struggle! Anyway, I drop my wallet into the pocket of the arm rest just under the door handle and am about to do the same with my phone, when I notice it's lit with a notification. It's a notification from AphroDATEme. I swear, if it's a message from Rudy, I'm not in the mood to deal. But to my surprise, it's not. It's a message from someone with the username PocketSizedPrince. I tap on the profile picture and see it's this bright-eyed guy with the biggest smile. He looks to be on the younger side, but who am I to talk? I'm barely legal myself. I scroll through his other pictures and find one of him at what looks to be a gym. It's one of those full-length mirror selfies that fitness influencers are always posting. Judging by his pictures, this guy looks tiny, but he's in good shape, unlike *some* people. Then I navigate to his bio, which confirms it. The first line reads:

> *4'11" menace to society.*
> *Try to tame me. I dare you.*

Challenge accepted.

I navigate back to my inbox and open the message from PocketSizedPrince.

"Free tomorrow?" is all it reads. Without even giving it a moment's thought, I type in my response.

"Time and place?" I message back. Paul might've been a bust, but that doesn't mean the next guy will be. And I'm intrigued by this allegedly four-foot eleven menace.

"Not everyone's gonna be a good fit for your team. Maybe this one just wasn't for you," I hear my dad's words echo in my mind. The fact that I have another guy waiting on the bench, itching to play, right when the one I'm playing with pulls himself from the game, says to me that someone or *something* is looking out for me and my romantic dealings. I'm putting my money on the slutty one.

Also, fuck Paul.

Or, in this case, don't fuck Paul. He doesn't want it. I already asked.

chapter fourteen

It's a little before noon. I'm waiting in my mom's car near a coffee shop just outside the local mall. Not the good mall in the neighboring city, but the mall in town that's barely staying afloat. Aside from the 24-hour gym and a bougie chain department store, the place is pretty much a ghost town. All the good shops inside closed down and they even took out the fountain that was the main draw for kids to hang out at. If I remember right, they replaced it with an Orange Julius, which was cool until that closed down too. Everything closing down up in there. But I haven't been inside in a hot minute, so whatever. The mall's not why I'm here anyway.

I get a notification from AphroDATEme. It's a message from one PocketSizedPrince.

"Hey, I'm here. Where you at?" the message reads.

"Parked under a tree by the coffee shop drive thru," I message back. I look around the parking lot through the windshield to see if I can spot him. Should be hard to miss. I mean, I don't know too many guys under five-foot, so — actually, that might make him easier to miss. I scan around and spot a small guy in gray sweatpants standing on the curb in front of the entrance to the coffee shop. "That you in the gray sweats?" If that is him, thank God I didn't get dressed up for this. I'm dressed in a pair of burgundy basketball shorts and a loose-fitting gray tee. I figured since it's a morning coffee date that I should look relaxed. Don't want to come off like a tryhard, you know?

"Yeah. Where are you?" he sends.

"I'll come to you," I reply.

"No. I'll come to you. Flash your headlights." So I do. Why he doesn't want me to just go to him is beyond me. I mean, aren't we gonna go inside to get coffee? Whatever. I see him start to make his way over to me and I think nothing more of it. I wave to him as he approaches. When he gets to my car, before I can get out to greet him, he opens the door to the backseat and hops in. Yeah… I have no idea what's happening.

"Andrew, right?" PocketSized asks.

"Uh, yeah," I reply.

"Charlie." We go silent for a moment, and I take a good long look at him from the rearview. He's cute. Smaller than I imagined. Like, I knew he'd be short, but I dunno, his pictures made him seem bigger. It's all about the angles, I guess. Still, there's something about his small stature that excites me. Is that gross? That's probably gross. Then I notice a smile forming on his mouth. "Are you gonna join me or are you just gonna sit there?"

"What? Back there?" I ask. As soon as I say it, I realize how stupid I sound. Of course he means back there. Where else, you idiot? Charlie shrugs, smiling, never breaking his gaze from mine in the rearview. I feel my heart start to pound, and immediately I open the car door, climb out of the driver's seat, and join him in the back.

"Good lord," he says, practically whispering. "You're so fucking cute." Our eyes lock together and it's like the world outside my mom's car just ceases to exist. I feel my breath start to grow heavy.

"You're so…" I begin but can't seem to find a word more appropriate than the thing I hear myself say, "small." He just laughs.

"Does that turn you on?"

"Yeah." And before I even know what's happening, his lips are on my lips, his tongue is on my tongue, and he's on my lap like it's Christmas and I'm Santa. Just add our names to the naughty list right now. We bump, and grind, and roll, and sigh. We steal each other's breath and breathe life into one another with every kiss, as if the air in this car were running out. Then, suddenly, Charlie slides off my lap and pulls the front of his sweats down, revealing himself to me. I can't say it's impressive. It's relative to his size, but still. Holy shit. Then, just like that, he pulls his sweats back up and goes back to kissing me, comfortably, as if he didn't just whip his dick out at me. Out of context, this would probably be hilarious, but right now, I'm into it. I'm into him, which is funny. Being a six-foot-tall guy, I always imagined I'd be with a guy close to my height, give or take a few, but I never imagined being with someone who could probably fit in one of my pant legs. Like, literally.

We kiss and kiss and let our tongues twist until we're both eventually out of breath. I'm spent, and we've only been at it for, like, fifteen minutes. I don't think I've ever made out with someone like this. Who knew just kissing could be so exhausting? And, since I didn't think to put the AC on before all this, I'm drenched in sweat and feel like I just spent the morning running hurdle drills and doing, like, a bajillion burpees.

"I gotta get going," Charlie says with a sigh. It kinda throws me.

"That's it? You're just gonna go?" I ask. I'll admit, hearing this does have me a little disappointed. I mean, you're just gonna take my breath away and run away with it? Really?

"I have to work," he explains.

"Well, how about we meet up after? Let me take you to dinner."

"That sounds nice."

"What time do you get off?"

"Six. It's a stupid four-hour shift."

"Great, so how about we meet around seven? I'll message you where," I suggest. He smiles and then kisses me softly on the lips.

"Okay," he agrees. "See you then." And with that, he opens the door, climbs out of my mom's car, and heads off. I watch him as he goes, and stare at his tiny little butt until I lose sight of him in the parking lot. I feel this uncomfortable sensation below the waist. I'm throbbing. As great as having a penis is, they're not always the most comfortable things to have. Especially in moments like this. I should probably get home to deal with it.

I have about sixty bucks left from the hundred I got for my birthday. And since I'm not about to go to the same diner two nights in a row, nor do I want to have random little things remind me of the Rude Fern, I decided on a bit of an upgrade for my date with Charlie tonight. We're going to Antonini's. I realize this might be more of a risk with Antonini's being a pretty popular place in town on the weekends, but unless someone I know is having a birthday, I don't imagine I'll be running into anyone. Not anyone of any consequence anyway.

I'm feeling pretty good. Considering me and Charlie already made out and he's shown me his pork sword, I don't see any way that tonight could go south like the way my date with Paul did — fuck Paul. Anyway, I'm feeling pretty confident. I got a couple condoms I stole from my dad's underwear drawer in my back pocket, and I'm all dressed up in his white button up, a red hoodie, and jeans. I kinda look like that one dude from those old, old movies that everyone references, but no one's ever seen. You know, unless you're a film buff, which is, like, super pretentious. Actually, come to think of it, I think I know the reference because my brother might've watched it. That nerd. Speaking of, Art's supposed to be coming home for the summer next weekend. Ugh, I don't even want to think about that.

When I get inside Antonini's, the place is already crowded. I fall in line behind a group standing near the host stand, then pull out my phone to check the time. 6:54pm. I'm a bit early, but it's fine. Judging by the fact that there are no open seats in the entrance lobby for-yay — foy-er? area, I'm assuming the wait might be a while. When Charlie gets here, I'm sure we can find something to keep us occupied. Wink. Wink. Nudge. Nudge.

"Hi, how many — Oh… It's you…" I hear a somewhat familiar voice greet me in the most unenthusiastic tone. I look up and see Molly/Miranda… Monica? You know, What's-her-face. Erik-Potato-Park's friend.

"You're working tonight?" I say. It's not really a question. It's more of a statement of my annoyance. Like a sigh, but with words.

"No, I just do this for fun." The sarcasm is strong with this one. She narrows her eyes with so much hatred, I can't help but flinch.

"Uh, table for two," I mumble. She stares at me for a moment, almost as if she's trying to figure out if I'm just here to fuck with her. If that's the case, I'm not. I'm just trying to go on a date, walk out of here with a boyfriend, and maybe get laid. Maybe not in that particular order, not that it's any of her business.

"Wait's gonna be about forty minutes," she says, still narrow-eyed, still staring.

"Okay."

"And your whole party has to be here before I can seat you."

"Okay."

She then flashes me the most pleasantly hostile smirk I've ever seen. It's like looking into the face of the devil. I back away slowly, keeping my eyes on her as I go, in case she gets the urge to stab me with her pen, or something. Also, what the hell is her name? Mileena? No, that can't be right. Though, she does have eyes like daggers. And she could probably eat me alive.

I head outside to wait for Charlie. It's warm out with a gentle breeze. I roll up the sleeves of my hoodie and check the time. My phone reads 6:58pm. He should be here pretty soon. Until then, I open the piano app on my phone and start plucking out the all too familiar starting notes of *Moonlight Sonata.*

G hashtag, C hashtag, E normal.

G hashtag, C hashtag, E normal.

What is the note that comes next after this part? I guess I'll just repeat the same three notes over, and over, and over… Man, I wish I could play this with both hands right now. With the sun just starting to set like it is, everything sorta has this orange glow about it, and this would be the perfect song to have playing in the background. Just picture it, the world all bright and orange, and over the course of the song, it slowly changes to pink, then purple, until eventually everything's covered in the dark blue of the nighttime. Sick. That sounds romantic as fuck.

Speaking of romance, what time is it? 7:09pm. No biggie. What's-her-face said it'd be a forty-minute wait. I'm sure Charlie's on his way. And when he gets here, we'll have some time to kill. Since I can't remember what comes after the first couple measures of *Moonlight Sonata* — which is super difficult when you're only playing with one hand 'cause it all sounds the same — I decide that's enough piano for now, and open AphroDATEme. I navigate to my inbox and tap the conversation I had with Charlie earlier.

GoldenBoy513: Hey, you're probably busy at work, but I'm thinking maybe we do Antonini's. You know it?

PocketSizedPrince: I love Antonini's!

GoldenBoy513: Great. So see you at 7?
PocketSizedPrince: Sounds good.
PocketSizedPrince: Oop. My break's up. Ttyl.

I'm debating whether or not I should message him. Would that be weird? I don't want to come off as needy, you know? It *has* only been, like, ten minutes from the time we agreed to meet. Hmm… To message or not to message? I think I'll wait.

7:24pm.
Still no sign of Charlie.
"Hey, where you at?" I message him. I wonder what could be holding him up. He said he'd be here. I can see the short conversation we had about tonight floating above the message I just sent. I'm not crazy, right? He did say he'd be here. I read our conversation again. Huh, well, he didn't say he'd be here *exactly*, but he did say, "sounds good," and that's basically the same thing. I figure I should head inside and check in with What's-her-face about our table.

"You're still here?" What's-her-face says when I approach her at the host stand.

"Just checking where I am on the list," I explain, trying to seem as friendly as possible. She rolls her eyes and checks the tablet she's got sitting on the host stand. Antonini's been upgrading. I remember when they used to use just a clipboard and some dry erase markers on a clear sheet of plastic with the table layout printed under it. They must've saved a bunch of money on not having tablecloths.

"So, you're actually next," What's-her-face tells me. "But I can't seat you until your entire party is here."

"Right. But what if he's late? Like, do I lose my place in line, or do I get bumped to the bottom, or something?" She narrows her eyes, a little less hostile this time, then cocks her head to the side.

"Are you on a date?" she asks. "Are you, like, trying to seem impressive or something?"

"That's none of your business."

"I'm just asking. By the way, can you move so I can help the next guests?" She waves her hand, shooing me away, so I take a step to the side. That's when I notice the "guests" who were standing behind me. It's a couple. It's Erik Park and his hot-fucking-boyfriend. Really, Universe? You're gonna rub *that* in my face. Jesus must be pissed that I've been praising Aphrodite or something, 'cause this is just mean.

"Hi, Andrew," Erik says, offering me a small half-hearted smile that makes him look super uncomfortable.

"Hey," I reply, trying my best to seem unbothered. "You guys, uh, here on a special occasion?"

"Nah, I just wanted pasta," Nick says, jumping in. His tone is friendly enough, but his expression is blank. "You?"

"I'm here… on a date," I explain. "Well, I'm waiting on my date. Should be here soon. The wait here's crazy though."

"Yeah, these places always are on the weekend," Nick replies. "That's why I called in a reservation." He pats me on the shoulder, then turns to What's-her-face, who then has them follow her into the dining room. As they go, I watch Nick place a hand on the small of Erik's back. Seeing that tiny gesture takes my breath away in a way unlike how Charlie took my breath in the backseat of my mom's car. I want *that*, those tiny gestures.

"Good job, Mr. Park," I mumble to myself.

8:15pm.

I'm waiting outside now. It's too crowded to wait inside, so I'm watching the orange world quickly fade to blue in real time. It's faster and far less romantic than I imagined. And quieter too since I'm not in the mood to try to play the music for this scene.

Charlie said — well, he *implied* — that he would be here. I sent a couple more messages, just checking to see where he was at. I'm still waiting to hear back. I guess I'll just keep waiting.

8:47pm.

It's dark out now. I'm staring at one of the lights that's posted on either side of Antonini's entrance and counting how many gnats there are circling around it. There are one, two, three, four, five… Actually, I think I might've counted that one already. Let me start again. There are one, two, three… Forget it.

I pull out my phone and check my messages on AphroDATEme. Still no response from Charlie. What gives? I thought we had something. I thought he was into me. I thought he was gonna be here. I got all dressed up and for what? So I could stand outside counting bugs dancing around a light fixture? Shoot, the bugs are having a better time than I am tonight.

Five more minutes.

I'll give him five more minutes.

8:56pm.

I managed to find a seat inside. The waiting area by the host stand has cleared out. Everyone waiting before me has probably already been seated. I'm the only one around. Not even What's-her-face at the host stand is here at the moment. I've got my phone open to the message box I shared with Charlie and I'm staring at our conversation. It's been about two hours. What a fucking douchebag.

"Ugh, you're still here? I was hoping you'd left,"
I hear What's-her-face say. I look up to see her coming
back from the dining room. She makes her way to the
host stand and leans onto it, letting her chin rest in the
palm of her hand.

"Nope. Still here," I answer, shutting off my
phone and slipping it into my pocket.

"So, what? Your date just never showed?" I
shrug. "I'm sorry," she offers, though I'm not sure she
means it. Her delivery is so dry and emotionless, it's hard
to take her as anything other than sarcastic.

"Well, I should probably get going," I say, getting
up. "You can take my name off the waitlist."

"Yeah, I already did, like, an hour ago." I nod and
give her one of my awkward tight-lipped smiles, then turn
to head for the door. It's pitiful. Like, I got all dressed up
to sit around and wait for nothing for two hours. I feel
like an idiot. I put in all this effort just to get stood up.
Last night, I put in all this effort just to get shot down.
And the week before, I put in all this effort to walk away
with blue balls. And then there was that whole thing with
Rudy. It's like I can't win. Why can't I win? Guys like Erik
Park can win and he's a potato. He's probably in that
dining room right now, gorging himself on fettuccini
alfredo, and playing footsies under the table with a guy
who is so clearly out of his league. Meanwhile, I'm over

here waiting on a four-foot eleven midget with a tiny penis who never showed up, and I can't even get a table.

Wait…

Can I get a table?

I mean, I know it's sad, but I'm all dressed up. Why not? I'm at the door, my hand's literally holding onto the handle, when I decide to turn around and walk right up to What's-her-face at the host stand. She seems genuinely surprised by this.

"Can I get a table for one?" I say immediately, without giving it another thought. I came here to have dinner, damn it, and I'm gonna have dinner.

"No," What's-her-face replies, her nose scrunching up as if she just got a whiff of a fart. God, even at work, she can't manage a friendly face.

"Why not?" I ask, feeling almost offended.

"Because this whole thing is pathetic."

"Give me a table for one or let me speak to the manager."

"Okay, Karen," she says, wearing the most blank expression. There's no intimidating this girl. She's staring at me with this sort of bored-ness that's just so unaffected, I'd almost find it impressive if it wasn't so obnoxious. But I'm determined to not end this night on a bad note. "Look, I'll tell you what," she then says, "my shift's about to end. I haven't eaten yet. So, if you want, you can join me at the 24-hour diner across the freeway in, like, fifteen minutes." Well, this is surprising.

"Why don't we just eat here?" I ask.

"Because I work here. I don't want to spend any more time here than I have to."

"Fair enough." I'm about to turn around and get going when something occurs to me. This girl — whatever her name is — doesn't like me. I *know* she doesn't like me. Why is she inviting me to dinner? "Wait. Is this some kind of joke? Because I just got stood up and I'd really rather not get stood up twice tonight."

"Why would I stand you up?" she asks.

"I mean, we're not exactly friends."

"Let's just say I have a soft spot for pathetic gay boys." She gives me a narrow-eyed smirk. I take this as her telling me to just accept the invite and leave, so I nod and turn to head for the door. I'm just about to pull the door open, my hand, once again, is literally on the handle, when I remember something I forgot.

"Oh, um… Can you remind me what your name was again?" I say, trying my best to not seem like an asshole. Her jaw practically drops to the floor.

"Oh, my God!" she exclaims just loud enough to sound agitated, but not loud enough for her voice to carry.

"Yeah, sorry. I'm joking. I'll just, uh, meet you at the place. See you there." And just like that, I see myself out, cross the parking lot, and hop into my mom's car. I'm sure at some point over dinner her name will come up. I hope. That is, if she even bothers to show up. Lord knows tonight hasn't exactly gone well for me, so I'm not holding my breath.

chapter fifteen

Here I am sitting in a corner booth at the same diner that I told myself I wasn't gonna go to two nights in a row — for reasons — blowing bubbles in my root beer through a straw. I needed something to take the edge off and I'm too young to be served alcohol here, so the sugar will have to do. I don't know what I'm expecting. Do I really think What's-her-face is gonna show up? I mean, she wouldn't even tell me her name. If I get stood up twice tonight, it'll be my own fault.

I check the time on my phone. It's 9:24pm. I've been sitting here for a little over ten minutes, lazily flipping through the menu. My server tonight is the same angry middle-aged dude that waited on me when I was here with Rudy. Great… He hasn't been back to check on me since handing me my root beer, and now I'm starting to run low. I guess I should probably figure out what I'm gonna eat. I haven't had dinner yet, so I might as well, whether What's-her-face shows up or not. I'm probably just gonna default to a burger and fries like I always do. It's comforting. I just gotta figure out where my waiter is. That's when I see What's-her-face making her way towards my booth. She's taken off her faux fancy Antonini's work shirt — which is really just a black button up — and is dressed in a plain black tank. She's also let her hair down. Before, it was in a side braid, but now it's more relaxed. She looks more relaxed. But I guess anyone would after getting off work.

"Were you being serious?" she asks as soon as she gets to my table.

"About?" I reply.

"Do you really not remember my name?" I shrug. I feel like this is a trap, or a test, or something, and I already know I'm gonna fail. "Ugh." She rolls her eyes before plopping herself into the booth across from me. "It's Mackenzie. I'd say it's nice to meet you, but you're an asshole and I hate you."

"Yeah, why is that?" I ask. I'm genuinely curious. What happened between me and Erik is in the past. *He* seems to have gotten over it. At least, enough to be able to have civil interactions with me. Why can't she?

"Oh, where do we begin?" Mackenzie says. "You hit on my best friend, Erik, then told him you were out of his league when he wouldn't sleep with you."

"That was last year," I defend.

"That was *September.*"

"Of *last year.*" She scoffs at this.

"You are incredible."

"Thanks."

"That's not a compliment," she says without an ounce of humor in her tone. "You also inserted yourself into our conversations, eavesdropped on us, and threatened him with your internalized homophobia."

"You make it sound way worse than it was," I mumble, starting to feel guilty.

"You sent him a note telling him to kill himself."

"That… that wasn't my idea. That was my friend, Jacob's, idea. It was stupid and mean. And I already apologized to Erik about it last year." Mackenzie stares at me silently, seemingly unaffected. "Besides, me and Nick already got into it about that, but I wasn't gonna fight the dude."

"Smart choice," she says. "He would've beat your ass."

"No, he wouldn't."

"Oh, please. Even *I* beat your ass."

"You slapped me once."

"And yet, you couldn't remember my name."

"Can we just move on?"

"Fine." Just then, our waiter, Mr. Middle-aged Mean Face, arrives at our table.

"Can I get you a drink?" He asks Mackenzie.

"Water's fine," she answers.

"Can I get a…" I start to say, but the man walks off before I can get to the word "refill." Never mind then. I turn to Mackenzie, hoping we can move past all the drama. That was a different time, a different story. Do we really need to rehash that? For a moment, neither one of us says anything. We just stare at each other, both of us waiting for the other person to say something and save us from this awkward silence. Finally, after what feels like forever, she makes a move.

"Look, I didn't invite you out to give you a hard time," Mackenzie says. "I just know how it feels."

"How what feels?"

"To get stood up. I just thought, like, even though I hate you, *that* sucks. And, I don't know, maybe it'd be nice to have dinner with someone and just talk, you know?"

"What do you want to talk about?" I ask, my mood starting to lighten a bit.

"Well, I would like to know what kind of guy can get you, Andrew Logan, star of the… sports… ball team, waiting for two hours for him," she says. "Does he have, like, a magic penis or something?"

"It was actually really small," I reply. And for the first time in, probably, the entire time I've known her, I see Mackenzie crack a smile. Not, like, a demon-y smile, but an actual smile. I didn't think it was possible.

"Now I really want to know what kind of guy this was," she says.

"Aside from him being super short, I actually don't know," I explain.

"What do you mean you don't know?"

"Well, I've been going out with a lot of guys lately."

"Oh, I'm gonna have to hear about *all* of this." I notice a twinkle in her eye, and I can tell that she's genuinely interested. At least, I hope she is. I hope that I can trust her. I *want* to trust her. I mean, I have no one else that I do, so why not her? She's been known to roll with gay guys. I'm sure she'll understand.

"Figure out what you want to eat then," I say. "We're gonna be here a while."

Mackenzie orders a nacho plate and I ask for a refill — I'm not about to let Mr. Middle-aged Mean Face gyp me on a three-dollar soda — before defaulting to my burger and fries order. Mackenzie takes a sip of her water, and I wait until our waiter is out of ear shot before continuing our conversation.

"Let's see… It all started when…" I begin, my voice trailing off for a moment. I suppose I should just start at the beginning. "Well, Becca — you know Becca, right?"

"Ugh, Becca," Mackenzie comments, rolling her eyes. "That girl is about as flavorful as mayonnaise on white bread."

"I like mayonnaise on white bread."

"You fuckin' would."

I let out a chuckle. Mackenzie takes another sip of her water. She probably needs to hydrate with that dry delivery of hers.

"Anyway, Becca asked me out, and I had to reject her, and my buddies, Riles and Jacob were like, 'Why don't you want to go out with her?' and I'm not out, so I was like —"

"Oh, my God, I don't care about your playing it straight bullshit drama. Get to the good part. I came for boy love and penises. Give me the penises!" She says "penises" way louder than I'm comfortable with that, in a reflex, I duck down in the hopes that nobody will notice me. Meanwhile, Mackenzie sits there all stoner-faced and serious, taking yet another sip of her water. I almost wish she'd choke on it. Luckily, it's not exactly busy here at the moment. "So, how are you meeting these guys you mentioned going out with?" she asks. "You just hooking up with them at the park or something?"

"Do guys do that?"

"God, open a book," she says. I swear, she makes me want to rethink opening up to her. Is it possible for someone to be supportively judgmental? Is that a thing? Does that make sense?

"I meet up with them through this dating app, AphroDATEme."

"A dating app? Are you, like, jail baiting people? Aren't you supposed to be eighteen?"

"I am eighteen. I got held back in kindergarten. They said I was emotionally underdeveloped."

"Oh, that explains a lot," she says. See? Supportively judgmental. "So, what? You haven't had any luck with it?"

"I thought I did with the first guy. We had, like, this genuine connection. At least, I *thought* we did, but then he didn't want to kiss me. So then I went out with the second guy. We made out but he didn't want to do anything else. Then the third guy was nice, but he wasn't really interested in doing stuff. And then the fourth guy made out with me, showed me his dick, then stood me up. And now I'm here with you, feeling sorry for myself."

"Why are you feeling sorry for yourself? It sounds like you've been having a great time."

"Because… it's not right," I explain. "You know, I look at people like your friend, Erik, and no offense, but he's not exactly the best-looking guy out there. And yet he's got a guy like Nick taking him out to dinner, putting his hands all over him, claiming him as his own. And what do I got? Nobody's claiming me."

"Do you want someone claiming you?" Mackenzie asks. "Like, honestly?"

"Yeah."

She stares at me for a moment with an expression that's surprisingly soft and sympathetic. Her eyes narrow as they focus on mine, as if she's trying to find something in them. What that is, I don't know.

"I don't think you do," she then says.

"You don't even know me."

"Yeah, but I can tell just by your story that you weren't trying to find someone to claim you. You weren't looking for a relationship. I mean, you dropped the one guy you said you felt a genuine connection with because why? He wouldn't kiss you? Poor Andrew."

"Huh… I didn't really think about it that way," I say. Could she be right? Was I *not* trying to find someone to claim me? Was I *not* looking for an actual relationship? No, that can't be right. That *is* what I want. That *is* what I'm looking for. I'm looking for somebody to love. I'm looking for somebody to love me. I know I am. Still, having that questioned is a little jarring. It makes me second guess myself. Mackenzie's giving me a lot to think about. But it's kinda nice. I don't talk like this with anyone. The last time I had a conversation as deep and as open, it was with Rudy, but it was different because there was a potential relationship at stake there. There was the pressure to be flirty, to be cool, to be impressive. With Mackenzie, there's none of that. Probably because I know she hates me, so really, it can only go up from here. "Hey, do you mind if I get your number?" I ask. "I don't have anyone to talk to about this kind of stuff."

"Sure," she replies, and surprisingly without hesitation. "As long as you never call me about something that could've been a text."

"Noted." I then pull out my phone, unlock it, and hand it to her so she can input her contact. While Mackenzie's adding her info, Mr. Middle-Age Mean Face arrives with our food. "Can I get a…" and again, he's off before I can get to the word "refill." Bitch…

"Yeah, I don't think he's very happy about having our table," Mackenzie says, handing me back my phone. "He probably thinks we're not gonna tip or something."

"Well, I'm definitely not now," I reply, raising my voice a little, hoping our waiter might hear. Mackenzie chuckles and begins unraveling the paper napkin from her silverware. I find it a bit odd, considering she ordered nachos. I can't help but ask, "You eat nachos with a fork? Why not just use your hands?"

"Why don't you just come out of the closet?" she quickly fires back. "You see? We all have our reasons for why we do what we do." Just when I was starting to think

I could see her as a friend… She looks at me, all smug, and pops a chip into her mouth with her fingers. Why even unwrap the fork then? I swear she's just doing this to mess with me. "I like the crunch," she says.

Crunch…

Crunch…

Crunch…

Yeah, I hate her.

chapter sixteen

No plans today.

I'm lying on my bed, bored, scrolling through AphroDATEme. I'm thinking I might find some decent conversation, or another date, but no luck. It's just oldies, uggos, and a few guys who look like they haven't seen their toes in a couple of years. I know weight isn't something I should concern myself with, but, like, if I'm gonna date a guy, he's gotta be able to keep up with me, you know?

. . .

Okay, yeah, I know I'm a terrible person, but shit. Can't I just like what I like? I just want a guy who's pretty, close to my age, isn't a complete nerd, who's not a prude about sex but can do the whole romance thing, and preferably close to my height, who stays active, and isn't too bougie to order off the value menu. Is that too much to ask? I mean, come on, I deserve it. I'm built like a freakin' stallion. And hung like one too. Wink. Wink. Nudge. Nudge. I guess it doesn't matter though. I'm not having any luck on this app today.

I set aside my phone and stare at the ceiling for a minute. What to do? What to do? Hmm… I look over and see my mom's janky old keyboard on my desk. I suppose I could mess around with the piano for a bit, so I pull myself out of bed, sit myself at my desk, and turn the thing on. I haven't played with it much since the day I set it up. The missing Middle G was enough to turn me off to it, so it's just been collecting dust like it has been all these years. The keys feel grainy. Better than nothing, I guess. What else am I gonna do today?

Suddenly, my phone chimes. Thank God. I immediately abandon the keyboard, grab my phone, and plop back on my bed. It's a notification from AphroDATEme. New message. Yes! Let's see if whoever sent this is worth responding to.

Loading…

Loading…

Come on, phone!

Loading…

Uggo.

Damn it!

I back out of the profile to my inbox. Maybe there's a message I missed from someone who's not an uggo. I doubt it, but it couldn't hurt to check, right? At the very least, I can clear out some of these messages. I go ahead and start deleting messages, and then come across the message thread I had with Charlie. Deleting that. Then there's the message thread I had with Paul. Deleting that too. Right under Paul is my message thread with Rudy. Huh. I'm thinking I should just delete it, but something stops me, and I remember the talk I had with Mackenzie last night. Maybe I made a mistake.

Hmm…

After a brief moment of thought, I decide I should send Rudy a message.

"Hi," I send. It's all I can come up with.

Monday. June 2nd.

There's only a week and a half left of school, which means that a lot of my classes are gonna be having finals and what not. I'm not worried though because I think I'm pretty solid in my classes for the most part. I don't have a final in Piano, I already turned in the final essay I bullshitted for English, US History is open book,

P.E. is P.E., so really, I only have to worry about Algebra and Bio, and who needs those besides nerds? So long as I'm passing, it's all good. Should be smooth sailing to the summer.

I'm standing at my locker, sorting out my backpack, when I feel my phone vibrate in my back pocket. I pull it out and see it's a notification from AphroDATEme. Then my phone vibrates again. Another notification from AphroDATEme. And then another. I go ahead and open the app, head straight to my inbox, and see the message thread I shared with Rudy highlighted in bold. To be honest, I'm a little surprised by it. He didn't respond to my message last night, so I thought he might be mad. Or worse, not interested.

> **RudeFern69:** You sure like to keep a guy waiting.
> **RudeFern69:** How you been? How was your weekend?
> **RudeFern69:** I've been thinking about you. Hoping I could see you again soon.

Reading this makes me realize that I have no idea what I'm doing. I messaged him last night impulsively, out of boredom. But now that I'm not laying in bed, bored out of my mind, I'm not really sure if his response is something I should be happy about. What do I say? I'm trying to think of something, anything, but the only thing my mind lands on is the disappointment of that failed kiss attempt, and how stupid it made me feel. My thumbs hover over the keyboard, suspended. I'm drawing a blank, and I can feel myself hesitating, talking myself out of this. "Not everyone's gonna be a good fit for your team. Maybe this one just wasn't for you." But then again, maybe this one was. I need someone to talk me down.

"Mackenzie!" I call out as I approach. She's standing with Erik and Nick beside Erik's locker, which is just down the hall from mine. The three of them look at me with such surprise you'd think I yelled out "PENIS!" inside a church and burst into flames or something. But that's why I'm non-practicing. Nothing that exciting ever happens at church.

"Uh, Mackenzie, why is Andrew Logan coming over here to talk to you?" Erik Park asks when I step up to them. "Did you get in another fight with him?"

"Please, Erik. If I got into a fight with him, he wouldn't be walking straight. Not that he could anyway," Mackenzie explains to him. I glance over at Nick, who's leaning against the locker behind Erik and staring at me all suspicious. I feel super awkward. He's so pretty, even when he's looking at me like I'm a total weirdo. Why is he so pretty? "What do you want?" Mackenzie says.

"Huh?" I respond. I was lost in Nick's dark eyes, I totally zoned out. I notice Mackenzie looking at me all sideways, and now I just feel really dumb. "Sorry. I just… spaced out for a moment."

"Uh, yeah, I think we should leave you guys to talk," Nick says abruptly. He places a hand on Erik's back and gently pushes him forward. "Come on, babe."

"Okay. Later, Mackenzie," Erik says, and with that, the two head off. I watch them as they go, and let my eyes linger on Nick's hand resting on Erik's back. Good job, Mr. Park. I'd be annoyed if I didn't want that too.

"So, are you just gonna stand there, or did you actually want something?" I hear Mackenzie ask. The impatient look she has on her face when I turn to her would be enough to scare even the bravest man away. Unfortunately, I have no one else to turn to, so…

"I need some advice," I explain. "Check this out." I take my phone and show Mackenzie the messages I got from Rudy on AphroDATEme.

"What am I looking at?" she asks. I look at her, she looks at me, I look around and see all these random people in the hall. Then I look at her, she looks at me, and we look at each other waiting for the other person to say something. Like, isn't it obvious what I'm showing her? What is she not understanding? Is she just messing with me? "Ugh, meet me at lunch behind the bleachers," she says finally. "And feel free to tell whoever that we're hooking up. It'll be fun to see the popular girls clutching their pearls."

"You're really mean, aren't you?"

"Why, I do declare," she says in the most stereotypical southern accent before walking away. I guess I'll see her at lunch then.

After fourth period lets out, I'm making my way down the hall, having just dipped out of Milano's cheese smelling classroom. I swear, the stench of him gets worse as the days get hotter. Think less melty mozzarella and more — I don't know, shitty? I would breathe through my mouth, but I try not to put things that smell weird in my mouth. I should probably get over that though if I'm being honest.

"Yo, Drewster! Wait up!" Fuck! It's Riley. I turn to see him hurrying towards me. He's probably expecting us to do the usual and meet up with Jacob in the cafeteria. "Dude, why you in such a rush?"

"Did you smell Milano today?" I ask.

"Yeah. I had to shove some tissue in my nose and breathe through my mouth."

"So you tasted him then?"

"Whatever, man," Riley says. We exit the annex and cross the street towards main campus. Somehow, I gotta figure out a way to ditch him without letting him know that I'm ditching him. And whatever excuse I come up with has to be solid enough to not make Jacob suspicious. What to say? What to say? I could tell them I'm hanging with a girl, but then they'd ask questions, and I'd rather not deal with that. The less attention there is on me, the better.

We're inside now, nearing the cafeteria when Riley says, "I can't wait till this school year's over. I just hope I pass Algebra." While he's talking, I get an idea. "I don't get why we need to know how to factor polynomials. Like, what's a polynomial anyway?"

"Yeah, about that. I'm actually not doing too well in Algebra," I say. "Um, I, uh… I gotta retake a test I bombed on, so…"

"Right, okay. Sure. Well, good luck." Riley pats me on the shoulder, and I nod before heading off to meet Mackenzie. Thank God for my BS-ing skills.

I make my way to the football field behind the gym and walk around the outside of the stadium to get to behind the bleachers. It's super out of the way, so unless people are smoking or boning, I think me and Mackenzie will be safe back here. I'm the first to get here, so I pull out my phone and look over the messages I got from Rudy while I wait. Is it stupid that I haven't responded yet? I've been thinking a lot about it and, keeping in mind what I talked about with Mackenzie, I'm starting to wonder if maybe *I'm* the fuckup. And if I am, I don't want to fuck this up.

"This better be good," I hear, and look up to see Mackenzie walking towards me, eating from a bag of chips. "You better not have me walking all the way out here for some nonsense," she says, popping a chip into her mouth.

"You know the first guy I mentioned, the one I had a connection with?" I begin. "I messaged him impulsively yesterday."

"And?" she pops another chip into her mouth.

"*And* he messaged me back." She looks at me unimpressed before, once again, popping another chip in her mouth. "Can you stop with the chips for a minute?"

"No. I like the crunch," she says, sounding almost bored. And *again*, she pops another chip in her mouth. God, I hate her. "Is that really all you asked me here for?"

"Look, I need help. I've been going out with all these random guys, on all these dates, and for what? What we talked about on Sunday made a lot of sense. And I don't trust myself to make good choices."

"What did we talk about on Sunday?"

"You know, how you didn't think I wanted a relationship. But I do."

She stares at me suspiciously, crunching on yet another chip, and I do my best to put on the sorriest puppy dog eyes I can manage. I think I might even be able to get a tear. How could anyone say no to that?

Crunch…

Crunch…

Crunch…

"Oh, my God, fine! Let me see the messages," she yells. Ha! I got her. And all I had to do was cry. I go ahead and hand her my phone, and almost immediately, her face drops. "Are you serious? The guy misses you. He wants to see you. Plan a date. Problem solved." She shoves my phone back into my hands and takes a step back. I'm scared she's gonna leave.

"Mackenzie, wait," I say. "I need you to help me through this. I have nobody else that I can talk to about this stuff."

"So come out of the closet."

"It's not that easy for me." We go silent for a moment. Mackenzie closes her eyes and takes a breath. Just when I thought I had her on my side, I feel like I'm losing her.

"Okay," she then says, now looking at me. "This guy better be cute. He'd better be worth it." So, I show her his profile picture and she laughs. It's almost like a cackle. Like a witch. "Why does he look like a scrawnier, alternative, hipster version of Nick?" I shrug. She eyes me all suspicious and amused. I don't know why. So maybe I have a type, is that so wrong? "Just talk to him," she says. "Tell him you've been stressed out at school or something — I don't know, make small talk — and go from there."

"Just like that?"

"Just like that," she nods, so I nod too. Then my eyes drift down to the bag of chips she's got, and I feel a bit of a hunger pang in my stomach.

"Can I have one of those?" I ask.

"No."

Later, in the afternoon, I'm sprawled out on my bed trying to review stuff for Algebra when I hear from Rudy. I sent a message earlier while I was with Mackenzie, but he didn't respond, so me and Mackenzie spent the rest of the lunch period arguing about whether I should or shouldn't let her see my junk.

"Well, I gotta get something out of this," she argued.

"I'm not showing you my junk, Mackenzie," I responded.

"Why not? You could be like that Charlie guy you went out with and just flash it real quick."

"Charlie stood me up."

"I almost did too!"

Yeah… I can't with her.

Anyway, back to Rudy. At lunch, I messaged him, "Sorry I been MIA. Been stressing with school. How you been?" He's just now responding.

RudeFern69: I'm ok. Just working. Semester's over, so I got more time if you ever wanna meet up again.

GoldenBoy513: Depends. Is you're hair the same color?

RudeFern69: No.

GoldenBoy513: Oh?

RudeFern69: I like change. Keeps the boys guessing.

GoldenBoy513: Boys?

RudeFern69: Well, one boy.

GoldenBoy513: And whose this boy.

RudeFern69: Your* autocorrect really doesn't like you today.

GoldenBoy513: ???

RudeFern69: You're very possessive today.

GoldenBoy513: How so?

RudeFern69: It's who's*

GoldenBoy513: Ast-a-risk of sounding dumb. What's who's?

RudeFern69: You're very cute.

GoldenBoy513: Thanks. I know.

RudeFern69: Not a compliment.

GoldenBoy513: Bitch. [Winky face with tongue emoji]

RudeFern69: How very feminist of you.

GoldenBoy513: You sound like my friend.

RudeFern69: You're friend sounds brilliant.

GoldenBoy513: Your*

RudeFern69: I gave you that one. [Winky face emoji]

GoldenBoy513: I figured.

GoldenBoy513: God, I missed you.

Yup. I let it slip. I miss him. I didn't realize how much until just right now. I didn't realize how starved I was for the conversation. I mean, I get this same kind of back and forth with Mackenzie, but it's different when you're actually trying to get with the person, you know? It's… exciting.

I don't think I'm gonna get much studying done tonight. Luckily, my Algebra final isn't until next week, and my teacher's allowing a cheat sheet.

Tuesday. June 3rd.

I texted Mackenzie in the morning asking if she wanted to meet up again at lunch. She agreed, so once again I have to come up with another believable and not-at-all suspicious excuse to give Riley when fourth period lets out.

"Hey, so I actually have to meet with my English teacher about my final paper. She gave me an incomplete," I explain to Riley as we're walking out of

Milano's class. He gasps for breath. I don't blame him. The cheese smell has been getting worse and worse.

"Sorry. I tried breathing through my mouth today, but you were right. I think I could actually taste him," he says. "Anyway, an incomplete? What does that even mean?"

"No idea. Probably cited my sources wrong or something."

"Ah. Well, good luck." That's one thing I've always appreciated about Riley. He takes what you give him and doesn't demand for more. You could feed him a bowl of lies and he'd scarf it down like a cereal called *Troots* and be totally satisfied. It makes my life easier. At least that part of my life.

I meet up with Mackenzie behind the bleachers and show her the entire conversation I had with Rudy last night. The whole time she's reading, I'm watching her reaction, expecting her to get happy, excited, maybe even giggle, but she doesn't. She's stoner-faced the whole time, and when she's done reading, she looks at me almost bored.

"You guys make me so dry," she says. "For two hot gay guys, you'd think you'd come up with something juicier than typos and grammar jokes."

"It's called wordplay," I defend.

"It's called *boring*. If you want sexy wordplay, write some erotica. I mean, you didn't even make a move. The guy is clearly pining for you —"

"Like a Christmas Tree?"

"Don't. Why don't you just ask the guy out?"

"You think I should?"

"Like, yesterday," she says. She's so matter-of-fact about it that I almost feel stupid. Still, I don't know. I'm hesitating. I guess I just don't want to be disappointed again. "You know what you need? Something to take the edge off," Mackenzie says, suddenly pulling out a joint. "You smoke?"

"Got a light?"

Yeah… This probably isn't a great idea at school, but I'm coming to accept the fact that I'm not exactly the model of someone who makes good choices.

Wednesday, June 4th.

Late last night, I got to talking to Rudy, and I somehow mustered up the courage to ask him out. I just kept thinking about how Mackenzie made it seem stupid of me not to, so I just bit the bullet. Actually, what does that saying even mean? If you bite a bullet, wouldn't it, like, kill you? Or is it that you bite the bullet after it's already been shot? Maybe the bullet isn't even being shot? But then, like, why would you bite it? English is weird.

Anyway, during fourth period, Riley got in trouble with Mr. Milano. Milano gave us the period to read and review for the final on Tuesday. Tim Martinelli was playing with this little fidget toy he'd brought to class and Riley asked to see it.

"No, you're not gonna give it back," Martinelli said.

"Yeah, I will," Riley defended.

"Like you gave back the Rubik's cube you stole from the teacher?" I guess Riley wasn't as slick as he thought. Sucks to be him, but lucky for me. I'm meeting up with Mackenzie again today and that's one less excuse I had to come up with.

Before heading over to the bleachers, I decide to stop by my locker to drop off my History book, and end up running into Mackenzie in the hallway.

"Hey," I greet her as she approaches me at my locker.

"Hey," she replies. "So, what kind of baggage are we unpacking today?"

"Actually, I think you'll be very proud of me."

"Oh? Are we planning a date?"

"That we are. I was thinking about doing Antonini's. I want to do something fancy this time around," I explain. Mackenzie cackles. "What? Antonini's is fancy."

"Sure. Whatever you say. What do I know? It's not like I work there."

"Hey, I'm trying here," I defend. I don't care what she says. Antonini's *is* fancy. "So, do you think you could get us a table?"

"Depends. If you do it on a weeknight, I can probably make it work."

"Cool. I'll let you know."

Since it's the last week of school, we're not dressing for P.E. anymore. What used to be a *kind of* free period is now a real free period inside the gym. As long as we show up and stick around the whole period, the teachers don't dock our grade.

I'm sitting on the bleachers — the ones inside, not the ones you have sex behind — at the start of class, typing out a message to Rudy, when I notice Riley and Jacob walking across the basketball court towards me. I hit the power button on my phone and shove it into my pocket. Probably not smart to have it out with them around.

"Hey, man," Jacob says as he and Riley take a seat on the tier just below me. "Long time no see. Where you been?"

"I been around. Just dealing with some school stuff, making sure my grades are good. You know how it is," I explain. "So, uh, Riles, how'd it go with Milano?"

"It's whatever. He said he didn't want to reprimand me this close to the end of the year. I just gotta give back the Rubik's cube," Riley says.

"So, anyway, we ran into Becca at lunch," Jacob says, cutting in. Huh. I wonder why he's bringing her up. "She said she saw you in the hallway with that one chick. You know, that one who hangs out with all the gay dudes." Shit…

"Yeah. That's, uh, Mackenzie," I say nervously. I knew this would happen if they found out. I knew they'd ask questions. What do I do? What do I say? Should I just tell them what's going on? No. I'm not ready for that. I don't know if *they're* ready for that yet either. No. I've gotta think of an excuse. Think of an excuse, Andrew. Think. Think!

"You guys hookin' up or what?" Jacob asks. That's it! That's what I'll tell them. I'll tell them that I'm hooking up with Mackenzie. If I remember right, even Mackenzie told me to use that excuse. And in a terrible southern accent no less. I open my mouth to say just that, to confirm that I'm banging Mackenzie — ew, I would never — but… nothing.

"Uh…" I start to say. That's all that comes out. Jacob then turns to Riley, looking all sorts of excited.

"Bro, I bet she sucks some good dick hangin' with all those faggots," he says, laughing like it's the funniest thing in the world. Riley joins him. My heart sinks.

Just tell them that you're sleeping with her, Andrew. Go ahead. But hearing them laughing their asses off about her sucking dick, and faggots, and stuff… How long can I go on listening to this kind of thing? How long can I just keep quiet about it? I can't. I can't do that. I can't let Mackenzie take the fall for me. Even if she's willing to. Especially because she's willing to. Then again, I know the rumor mill can be vicious, and who's to say if Mackenzie was being serious when she said I could use boning her as an excuse. That might just blow up in my face and I can't have that. I need her.

"No. We're just friends," I say. I'm trying to sound tough about it, but I don't feel like I am at all. I feel like a little boy who did something bad and was caught red handed but is too afraid to admit his guilt.

"So what's going on then?" Jacob asks. "What're you hanging out with her for?" Am I really gonna do this? Am I really gonna come clean to them? I think about my newfound friendship with Mackenzie and how easy it's been — relatively speaking — even though we don't exactly see eye to eye. I don't even know if we necessarily like each other, but even then, it's been easier than my friendships with Riley and Jacob. Maybe it is time I tell them.

"Why don't you just come out of the closet?" I hear Mackenzie's voice echo in my mind. Why don't I? What am I afraid of exactly? I look at Jacob and I look at Riley and I think, these two are supposed to be my best friends. Let them be your best friends.

"I'm…" I start to say. "I'm… Uh…" but I can't do it. I can't bring myself to say it. Not out loud. "Here, I'll just text you." I pull out my phone, set up a group chat, and type in the words, "I'm gay." Then I take in a deep breath, hold it, and hit send.

chapter seventeen

"Dude, quit joking," Jacob laughs after reading the text I sent. Riley's smiling, but he looks unsure about it. I just look at them, holding my breath while I wait for it to sink in. "You're joking, right?" Jacob asks when he settles down. I shake my head. None of us say anything for a while which, in a way, is good since we're surrounded by everyone in fifth period P.E. but it's really uncomfortable.

Eventually, Jacob gets up and starts making his way down the bleachers.

"Where you going?" Riley asks.

"I'm just gonna, uh, make sure that I cleaned everything out of my gym locker," Jacob answers. And then he leaves. Riley turns to me and gives me a look of pity, followed by an awkward, tight-lipped smile. It's the kind I've become all too familiar with.

"I'm gonna go check on him," he says. "You know how he can be." And just like Jacob, Riley gets up, starts making his way down the bleachers, and leaves. I can't say that I'm surprised by their reaction. Really, I was stupid to think that it'd be anything different. I don't know. I guess I just hoped that because things seemed to be looking up for me that I'd be wrong about them.

Telling Riley and Jacob doesn't feel real. I'd been hiding, and denying, and lying to them for so long, that the truth doesn't feel like the truth anymore. It feels like a joke I made up for them to laugh at, or something to claim to scare them off. How sad is it that I can use my sexuality as a weapon, knowing it might hurt someone? How sad is it that people care that much?

That's why I prefer not to say anything.

On the bus ride home, I decide to message Rudy. I need someone to talk to about the whole Riley and Jacob situation. And considering how Mackenzie talks about coming out as if it's an easy thing, I don't really want to talk to her about it. I know I shouldn't be, but a little part of me is mad at her for putting the idea in my head. "So come out of the closet," she said. A brilliant idea that turned out to be.

GoldenBoy513: Hey. Question.

RudeFern69: What's up?

GoldenBoy513: How did your friends react when you came out to them?

RudeFern69: They already knew. Said it was obvious. So annoying.

RudeFern69: Why?

GoldenBoy513: I came out to my two best friends today.

GoldenBoy513: It wasn't great.

RudeFern69: Oh…

RudeFern69: Well, fuck 'em.

RudeFern69: Or don't. You can't threaten people with a good time.

GoldenBoy513: Lol.

RudeFern69: Are you ok?

GoldenBoy513: Idk.

RudeFern69: You will be.

RudeFern69: You don't need people in your life who aren't gonna value you.

RudeFern69: You learn that when you value yourself.

GoldenBoy513: Yea…

Stepping into Milano's fourth period History class is uncomfortable, to say the least, what with Riley in this class. Do you ever get the feeling when you tell someone something that suddenly the whole world knows your business? Because that's what it feels like right now. As I walk over to my seat in front of Riley, he doesn't bother to look up. No one does, which is weird because I feel like everyone's staring at me. Either I'm really paranoid or I'm just *that* conceited.

"Hey," I say to Riley before taking my seat.

"Hey," he replies.

"Uh… Are we good?" I really would rather not hash out my problems in the middle of class, but I know if I don't say something, it's gonna eat away at me. Riley looks up. He seems… I don't know, disappointed? I guess I can't blame him though.

"Yeah, we're good," he says. He *says* that we're good, but despite Milano giving us the period to brush up for the final again, me and Riley don't talk the rest of class. And when fourth period lets out, I decide I should wait for him, but he's out the door before I can put away my things.

Outside of Milano's class, I check my phone and see a notification from AphroDATEme. It's a message from Rudy. Thank God. After the cold shoulder I got from Riley, I could use a bit of warmth.

RudeFern69: How's school?
GoldenBoy513: Not great.
RudeFern69: Your friends being butts?
GoldenBoy513: They're not talking to me.
GoldenBoy513: The nice one isn't anyway.
RudeFern69: And the not nice one?
GoldenBoy513: I'm avoiding him.
RudeFern69: His loss.
GoldenBoy513: I guess. I still feel bad though.
RudeFern69: I know. Tbh it's probably gonna hurt for a while. It's never fun to lose a friend.
GoldenBoy513: This sucks.

At lunch, I'm leaning against one of the support beams of the football field bleachers and messaging Rudy when Mackenzie shows up.

"Hey," she says, unwrapping the foil from a cafeteria burger as she approaches. "Who you talking to? Doppelganger Nick?"

"His name's Rudy," I reply. My voice comes out all sad and depressing. I don't mean for it to. It just does.

"What's up? Something wrong?"

"I don't really wanna talk about it."

"Okay."

"I came out to my friends. Did what you told me to do."

"I was joking."

"Yeah, well, they didn't take it well."

"I'm sorry." We go quiet for a moment. I don't know what to say. I mean, I can't really blame her. She gave me an out — whether she was serious about it or not — and I chose not to take it. Still, I can't help but be a little bit mad at her. "Do you want half of my burger?" she then asks. "Would it make you feel better?"

"You're a fuckin' idiot," I chuckle. I don't know what it was. Maybe it was her dry, uncaring delivery but the question makes me laugh. Like, really, Mackenzie? She just shrugs.

"You know what might actually make you feel better? We should plan that date."

"Yeah. Um, I'm thinking maybe once the school year's over. Like, Wednesday or Thursday. I gotta see when he's free."

"Sure. Yeah, let me know. I'll put you guys down on the reservation list," Mackenzie says. I watch her take the first bite out of her burger, and I suddenly regret saying "no" to half. I'd been feeling so down today, I didn't have an appetite for breakfast. I'm paying for it now.

"Actually, can I have half of that?" I ask.

"You're so annoying," she says, and rips me off a piece of her cafeteria burger.

Thank God it's the weekend. Friday was more or less the same as Thursday. Riley was still closed off and distant, and I haven't spoken to Jacob since I came out to them. Mackenzie had plans with Erik and Nick for lunch. She mentioned they wanted to go off campus to celebrate the last full day of school — next week, it's all half-days. She invited me along but given my not-so-great history with her friends, I didn't think it was a good idea. So actually, Friday was worse.

I know people see me as a "popular" guy. You know, I'm on the football team, people know me, and if they don't know me, they know *of* me. That comes with this idea that I'm never alone. That I never not have someone to hang out with. But the thing is, once you're in a group, that's your group. And if, for whatever reason, you're not part of that group anymore, then you're on your own. So, I spent the lunch period wandering aimlessly through the halls, trying to seem like I had somewhere to go, so I wouldn't look like a loner. Sure, there were a couple of people who stopped me to say, "What's up?" and whatever, but I wasn't in the mood to be around people.

What?

I wanted to be alone. I just didn't want it to look like I had no one to hang out with. Being a loner and *looking* like a loner are two entirely different things. It's a lot to juggle. Lots to think about.

God, I can't wait till school's over.

It's around 10:00am. I'm lying in bed, scrolling through my social media, trying to wake myself up. I'm exhausted. This last week really took it out of me. All I want to do is lay here and do nothing. Or maybe I'll watch TV. Maybe I'll rub one out. I don't know. I just don't want to think about anything today.

I hear a knock on my door.

"Come in," I say, and in comes my mom, all dressed up in capris and a short-sleeve button up.

"Andrew, you're not dressed?" she asks. I look at her confused, half of me still buried under my covers.

"What for?"

"We're picking up your brother today. Don't you want to come?" It hits me then that Art is supposed to be coming home today for the summer. I'd completely forgotten, mostly because I don't care. I don't want him here. As if his presence isn't constantly felt from the mantelpiece shrine in the living room. Can't he just take his overachieving ass to summer school or something?

"Mom, it's been a really long week," I say, trying to come off as tired as possible. "Can I just stay home?"

"But we were gonna make a day out of it," she replies. She sounds disappointed and I feel bad, but it's Art. Ew. "I was thinking we could grab dumplings from that fancy dumpling shop by his school."

"Please? I still got finals to study for." Mom takes a moment and lets out a sigh.

"I'll tell your dad to leave you money for pizza." And with that, my mom steps out of my room, slowly shutting the door behind her. My mind lingers on the thought that my brother is coming home today.

Art is coming home today…

As if my life weren't complicated enough, now my brother's going to be here to make me feel bad about myself. He's probably gonna have perfect grades, hilarious stories about his stupid roommates, positive vibes from his smoothie shop job, and he'll probably want to go shopping for the perfect car, to complete the perfect image he's carved out for his perfect self, because he's so fucking perfect. Like, couldn't he just have dandruff or something? Couldn't he, like, gain a few pounds so I have the better body? Or better yet, fail a class? I mean, how is anybody supposed to measure up to him? I can't even measure up to a potato.

I don't know. Maybe I'm just overreacting. The last time he was here, he barely paid attention to me. So, maybe it won't be so bad. I need to just look on the bright side.

. . .

But seriously, if he could just get, like, a nose pimple, that'd be great.

chapter eighteen

On Sunday, my dad insisted that the whole family go out for a family lunch. He and Art spent the entire time talking about how great college is, his ridiculous roommate, this random girl he's *kind of* seeing, and blah-blah-blah-blah-blah-blah-blah. Art asked if I wanted to hang out after, but I told him that I had to study for my finals, which is actually true.

"Yeah, you should definitely focus on school. We can hang when you're on break," he said. Nerd. Anyway, he pretty much left me alone after that, just like he did when we were growing up. Don't know what I'm gonna tell him if he wants to hang once school's over though, but we'll cross that bridge when we come to it.

Speaking of school, Monday kicked off our last week and every day was a half day. How it works is that all of our classes are extended by an hour, but we'd only have to go to two classes a day with a half hour break in between. We do this for finals. I didn't have a final in Piano, so we spent the period doing what we do. I got some good practice in on the keyboard and Mrs. Dolittle again insisted I consider getting piano lessons when she caught me playing through *Moonlight Sonata*. It's fun and I like it well enough, but I don't know if Piano is really my thing, you know? My second class that day was Algebra II and that final kicked my ass. Even with a cheat sheet. Really, what I needed was a cheat poster. Or better yet, make it open book.

Tuesday was probably the easiest day and the hardest day of the week all at the same time. It was easy because I already turned in my final for English and Milano's final was open book. What was so hard about it though was the fact that Riley's in Milano's class and we're not really talking. I mean, I guess we're cool. He pretty much said so. But it doesn't feel like we are. He didn't even say anything to me before he left. It just reminded me of why I never wanted to come out to him and Jacob in the first place. Still, it sucks when you're not friends with your friends anymore.

Today at school was rough. Riley and Jacob both had P.E. when I had P.E. so it wasn't the funnest thing ever, but at least they had different teachers, so they weren't sitting anywhere close to me. In fact, if I didn't already know they were in P.E. I probably wouldn't have known they were there, there were so many kids in that period. Anyway, I passed the time by texting Mackenzie — I guess her fifth period was a bore too — and we just spent the whole class shitting on Riley and Jacob. It was pretty funny.

"They sound like incels," she texted at one point.

"What?" I replied.

"Involuntary celibates."

"Is that a dig at me? [Unamused face emoji]"

"I mean, it can be. But at least you can get it."

"Uh… Thanks?"

"I'd have sex with you." I can't with her. "It'd probably be really vanilla sex, but I would."

"Lol. Guess you'll never know."

"Your loss," she texted. Then almost immediately after, she sends, "Send a dick pic." Yeah… I really can't with her. I hate her. But I'm also starting to like her, so what can you do?

Lastly, there was Bio. The test wasn't too bad. It wasn't great either, but I think I did well enough to manage at least a B in that class. I won't find out for another week or so. But either way, I'm happy to be done with school. It's something I've been looking forward to for months now. But even more exciting than summer break, tonight I've got my date with Rudy.

I'm walking up the ramp to Antonini's entrance dressed in a short plaid button up, khaki pants, and some black sneakers. I wanted to look nice, but not all tryhard like the last time I was here. No need to give Mackenzie something to make fun of. Besides, knowing I was meeting up with Rudy, I thought it might be weird to dress up more than this, so I kept it simple. Though I did remember to tuck.

"What are you wearing?" Mackenzie asks from the host stand when I step inside. The lobby is empty right now, being that it's barely six o' clock, but I expect it'll pick up. Mackenzie smirks at me with hooded eyes, all amused. "You look like *Leave it to Beaver.*"

"Why would you leave anything to a beaver?" I reply. She rolls her eyes and shakes her head, then waves me towards her.

"I hope you're wearing something under this," she says, starting to unbutton my shirt. She pulls it up, so it's no longer tucked in, revealing the white tank underneath, then tousles my hair a bit.

"Hey!"

"You need to look more relaxed. You look like someone who says 'neato' and 'boy, howdy' when they get excited."

"You make me sound puritanical."

"Ah, I'm surprised you know the definition."

"I don't actually. I just try to speak with confidence."

"Confidence unearned is a lesson to be learned," Mackenzie says dryly.

"What are you, a poet now?" I reply.

"And you're a disaster waiting to happen."

"Eh, you're probably right. Boy, howdy." I give her a smug look. She scoffs. I notice her eyes shift over to something behind me. It sounds like someone just walked in, so I turn to step out of the way and immediately freeze up.

"Hey, you," Rudy says. It's been long enough since we last saw each other, seeing him now feels almost as if we're meeting for the first time. And with this version of him, it is. He looks different. The once silver parts of his hair are now a bubble gum pink. His lip ring has been changed out to a diamond-y stud. He's traded his oversized sweatshirt for a loose-fitting short-sleeve button up with a floral print, and his black jeans for a gray pant, rolled up at the ankle. The first time we met, he was dressed for comfort. Tonight, he's dressed for a date. And I suddenly feel like I should've tried harder.

"Uh, hi," I say, practically choking on the word. "You look… Wow, I feel underdressed."

"You told me we were going somewhere fancy," he replies, slowly moving towards me. I feel my heart pound with every step he takes in my direction. As he draws closer, my breathing gets heavy. And I feel this incredible urge to lunge forward and press my lips onto his, but the memory of the first time I tried that stops me. I think tonight, I'll let him take the lead. I mean, he seems to be playing this much smoother than I am so…

"If your whole party is here, I can go ahead and seat you," I hear Mackenzie say. Thank God. I could feel myself getting all caught up in his dark eyes. They're like two paintings of nighttime, each with their own moon, reflecting the light back at — what the hell am I talking about? I'm losing myself in him, aren't I? Snap out of it, Andrew. Now's the time to put on the moves. Stay focused.

Mackenzie leaves the host stand to take us into the dining area, when I suddenly feel something press against my lower back. Surprised, I turn to Rudy and realize it's his hand gently trying to lead me forward, the same way I've watch Nick Santiago do to Erik-Potato-Park. Are all Latin men like this? Because, uh, this has got me feeling kinda spicy. Like, it tingles. In a good way. But I can barely handle it.

We follow Mackenzie into the dining area, weaving through and around tables until we get to a booth tucked away in the corner. The girl pulls through with my request for privacy. Rudy takes a seat and I slide into the booth across from him. Mackenzie hands each of us a menu, and then her eyes lock into mine for a minute, having what I swear is a full-on conversation with our eyeballs.

"Oh, my God," Mackenzie's eyes say to mine. "If you don't get pregnant by him, I will."

"Uh, no, he's mine," my eyes reply. "And thank you for setting this up."

"Your server will be here momentarily," she then says aloud before leaving me and Rudy alone together.

"You guys know each other?" Rudy asks, casually looking over the drink section on the back of his menu.

"Yeah, she's a friend from school," I explain.

"I do that with my friends too. We have full-on conversations using just our eyes."

"We weren't —"

The way he's looking at me is smug, like he already knows I'm lying. I crack and start laughing awkwardly, embarrassed. If it wasn't obvious to him before, it definitely is now. He just smiles at me. I'm glad this is fun for him.

"So, what were you saying about me?" he asks.

"Uh…" I laugh again, nervously this time. Should I just admit it? Would that be, like, sexy? "Um, well, I think she thinks you're cute, but I call dibs."

"Oh? You're calling dibs now?" He chuckles. He then takes a breath and leans in. "Well, let me ask you. It's been, like, two — almost three — weeks since we last saw each other. What are you looking for?"

"I feel like we've talked about this before."

"Yeah, but it's been a while. Things can change." I pause to give his question some thought. After all the guys I've gone through over the last couple of weeks, I don't know. I don't think anything's changed. I think I still want what I wanted before.

"A relationship, I guess," I say.

"You guess?" Rudy questions. I shrug. I feel like the answer to this question is obvious, you know? You go on dating apps to find a date, and you either hook up with or end up dating someone. Isn't that what they're meant for? Why does everyone keep questioning me about this? I'm not looking to sleep around. It'd be nice, but that's not my goal. "You are so dangerous, you know that?" Rudy says, leaning back.

"How?" I reply. "Do you not trust me or something?"

"It's not you I don't trust."

Suddenly, our server, a peppy girl who doesn't look too much older than me, arrives at our table.

"Thank you, guys, for waiting," she says, her voice is cheerful and bright. She seems like the type of girl who was probably a cheerleader in high school. "My name's Amanda, and I will be your server tonight. Can I get you something to drink?"

"Italian sodas for the both of us," I order before Rudy can get a word in.

"Sure thing." And with that, Amanda leaves.

"Italian sodas?" Rudy says to me when our waitress is out of earshot. "That's gonna go straight to my ass."

"Neato. That's where I want it to go," I say.

"Neato? What is this, the fifties? Can I be a housewife?"

"Why, yes, dear. I would like for you to be barefoot and pregnant."

"Please, if that's gonna be my life, I insist on wearing heels," he laughs. I laugh along with him. We laugh together until the laughs fade to a quiet and we're just smiling stupidly at each other. "I'm a mess, Andrew," Rudy says softly after a moment.

"Well, some messes are beautiful," I reply. He eyes me suspiciously, but in a way that says he's amused.

"You're really corny, you know that?"

"Well, then spread on some mayo and put me on a stick."

"Ah, I love elote!" he exclaims excitedly, which catches a passing waitress — not Amanda — by surprise. I bite my lip to try to keep myself from laughing, at least until she's gone, but it's really hard to with Rudy smiling at me like an idiot.

We talk throughout dinner, losing ourselves in conversations about whatever. We talk, we laugh, and when we run out of things to say, we make gross sex faces while eating our food, trying to make the other one choke on theirs. It's stupid and childish, and I'm loving every second of it. The time passes so quickly when I'm with him. It's like I'm on a roller coaster, and the ride's coming to an end when the bill arrives. All that track and it's suddenly over, but I don't want to get off. Not yet. Rudy offers to pay since I ended up paying last time. At first, I feel a little bad about it because, of course, I want to be the man, but then I see that the bill is more than the forty or so I've got left in my wallet, so I take the L. Besides, we're both dudes, so I'm still the man.

It's crowded now inside Antonini's and there are enough people celebrating — probably graduating seniors — that it's gotten pretty hard to hear over the noise, even in our little corner of the world. Rudy and I decide to step outside for some fresh air and quiet. On the way out, we pass Mackenzie at the host stand. She's too busy to talk, but our eyes meet for a second, and I just know she's gonna want to hear all about how this date's going. But we'll talk later.

Antonini's is nestled on the outer edge of a long shopping center, right next to a faux fancy seafood restaurant. If you can't get into Antonini's then you go there, and if you can't get in there, you go to Antonini's. And if you can't get into either, then you're shit out of luck. I mean, there's always the fast-food places across the street, but those are a little too casual for the first couple dates. Then again, who am I to talk? My first date with Rudy was at a 24-hour diner. And I showed up with my backpack. Whatever works, I guess.

It's dark out now. I take in the fresh air as me and Rudy make our way across the parking lot. Where we're going, I don't know. I don't think Rudy knows either. We're just two shadows floating, side by side, in the dark spaces between the light of the lamp posts.

"I'm having a lot of fun tonight," I hear him say. "Can I ask you though?"

"Hmm?"

"What took you so long to get back to me?" The question catches me off guard. I know the answer, but the more that I think about my answer, the more that I think about how stupid it is. I like him. I like him a lot. And yet I let myself be convinced that he wasn't "a good fit for my team." I think about it now and I realize that

that wasn't even my idea. But I let it get to me because…
I don't know. I guess disappointment seeks validation. It
seems to be great at finding it in even the most
encouraging places. Like, you could play the most
beautiful song, but one sour note will tell you it's not
good enough. And so, you tell yourself that *you're* not
good enough. "I guess, I was protecting myself," I say.
Rudy lets out a slow breath and then smiles.

"Aren't we all?" he replies.

The two of us fall silent. In the darkness, we
wander slowly, staring up at the black and violet sky,
quietly enjoying each other's company. Then I feel
something brush against my hand. It's his fingers,
weaving through and lacing themselves in between mine.
My heart jumps. In a reflex, I quickly glance, checking to
see that no one's around. We've found ourselves in an
area of the parking lot where there are almost no cars,
nobody around, yet I still feel so exposed.

"Relax," I hear him say. "No one will see. And if
they do, they won't care."

"How do you know that?" I ask.

"Would it matter if they did?" I think on it. *Would*
it matter if someone saw? And if they did, *would* it matter
if they cared? I know the answer should be "no". It's just
hard for me to commit to that when I've spent my whole
life hiding. I want to let go of those cares. I want to let go
of those worries and surrender myself to the moment.

But that's like asking me to switch positions and run a play that wasn't mapped out. How do I know that anyone will be there to catch my throw?

I feel Rudy's hand gently squeeze mine as we slowly wander toward a nearby lamp post. We don't speak. We don't say a word. When we reach the edge of the light cast from the lamp post, we stand in silence, staring into the little bright spot of the parking lot. There's something calming in this quiet. It's like the world has slowed down. I think about the moment when I put my fingers on the keys of a piano, that moment before I start to play. It's that moment that I decide what I want to do. That moment when anything is possible. In my mind, I can hear the music that I want to play. I take in a breath, preparing myself for that first note, and step forward.

"But what if somebody sees?" Rudy says from behind, still lingering in the dark. I turn to him. I can just make out his face outside the lamp light. He's smiling, from what I can see.

"It... doesn't matter," I reply. The words come out hesitant. It's funny though, they feel good to say. Like a weight's been lifted. If it could feel like this all the time. I let go of his hand and walk up to the lamp post, where the light is brightest. I nod for him to join me, but he just stands there smiling. I wish I could know what he's thinking. I wish I could know what he's smiling about. I guess for now, I'll settle for the silence. Because this silence, this moment between us is… everything.

chapter nineteen

It's right around ten o'clock.

We're standing next to Rudy's car. He's got the door open, ready to climb in once we've said our goodnights.

"It was great seeing you," he says, smiling.

"You too," I reply.

"Well, I should get going." Rudy then steps forward, places his hands around my waist, and pulls me into a hug. It's a bit surprising, if I'm being honest, but I like it. He lets his head rest against my shoulder, his face fit perfectly against my neck. "Mmm… You smell nice." I wrap my arms around him and hold him tight.

"I don't want you to go," I whisper.

"Me either, but I have to work," he says, pulling away. "Thank God it isn't the opening shift though, right?" I nod. Our eyes meet and I linger in them for a moment, losing myself in my thoughts. Kiss him. Kiss him, Andrew. He's looking at you like he wants you to. Like he's begging you to. Do it.

But I don't.

I decided that I wanted him to take the lead tonight, so that's what I'm doing. As much as I want him to touch his lips to mine, as much as I want to taste his mouth, and feel that little diamond-y stud, he doesn't give me the satisfaction. He just smiles and climbs into his car.

"Good night, Golden Boy," he says.

"Mmm, I don't know how I feel about that," I reply. "Did I tell you that my brother's home now?"

"You did not."

"Yeah, he's home for the summer."

"You don't seem happy about that."

"Eh, I'm happy about *this*." I nod towards him.

"You're laying it on real thick there, buddy. You trying to get in my pants?"

"Is it working?

"I have to go," Rudy laughs.

"Drive safe," I tell him.

"Good night, Silver Boy." And with that, he turns his car on, shuts his door, and heads out.

The fact that tonight didn't end with a kiss is disappointing, for sure, but it isn't frustrating or embarrassing, not like the first time. Maybe because I didn't make a fool of myself this time around. But tonight, him not kissing me feels less like a rejection and more like a moment that we're slowly building up to. And I think I'm okay with that.

But fuck, I really want to kiss him.

I'm sitting in a booth inside the 24-hour diner, nursing a glass of water. Me and Mackenzie agreed to meet up after she gets off work so I can tell her all about how the date went. It sucks that she has to work the closing shift, but that's how it goes when school's out, I guess. They can keep you for forever.

It's already past 11:00pm when Mackenzie walks in. She climbs into the booth across from me and starts to undo her braid.

"How was your night?" I ask as she's letting down her hair. She looks at me sideways, like I've just asked the most offensive thing. "That bad?"

"Don't get me started," she replies. "All these newly graduated high school kids and their entitled ass families. One lady had the nerve to complain that the wait time was ridiculous and that her child was hungry. Like, boo-hoo, everyone's hungry. That's why the wait time's so fucking long, duh! It really made me want to punch her and her kid in the face."

"Wow, you're brutal."

"It's a public service. I'm curbing entitlement." Just then, our waitress, Doris — good ol' Doris — arrives at our table.

"Can I get you anything to drink, sweetie?" she says to Mackenzie.

"Would you willingly serve alcohol to a minor?" Mackenzie replies. Is she for real? "It's been a long day."

"Not while I'm on the clock, but don't tell my boss that." Doris winks. "How about a Shirley Temple?"

"Lovely." Doris heads off and Mackenzie turns to me.

"You're ridiculous, you know that?" I say.

"What? It doesn't hurt to ask." She then leans in. "Anyway, enough about me. How was the date? How'd it go? Are you pregnant yet? Did you kiss?" I shake my head. "Really? Not even a kiss?"

"Nope. I didn't even try."

"Why? Did the night not go well?"

"It did. It went really well actually. It's just… I guess I wanted him to be the one to make the move tonight, you know? I like him and I want to know that he likes me. I don't want to force anything."

"That's not exactly your MO," Mackenzie says.

"And what is my MO according to you?" I reply.

"You're a fuckboy."

"I am not a fuckboy."

"Oh, you are such a fuckboy. And not a very good one."

"How am I a fuckboy?"

"Just look at your dating history," she explains. "You tried to start a 'relationship' with a guy so you could get in his pants, and you didn't even like him. You scared off another guy because you couldn't stop talking about sex. And then you got stood up by a guy who flashed his penis at you in the backseat of your mom's car."

"To be fair, he did that on his own. I didn't ask him to do that," I reply. Mackenzie cocks her head to the side, looking at me like I'm all sorts of stupid. "Oh, come on, give me some credit here," I say, all defensive.

"I did. I said it wasn't your MO."

"And what is an MO exactly?"

"Modus Operandi. It's like your way of operating. God, I cannot with you." She presses her fingers to her temple, and I just sit here awkwardly, almost wishing I had bothered taking Spanish when I had the chance. Modus Operandi is Spanish, right? Or is it Italian? Either way, it's like a whole other language to me.

"Well, maybe I'm growing up," I reply.

"Just stop talking," she says. Doris then returns with Mackenzie's drink, a Shirley Something. I don't even know what it is, but Mackenzie doesn't bat an eye. I swear, she's into all sorts of weird old people things. She's probably the kind of girl who has one of those old phones where you turn the little spinning thing to dial the number and calls it "vintage."

"Can I get you kids anything else? Any food?" Doris asks.

"The drinks are fine for now. We're gonna hang out for a bit," Mackenzie replies. Doris nods then heads off. "So, you and Rudy. That's exciting. You guys are cute together. You're gonna make some really cute babies."

"Babies? It's a little soon for that, don't you think?" I say. She shrugs.

"Eh. You'd be surprised how quick things move when two people are on the same page. Before you know it, you'll become *official,* you'll be hanging out, meeting each other's families. You won't have time for anything else and that'll be that. A beautiful love story." I'm not sure, but I'm getting the sense that Mackenzie's not talking about the possible future here. Her delivery is easy, unbothered, but there's something in her tone that I'm hearing. It's the tiniest hint of… sadness, maybe? She grabs the little dessert menu that's been displayed against the wall on our table and looks it over.

"Yeah, that's not gonna happen," I say, thinking about what she just said. "I'm not just gonna forget about everything — or about you — just because I get a boyfriend."

"Yeah, you will."

"No, I won't."

"*Yeah. You will,*" she insists, still looking at the dessert menu. "Trust me. If this thing works out between you and skinny hipster Nick, you will." She then sets the dessert menu down and looks me straight in the eye. "And I want you to. Whether you believe it or not, I do actually want you to be happy." Mackenzie stops for only the slightest moment to let the words settle before immediately switching gears. "Hey, have you seen our waitress? I decided I want dessert." How quickly she changes the subject is enough to give someone whiplash. She manages to get Doris' attention, and the nice old lady starts to make her way over.

"You need something, doll?" Doris asks when she gets to our table.

"Can I get a slice of apple pie?" Mackenzie replies.

"Sure, are you two sharing? Do you want one spoon or two?" I open my mouth to say, "two," but Mackenzie beats me to the punch.

"Just one. He's gay. He doesn't eat pie." My jaw literally drops.

"Oh, honey, that didn't stop my first husband," Doris laughs as she heads off. I stare at Mackenzie in complete and total disbelief. Did she really just say that to our waitress? And so casually? What the hell?

"Are you serious, right now?" I say, my voice coming out a little louder than intended. Luckily there are only, like, two or three other tables and no one seems to be paying us any attention.

"What?" Mackenzie responds, without a care in the world.

"You just outed me to our waitress now."

"Oh, come on, like she cares."

"*I* care. That's not something you just say to people. That's not their business, and it's not your business to tell." Mackenzie pauses for a moment, hopefully to think about what she's done, then takes a breath.

"You're right. I'm sorry," she says. "Can I ask you though, why are you so against people knowing? It's not like these random people affect your life in any way. Are you, like, scared that someone's gonna say something or try to hurt you? Like, what's your deal?" The question gets me to thinking. Why *am* I against random people knowing? I mean, she's right. Whether strangers know or not doesn't make any difference to my life. And I'm not exactly an easy target, being a six-foot-tall athletic type. So, why am I against it?

"I guess…" I start to say, though I'm not entirely sure what I'm about to say. I've never had to say it before, so it feels like I'm figuring it out just as the words are leaving my mouth. "I guess it's because… I'm not supposed to be gay. Like, the kind of guy that I am isn't supposed to be gay."

"And what kind of guy are you?"

"I'm a sports guy. My dad played sports, my brother plays sports, I play sports. Guys like us are supposed to be strong. We're supposed to be manly."

"Wait, are you saying gay guys don't play sports?"

"No. What I'm saying is I'm supposed to be a man. I'm supposed to be, like, a *guy,* you know? But I… I want a guy to text me just to tell me he's thinking of me. I want a guy to show up at my door with flowers. I want a guy to put his arm around me and make me feel… safe. I want to be treated like a girl."

"Okay, that's very sexist of you," Mackenzie says, which isn't exactly the response I was hoping for when I'm over here baring my soul. But she goes on, her tone a little more understanding. "You know you can want all those things and still be a guy, right? All this macho man stuff, it's all fake. Some dude-bro with a fat ego and little dick energy made it all up. And the whole world bought into it because people are stupid."

"Easy for you to say."

"Yeah, because I'm not an idiot." Somehow, I knew that Mackenzie wouldn't get it. As great as she is, and as much as she might want to understand, she's not a guy. Being a guy, there's this expectation for us to be a certain way, to act a certain way, and if we don't, somehow it makes us less than. It almost feels like I'm not allowed to be anything other than whatever it is I am. Or… I don't know. Maybe she's right. Maybe I am just an idiot who bought into it. I guess I just wanted to fit in. All these thoughts that I'm having must be written all over my face, because Mackenzie looks at me with a sort of pity. It's kind of awful. "You know what might make you feel like a man?"

"What?" I say, though knowing her, I'm not sure I want to know the answer.

"Do you want to eat my pie?"

"Oh, it's a good thing I brought you two spoons." Doris suddenly appears at our table with Mackenzie's dessert order. God, how fucking embarrassing. "You kids enjoy now. Let me know if you need anything else." I nod, biting my bottom lip to keep myself from laughing. Doris just smiles and heads on her way. I look up at Mackenzie, who's got the most self-satisfied smirk plastered all over her face.

"Did you know she was right there when you said that?" I ask, finally letting out the giggles.

"Don't hate me for being observant," Mackenzie replies, picking up a spoon.

"Yeah, that's not why I hate you."

Mackenzie takes a spoonful of pie then slides the plate towards me. As good as the pie looks and smells, I hesitate for a moment. This whole innuendo is a total innuen-*don't* for me. Still, once I get past it, I have to admit; it is pretty delicious. The pie, not... You know what? Never mind.

chapter twenty

It's been sort of an uneventful week. I haven't really been doing much of anything lately besides sleeping in, working out, and falling into YouTube rabbit holes of commentary videos and fail compilations. I tried texting Mackenzie a couple times earlier this week, but she was either working or already had plans to hang out with her other friends, Erik and Nick. Personally, I wouldn't want to play third wheel to a couple. But I guess she was friends with them before she was friends with me, so I can't really blame her. Still, I don't imagine she'd have a better time with them than with me. I can just picture her sitting there on her phone while the two of them canoodle right in front of her. Poor girl. If I'm being completely honest though, I'd love to see that. Is that weird? Is that, like, kinky? God, I need a boyfriend.

Speaking of boyfriends — or at least, people who could *become* boyfriends — Rudy and I have been messaging each other pretty much every day. We haven't been able to plan out another meet up just yet. Like Mackenzie, he's been working a lot, and when he's not working, he's doing something or another. I mean, he lives kinda far away and I don't expect him to stop his life for me at all. But I'd be lying if I said it wasn't a little disappointing. So much for him having "more time." I can't wait till we can get together again though. If only he wasn't so busy. Seems like everyone's always busy these days. Even my brother's always busy.

Art managed to get himself transferred to a local smoothie shop for the summer. They started him last Friday and he's been working most days ever since. Dad likes to comment about how proud he is that Art's a "working man" now and pretty soon he'll be "livin' it up like Gatsby." Must be nice having the golden boy back in the house. He's got so much going on for him. Maybe I should get a job. Everyone else has got a job, so why not? It's not like I'm doing anything else.

. . .

On second thought, never mind. If my parents are any indicator, work is probably how I'll spend the rest of my life. Why would I want to rush into that? Children are stupid. They all want to be adults.

It's a little past 10:00am. I'm sitting in bed, scrolling through my recommendeds on YouTube. We subscribe only to the highest quality content here: meltdown analysis videos and people falling. That's the good stuff. I'm about to start a commentary video I can listen to while I get in a morning workout when I get a notification on my phone. It's a text. From Riley, of all people.

"Hey." That's all it says. One word. I don't really know what to make of it. It's been over two weeks since I came out to him and Jacob. Is this really all he has to say to me after he basically left me hanging? I stare at the message blankly. I don't want to honor it with a response, but I almost feel like I should. I'm tempted to. I don't know, maybe I'm just bored. Since everyone's got their own thing going on, I don't really have anything to do.

The last two summers, most of my time was spent with Riley and Jacob hanging at a park, tossing around a football, and then wandering through one of our neighborhoods getting into all sorts of crap. I remember one time we were walking around Jacob's neighborhood and Riley jumped into a bush for no reason other than Jacob dared him to. I don't know what we were doing, but it was the funniest thing at the time. After, we ended up at Jacob's house and his dad made us a tray of nachos with some burnt shredded cheese. It was the best worst meal ever. It sucks to think about times like that and realize it's all in the past. But it *is* all in the past.

I let out a sigh and toss my phone aside. What would I have to say to Riley? What *could* I say to Riley? I mean, I wasn't good enough for him not to ditch after coming out, so why bother?

I'm not in the mood to workout anymore. Riley's text has me feeling some type of way. I decide to head into the kitchen and find something to eat. Hopefully some food will make me feel better. On my way to the kitchen, I catch a glimpse of the mantelpiece devoted to Art. It's something I've gotten used to and pretty good at ignoring most days. Except when Art's actually here, because then he's not just confined to the mantelpiece in the living room. And as luck would have it, he's standing at the counter, pouring himself a bowl of cereal when I get to the kitchen.

"Hey," he says.

"Hey," I reply. I head over to the cupboard to grab a bowl. At the same time, Art crosses to the fridge and pulls out the milk. I grab a couple of spoons out of the utensil drawer, hand one to Art, and then pour myself a bowl. The whole time, neither one of us say anything. We just go about our business separately together. That is until Art breaks the silence once he's taken his first bite.

"So, uh, I'm off tomorrow," he says, chewing on his cereal.

"That's nice," I respond, taking a bite of mine. "Big plans?"

"Actually, I was planning on going to the car dealership with Mom and Dad. Thought maybe you'd want to come."

"Why would I want to do that?"

"I don't know, to hang out? We haven't really hung out since I got home. I thought we could make a day of it. Catch up."

"You know, if I'm being honest, that sounds more like a *you* thing. I don't really want to get in the way." Thinking that's the end of it, I turn to leave, hoping to eat my cereal in my room in peace.

"Well, what about after?" he asks. Damn it. I stop in my tracks and turn back to him. "We can go and grab dinner or something. My treat," he offers. I have no idea what I'm going to say to get out of this. I don't want to be an asshole, but I don't want to hang out with him either. What do I say? What do I say?

"Yeah, maybe." Fuck. The words slip out before I can think to stop them, and I immediately regret it.

"Cool." Art nods, so I nod. Then I turn around to hole myself up in my room. If I stay in there for the next 48 hours, maybe he'll just forget this conversation ever happened. *I* would like to.

I decide to message Rudy. I need someone to vent to and he's the first person that comes to mind. Thankfully, he's not currently at work.

GoldenBoy513: Hey. Wyd?
RudeFern69: Running errands for mi madre.
GoldenBoy513: No work today?
RudeFern69: Later. Closing shift [Disappointed emoji]
RudeFern69: What's up?
GoldenBoy513: My bro wants to hang [Eye roll emoji]
RudeFern69: Why don't you want to hang with him?
GoldenBoy513: He's annoying enough when he's not here. Even more so when he is. Idk. I just hate how he's been put on a pedestal.
RudeFern69: Is that his fault?
GoldenBoy513: Yeah [Eye roll emoji]
RudeFern69: Lol.
RudeFern69: Why not just hang out with him?
GoldenBoy513: Who's side are you on?
RudeFern69: Whose*

RudeFern69: And I'm on yours. That's why I tell you how it is. It's not his fault he's on a pedestal. You gotta get over it. He is your brother. Would it be so bad to hang out with him?

GoldenBoy513: I guess not.

RudeFern69: Babe, you gotta give people a chance. You never know. They might surprise you.

GoldenBoy513: Babe?

RudeFern69: You are a babe.

GoldenBoy513: You like me [Smirking face emoji]

RudeFern69: [Winky kiss emoji]

RudeFern69: Anyway, driving now. Talk later.

God, I miss that guy. He really knows how to get me excited. It must be a Latin thing. I'm finding I have a thing for Latin men. Is that racist for me to say? That's probably racist. Oh well, I like what I like. Cancel me.

Sunday. June 22nd.

With Mom, Dad, and Art out car shopping, I got the house all to myself. I decide to spend the day on the couch, posted up in front of the big screen. The plan is to stream a whole bunch of horror movies and binge on microwave chicken nuggets, potato chips, and Oreos.

The first movie on the list is this movie about these poor people bamboozling these rich people into hiring them as the help, only to find a big secret locked away in the basement. It's a really good movie. I wouldn't call it scary, but it does get pretty crazy towards the end. It goes from like "Oh, shit," to "*Oh, shit!*" Good stuff.

The next movie I put on is about this pregnant woman who lives out in the country with her husband, and then these random people start showing up and destroying their house. And the husband lets them! I wouldn't exactly call this movie scary either. It's more like "What is happening right now?" But the last bit… Yeah… No. Big nope. The last bit made me want to spit out my Oreo. You know something's gone too far when it makes you want to spit out an Oreo. I'm thinking maybe I should switch gears.

I'm scrolling through the channel guide to see what's on and find there's a marathon of that home buying show that my parents like to watch. How much you want to bet that one episode will have a couple who makes jewelry out of hamster droppings and has a budget of ten million dollars on it? They'll probably want a starter home with eighteen bedrooms and room to "entertain." Like, bust out the accordion, Linda, we're doing some clogging.

It's about six, maybe seven o'clock, when I start to get bored of watching uppity people argue about whether going over budget for a turnkey is better than saving 50k on a fixer upper. First world problems, am I right? I decide to text both Mackenzie and Rudy to see what they're doing but neither one of them respond. I'm guessing they're both working, or busy, or whatever. I let out a sigh. What to do? What to do?

I'm scrolling through YouTube, searching for any old video to potentially fall into a rabbit hole with, when I hear the door to the garage in the kitchen open and my mom's voice calling out.

"Andrew, honey, we're home," she says as she appears from around the corner and enters the living room. "Did you spend the whole day in front of the TV?"

"Not the whole day," I reply. "I was also on my phone." Mom lets out a slight chuckle, shaking her head.

"Well, your brother bought a car."

"Good for him."

"It's really nice. You should see it. It's a hybrid," Mom says. I fight the urge to laugh. Sorry, but how pretentious can you be? It's like, "Look at me. I'm responsible. I save money on gas while also saving the environment." That nerd. Still, Mom seems impressed. Maybe I should be too. It's just… It's such an Art move. A hybrid? Really? Why couldn't he just get a normal car? Why'd he have to be all fancy about it? I know something like this shouldn't annoy me, but it does. So, when Art comes into the living room with Dad, I'm just like, "ugh!"

"Man, that thing drives smooth," Dad says to Art.

"Yeah, and it's gonna save a ton on gas," Art replies. Dad pats him on the back.

"You did good, kiddo. Can you believe it, Liz? Our son's a car owner. We raised a good one." I clench my jaw at this. Out of the corner of my eye, I notice the mantelpiece and suddenly I don't feel so great. I get up and start making my way to my room.

"Hey, Andrew," Art says. I stop and turn to him. I'd really rather not deal with him right now, but I'm not about to be a dick to him in front of my parents. "You wanna go for a drive with me? Test out the ride?"

"Uh, I'm actually not feeling too hot right now. I think I might've ate too much," I say, rubbing my stomach for maximum effect.

"Oh, okay. Uh, yeah. Another time then."

"Sure." I then excuse myself and hole myself up in my room for the rest of the night.

Wednesday. June 25th.

It's a little past 5:00pm. I'm heading into the kitchen, hoping to swipe a beer from my dad's stash before dinner. It's been a quiet week so far, and I'm getting so bored. I spent most of the morning scrolling endlessly through social media. I had nothing better to do. I'm not friends with my friends anymore and the friends that I do have seem to have other friends and lives of their own. And to think I was looking forward to the summer. Now, I want to escape it. Frankly, I could use the buzz.

When I get to the kitchen, I head straight for the fridge. There, I notice something new has been put up as I reach for the door. It's a printout of Art's grades. And of course, it's screaming his praises. AAAAAA!!! I can't help but roll my eyes. Is this a normal thing that people do with report cards or is my family just weird? I feel like decorating the fridge door with schoolwork and stuff like that stops being cute when the kid hits puberty. But then again, I wouldn't know. The last time I had anything make it onto the fridge door was before I hit puberty. Whatever.

I manage to find half a case of beer tucked behind a jug of OJ and help myself to a bottle. Just as I'm popping the beer open at the counter, Dad comes in from the garage, carrying a stack of mail. Seems he's just getting home from work.

"Drinking my beer again," he comments, not all that concerned.

"You keep buying them, I'll keep drinking them," I reply.

"I buy that for me, smart ass," he laughs. Then, he hands me an envelope from the stack of mail he brought in. "Here, you got something from school." My stomach twists at the sight of it. Fuck.

"Must be my report card," I mumble quietly to myself. Dad's attention is carefully on me like a nosey neighbor. Honestly, I didn't do too bad this last semester. At least, I don't *think* I did. But after seeing Art's grades, I know there's no way mine can compare. I sigh. Here goes nothing.

CLASS	INSTRUCTOR	GRADE	NOTES
PIANO	A. Dolittle	A-	Easily Distracted
ALGEBRA II	M. Castellano	C-	
ENGLISH	D. Maple	B-	
US HISTORY	R. Milano	B	
P.E.	A. Burke	A	
BIOLOGY	L. Reed	C+	

I stare at my grades for a moment. A part of me thinks that this report card isn't that bad. But then I hand it to my dad and see the almost confused look on his face, like he doesn't understand how my grades are like this, and it feels like a punch to the gut. I just imagine him wondering how he managed to have one perfect son who's winning at life, doing good in college, has a job, and can afford the monthly payments to buy a fuel-efficient car that's *also* good for the environment, only to turn around and have a kid like me. I'm the kid that got held back in kindergarten and couldn't pull out an A in history when the final was open book. The answers were right there! Ugh, I cannot deal. And I think Dad can tell.

"Hey, at least you're passing," he offers.

"Yeah?" I scoff. "Why don't you hang it up on the fridge?" And with that, I take a swig of my beer and walk off, heading right back to my room.

I'm sitting on my bed, drinking my beer, hoping for a buzz to set in. I keep having these thoughts about my brother being better than me, and I'm starting to get really annoyed, which is annoying in itself. I mean, so what if my brother is doing well? That's a good thing, right? So what if my dad is proud of him? That's a good thing, right? These are good things… Good things for everybody else. I down the rest of my beer and let out a sigh. I want to stop thinking like this. I hate that I'm getting so mopey over something that shouldn't even bother me. I need another distraction. The alcohol isn't cutting it.

My eyes drift over to my mom's keyboard sitting on my desk. I haven't touched that thing in a while. I wonder if I still remember how to play. I go ahead and take a seat at my desk, gently placing my fingers on the dusty keys. I can already hear *Moonlight Sonata* starting to play in my head and allow my fingers to follow along to the silent music in my mind.

G hashtag, C hashtag, E normal.

G hashtag, C hashtag, E normal.

I'm starting to get back into the groove of playing, stroking the same three keys repeatedly over, and over, and over again.

G hashtag, C hashtag, E normal.
G hashtag, C hashtag, E normal.

Eventually, it starts to dawn on me. I've forgotten what comes after this part. That, or I never learned it. I can still hear the music playing in my mind, but I can't for the life of me figure out which key to hit, so I just stop. I'm kind of regretting not listening to Mrs. Dolittle and practicing more when I still had access to the piano book. Oh well, I guess I could always work on some scales. I decide to start with the C Major scale. No way I would've forgotten that.

C, D, E, F, G — Blaaang!!!

The keyboard screams at me, and I tense up. Oh yeah, I totally forgot about that broken Middle G. That's gonna put a damper on this whole piano thing. I let out a disappointed sigh. What now?

Just then, my phone, which I'd left sitting on my bed, goes off with a notification. I go to check it and see it's from Rudy.

RudeFern69: Hey. Wyd for pride?
GoldenBoy513: Idk. When is it?
RudeFern69: This weekend. You going?
GoldenBoy513: I wasn't planning to.

RudeFern69: Why not?

GoldenBoy513: Idk. I never been.

RudeFern69: Well, do you wanna go?

RudeFern69: I was planning on going with some friends but I work till 5 and they wanna go earlier.

GoldenBoy513: Yeah. I'd love to.

RudeFern69: Perfect.

RudeFern69: How about we meet at BART? We can meet at a station between us.

GoldenBoy513: Sounds good.

RudeFern69: Great. See you then, babe [Winky kiss emoji]

And just like that, I've got plans for the weekend. My day's suddenly getting a lot better. I finally have something to look forward to. I'm going to Pride. I've never been to Pride. What do people do at Pride? Is it just, like, an all-day parade? Is it, like, a party or something? Maybe I should've asked. God, I have no idea how to be gay. And I'm not about to ask Rudy about this stuff, because how would that seem? *This lame high schooler doesn't know what Pride is.* I feel like there should be a pamphlet or a brochure on the basics of being gay. Like, the *Gaysics*… Nah, that sounds too much like "Gays sick." That probably wouldn't go over well with the community. You know, I'm just gonna ask Mackenzie.

"Hello?" she answers after the first ring.

"Mackenzie! What's up?" I say into my phone. "How you been?"

"I've been good. I'm just heading into work. What do you want?"

"I have some good news. Rudy just asked me to go to Pride with him."

"Oh, congrats. You realize this could've been a text, right?" Ha, she sounds so annoyed. Classic Mackenzie.

"Well, I actually wanted to ask you, do you know anything about Pride?"

"No, I've never been."

"What do you mean you've never been? You're an ally."

"And you're gay. What's your excuse?"

"Eh, you got me there." I'm honestly genuinely surprised by this. If there's anyone I know that would've been to Pride, it would've been Mackenzie. "I guess I'm just nervous. I don't really know anything about being gay, and the idea of going to Pride is like… What's the expectation, you know?"

"You'll probably end up pregnant." I let out a slight chuckle. It hadn't even occurred to me. Could sex be on the table? Is that something that happens at Pride, sex on tables? In public? Huh, I'm not opposed to it, but I should probably lose my virginity first before I start getting freaky about it. "Look, Andrew, I'm sure you'll be fine. It's probably just a block party, or a parade, or something to celebrate being your authentic self. Just go and enjoy it. Besides, you'll be with Rudy."

"Yeah, you're right." I miss Mackenzie. She's been such a good friend. Really, she's been the friend that I needed. I always felt like I was hiding from my friends before. With her, I don't have a reason to. "We really need to hang out."

"Yeah, we do. How about Monday?" she suggests. "You can tell me all about how your weekend at Pride goes with Rudy. I'll bring you a pregnancy test."

"Sure," I laugh.

"Oh, and Andrew?"

"What's up?"

"This whole conversation could've been a text."

"Noted."

"Later." And with that, she ends the call. She really is a great friend.

I hate her.

chapter twenty-one

I'm standing on the platform overlooking the freeway, waiting for Rudy's train to arrive. We agreed to meet up at MacArthur station; it's the first BART station on both our routes, so we figured it'd be easiest. I did have to lie to my mom to get her to loan me the car though. I told her I was going to hang with Riley and Jacob. Probably catch a movie or something. I mean, I wasn't about to tell her I was running off to the city for the night. She'd probably start asking questions, and that's not a conversation I'm in any hurry to have.

It's a little past 7:00pm. The sun's still up. I'm sitting on a bench, mindlessly tapping the keys of the piano app on my phone when a train pulls into the station. This must be his. At least, I'm hoping it is. I feel like it's been so long since I last saw Rudy, I can't wait to see him again. I'm curious to see if his hair has changed.

People start pouring out of the train as soon as the doors slide open. I get up to look around, searching for Rudy among the crowds. It's not, like, super crowded, but with the wave of people passing by, it'd be easy to miss someone. Especially when you're not sure what they might look like today. I don't know if I should be looking for a cute pink haired Hispanic boy or a silver headed one. For all I know, I could be looking for any color of the rainbow, which is fitting, considering the day.

"Well, what do we have here?" a familiar voice says from behind. I quickly turn and there he is, Rudy. His hair is a fiery red now, with hints of orange and gold. With his black roots, it looks like his hair's on fire, and I kinda love it. He's got this whole rebellious thing going on today, dressed in dark jeans, a plain white tee, and a black leather jacket. Meanwhile, I look all straightlaced by comparison in my pale blue short-sleeve button up, school letterman, and faded ripped jeans. Here I was thinking I looked cool and relaxed, but Rudy, he looks… *dangerous*. Which is funny, because today, he actually brought a backpack. Oh, how the tables have turned. The sight of him sends my mind back to my last conversation with Mackenzie, and a part of me is now hoping sex on tables is on the table. Then again, I probably shouldn't think about that until after we've had our first kiss, but we'll get there. One thing at a time.

"Hey," I greet him. "Wow, you look really nice. I feel like I look like a square."

"Not at all," Rudy replies. "You're perfect. I like that little flash of knee you're giving me. It's very risqué." I chuckle. He's stupid, but I'm into it. I'm into him.

As our conversation begins, we slowly start to wander aimlessly together. We've got a little bit of time before our train is set to arrive, and what else is there to do but talk and wander?

"So, Pride. What are we in for tonight?" I ask.

"Whatever," Rudy shrugs. "Saturday's are usually a massive street party. At least, it was every time I went. We'll have fun. We'll stop by a liquor store, get ourselves drunk, and we'll have the most amazing time."

"I take it you go to Pride a lot?"

"A few times," Rudy says. "It's really fun going with a big group. I would've hated having to go alone, so thank you."

"Would you actually have gone alone?"

"Probably not. So, again, thank you. I'm so excited about tonight. I cannot wait to get a drink in me and just turn everything off."

"Life's that bad?"

"Eh, no. I'm just complaining," Rudy says. We get to a round stone bench placed on the uncovered part of the platform. Rudy sits then pauses for a second. I take a seat next to him. "Do you ever feel like life just never slows down?" he asks. "When the semester ended, I thought I'd have more time, but then I started getting scheduled more at work, and now that I'm not in school, my mom wants me to do stuff, and I just… I just don't want to. I want everything to stop for a while, or at least, slow down, you know? What I wouldn't give to have no responsibilities."

"It's not all it's cracked up to be," I reply. "Since school let out, I haven't done anything with myself. I've been so fuckin' bored. I've been doing nothing but watching marathons of home buying shows and binging on junk food."

"That sounds amazing."

"We're like opposite sides of the same coin."

"Yeah, we belong together," he says with a light and casual tone. My heart about skips a beat. I turn my head to look out towards the freeway — I must look embarrassingly giddy smiling to myself right now — and watch the cars as they pass by. We've got a great view of all the ways the roads split; some going over, some going under, twisting in every which way. It's all so busy and loud here, and yet there's something almost calming about it. That might just be because there's no one else over here. It's just us. Like, on this little uncovered part of the platform, we're in our own little world. This gives me an idea.

"You want your life to slow down?" I ask. "How about now?" Rudy looks at me all sorts of confused. "We're here. Take it in."

"Take what in?" he asks.

"Everything. Look around. Enjoy the moment. Just chill."

"Just chill?" He smiles, then takes a breath. "Okay." We go silent. I wait for him to feel the moment and the setting the way I did. The way that I do. To see the cars passing by. To see the views of the splitting roads. To hear the calming quiet under all the noise. "This would be so much better high," he eventually says, and I can't help but burst out laughing. He laughs along with me. He may not feel it, but I could sit here forever with him, laughing about nothing.

We chat for a little while longer, mostly about stupid stuff. We're talking about how overrated avocado toast is — like, really, it's only a thing because bougie hipsters and pumpkin spice white girls said so — when a train pulls into the station.

"I think this is us," Rudy says. "Shall we?" We get up and head over to the covered part of the platform to rejoin the rest of the world. And together, we step onto the train. Next stop: the city.

I've always hated riding the BART through the underground parts. The train flying through the tunnel is so loud, it sounds like a scream. You can't talk to whoever you're with because you can't hear them, and you can't really use your phone for anything. You just have to listen to the sound. And it's not the kind of sound that you can block out either. It's like the train is begging to be let out. But because of how it's built, it has to stay down here to get where it's going. That's just how it is.

I'm not sure which station we're supposed to get off at. Truth be told, I've never gotten off anywhere past Embarcadero where the Ferry Building is. The only reason I take BART to the city is to hang out and do touristy stuff at Pier 39. Aside from that, much of San Francisco I've only seen from inside a car, when my dad would take us to random sites for a family outing. Driving around somewhere is totally different than walking through it. Really, tonight I'm just banking on Rudy knowing where we're going.

We end up getting off at 16th and Mission.

"You know, I don't think I've ever been to this part of the city," I say, stepping onto the escalator behind Rudy.

"I'm only ever here passing through," he replies.

"Oh? Do you come here often?"

"Is this you flirting with me?" Rudy smiles, playfully narrowing his eyes.

"Depends. Is it working?"

Rudy places his hand on my cheek, letting his thumb caress my bottom lip. I'd probably be really freaked out by this — being in public and all — if I wasn't so turned on.

"Ay, mi Güerito. Pudiera amarte, pero no ahorita." Fuck. I don't know what he said, but…

"That's hot," I say. Rudy chuckles.

"You're very cute."

It's looking like the sun's about to set when we get up to street level. Rudy steps off the escalator and immediately begins walking. I quickly follow, taking in the unfamiliar surroundings — the colorful fencing around the BART station entrance, the nearby storefronts, the buildings. About a block or so later, Rudy stops. I look and see we're standing right outside a liquor store.

"Wait here. I'll be right back," Rudy says before heading into the store. I know we just got here, and I know we haven't done anything yet, but I've got a good feeling about tonight. I feel like tonight is going to be a night to remember. I'm excited for what's to come. I mean, it's Pride. It's Rudy. It's us.

Just about a minute later, Rudy comes out of the liquor store carrying a paper bag. He nods to me, and we continue walking. Not long after, we come across a smaller street that feels more like an alleyway. Rudy ducks behind the building on the corner and pulls out two bottles from the paper bag: one's a bottle of OJ and the other's vodka. He wasn't kidding when he was talking about wanting to get a drink in him earlier. He opens the OJ bottle and pours half of it out. Then he takes the vodka and refills the OJ bottle with it. And I thought I was edgy for stealing beers from my dad.

"Screwdriver?" Rudy says, offering me the OJ bottle. I grab it and take a sip. I feel the alcohol burn in my throat as it goes down. How much did he put in this? My God. I have to take a second to regain my composure after. It's like I got punched in the throat. Rudy just giggles to himself, shoving the leftover vodka into his bag. He then takes the OJ bottle from me. "Cheers, love." And downs a massive gulp. "Oh, that's way stronger than I thought it was gonna be." I laugh, then take the bottle from him for another sip.

We step out of the alley-like street and start heading towards wherever it is we're going. I'm still not really sure, so I'm hoping Rudy's buzz doesn't kick in before we get there. As we're walking, out of nowhere, Rudy slips his hand into mine. He laces our fingers together. For a second, I feel that all too familiar sense of panic coming on, and I want to pull my hand away. But I look over at Rudy and notice him smiling to himself. I'm not sure if it's the alcohol or if it's us that's got him looking so happy. Either way, how could I ever let go of a guy like this? In a moment like this? I can't. I won't. So, I don't. Despite how nervous, or uncomfortable, or how scared it makes me, I don't let go. I don't want to. Fuck it. It's Pride.

Rudy and I walk for a couple more blocks. Eventually, we get to an area that's a little more crowded. We pass several groups gathered on the sidewalk, all decked out in rainbow flags. I look on ahead and see more and more people, many of which are spilling out onto the street. In the distance, I can hear the faint sound of music playing under the chatter from the drunk and half-naked crowds. And isn't it always a shame that the people who are half-naked are never the ones you want to see half-naked? But that's beside the point.

The sun's set now, but the street is still bright, lit up by all the city lights. There's a certain energy and excitement in the air, like when you're watching a football game with a bunch of people. They could be people you know, people you don't know, or people you barely know, and it doesn't even matter if you're rooting for the same team or not, so long as everyone's invested in the game. It's that kind of energy. It's that kind of excitement. I stop to take it in.

"You still got that drink?" Rudy asks. I hand him the bottle, and he takes a sip. I take another one too. The burn feels slightly better this time. "Don't lose that bottle. I'm just now starting to get a buzz. I'd love to go all the way." All the way? I immediately start thinking about sex on tables again. We're around our people, right? I should just kiss him now. And I actually try to. I take a step towards him, close enough so that our noses brush together. From the side, I hear a whole bunch of guys start to cheer: *"Woo!" "Yeah!" "Kiss him!"* Trust me, I want to. But just as I'm about to press my lips onto Rudy's, I feel his hand on my chest and him slowly pushing me back. "Careful, mi Güerito, calma."

"I have no idea what you're saying, but it's so fucking hot," I mumble, the alcohol starting to hit me. Rudy laughs. I can't say I'm not disappointed that he didn't let me kiss him, but I also can't say I'm surprised. I just don't know what he's waiting for.

"Come on, I want to dance." Rudy starts to walk on ahead. I turn to look at the guys who I assume were the ones cheering us on and see some grungy hipster guy with a manbun holding a bottle in a paper bag. Probably a beer. He raises it as if to toast and smirks at me. I flash him my awkward tight-lipped smile — no thanks — and jog to catch up to Rudy.

As Rudy and I head further down the street, the crowds start to get thicker and thicker. The music gets louder too. Whatever they're playing is real heavy on the bass, and it gets heavier with every step. It's so loud, I could swear I feel the ground shake. But then again, this is California. It could just be an earthquake. Who's to say? Suddenly, we come to a street where there are so many rainbow-dressed and half-naked people that I literally cannot see the street beneath them because everyone's packed together so tight. Something tells me this is where Rudy wants to be.

"Hold on to me. I don't want to lose you," Rudy says, practically yelling to be heard over the music. He offers me his hand. I take it, and before I can even think about it, he's dragging me into the thick of it. The thick of the crowd. The thick of the music and the dancing. The thick of the sweaty, squished together, half-naked — and in some cases, totally naked — excitement. The thick of freedom. Oh, what I wouldn't give to be like these people. And maybe I can be. Even if only for tonight.

Rudy pulls me along behind him. There are so many people around, and they're all huddled so close, it's amazing anyone's dancing here. I can barely move my free arm beside me. What's even more amazing is how Rudy's managing to get us through the crowd, pushing us past everyone bouncing and bobbing because bouncing and bobbing is all anyone has room for. I can kind of see over the crowd. From what I can tell, I think we're heading towards a stage. Eventually, we stop. We're right in the middle of the sea of people. All the body heat has got me covered in sweat, and I'm not sure it's even mine, but okay. I'm willing to surrender to the experience. Rudy turns to me as best as he can, places his hands on my shoulders, and starts bouncing along to the music. His mouth opens like he's yelling "Woo!" with excitement, but I can't hear him. The music here is so deafeningly loud that I can't hear anything but the bass. So, I just nod to the beat until I find myself bouncing along with Rudy and everyone else.

There's something about the music and the shared energy of everyone dancing that makes me feel really light and almost dizzy. It feels like I'm drunk, but I don't think I am. I haven't had that much to drink. Then I remember the bottle of OJ I've been carrying. I unscrew the cap and take a swig, letting the burn coat my throat and pour into my stomach. Rudy then takes the bottle and downs the rest of it. I smile, impressed. He throws the empty bottle to the ground and lets out another silent "Woo!" Cheers erupt from all around us. It's like they're cheering for him. I am. And then the beat drops. Everyone starts jumping like crazy. I doubt we're all in time, but it doesn't matter.

We dance and dance, losing ourselves well past the point of breathlessness. I have to stop for a moment. I feel like I'd just sprinted for miles, and I could use some air. It's stuffy around all these people though. I'm drenched in sweat. At least this time, I'm pretty sure it's mine. My whole body feels warm. I'm really regretting wearing my letterman tonight. But can you blame me? It's always a little chilly in the city. Rudy says something, but I can't hear what.

"What?" I yell. He leans in and talks into my ear.

"I said, 'Are you okay?'"

"Yeah, I'm fine. I just need a sec."

"You want to step out?" Rudy offers. I nod. He grabs me by the arm, and we quickly start to weave our way back out of the crowd. As soon as we reach a clearing, I rip off my letterman and take in the biggest breath I can manage, filling my lungs with all the freshness of pot smoke and gay sweat. It's much more relieving than it sounds. God, I never realized how exhausting dancing could be. I don't think I've ever danced this much before. Not even at homecoming or junior prom. Then again, I did spend half the time at those dances getting high in the bathroom off a joint me, Riley, and Jacob split with a few other guys from the football team. For as homophobic as those guys can be, they're perfectly fine taking hits off something we all put our mouths on. Makes no sense, but I'm not judging.

I toss my letterman onto my shoulder and walk a little bit to get away from the most crowded part of the street. Then I plop myself down on the curb. Rudy follows and takes a seat next to me. I look over at him and see his eyes are hooded. The guy looks drunk off his ass. I can't help but laugh.

"What?" he asks.

"Nothing," I reply, shaking my head. "I'm just happy I'm here right now. With you." He smiles, his eyes narrowing flirtingly. Flirtatiously? I don't know. Maybe it's just the alcohol. Either way, I'm enjoying his company. "Hey, do me a favor," I say. "Hang on to my letterman tonight, would you?" And I place my jacket on his shoulders, wrapping it around him the way you would a lover.

"I could kiss you right now," he says. My heart skips a beat. Suddenly, the world seems to fall silent. Really? Is he for real? I'm staring at him, wanting, waiting for him to come in for the kiss. Do it, Rudy. Do it! I want it so bad. But he just sits there, staring at me, smiling. What is he waiting for?

"So? Do it," I whisper, trying not to sound desperate, even though I am. I very much am. "Kiss me." Rudy goes silent for a moment. My heart beats faster and faster with every second he takes. Finally, he shakes his head.

"No puedo enamorame de ti ahorita." There he goes with the sexy Spanish talk again. If only I understood it. God, I should've taken Spanish as my elective.

"You know, you keep talking like that, and I have no idea what you're saying."

"It's probably better that you don't."

I suddenly get the urge to take a leak. That alcohol's finally run through me. When I get up, I feel a massive rush in my head, and I have to pause to make sure I've got my balance. I guess the drink that Rudy mixed together hit me harder than I thought. I look around, hoping to find somewhere that might have a bathroom I can use, and spot a row of porta potties just a little ways down the street.

"I'm gonna use the bathroom. I'll be right back," I tell Rudy.

"Have fun," he replies.

There's a bit of a line for the porta potties. There are about three people in front of me. Everyone smells of booze and a good time. Who am I kidding? I probably smell the same. At least no one around me is upchucking. I don't know if I could handle that right now.

One of the porta potty doors swings open. The person at the front of the line steps in. Just two more. I look around, tapping my hand against my thigh to pass the time. I see a wave of people approaching. It's looking like more and more are arriving for Pride. It's fascinating to see how people dress for this thing. Some people are dressed in normal streetwear, while others look like they're going to the beach, and some look like they've just stepped out of a sex dungeon. I noticed it before when we first got here and we were going to dance, but I didn't think much of it. But now that I'm standing here, watching everyone passing by, I'm just confused.

Another porta potty door swings open. One more person ahead of me. Not long now.

You know, when it comes to gay stuff, I always thought I wasn't the type of guy to be gay. I always thought that because I like sports and because I don't dress to make a big show of myself — I mean, half my wardrobe is stuff I stole from my dad — that I wasn't doing it right. That I wasn't being gay right. Sort of like how you can be less of a man for being gay. But seeing all these people dressed in all sorts of ways, from normal to formal to athletic to "Is that even legal?" has me wondering: What does it mean to be gay? They're just as different from one another as anyone else. Maybe I'm exactly the kind of guy to be gay. Huh…

Another porta potty door opens. The last person ahead of me goes in. I'm next. Thank God. I really have to piss.

While I'm waiting for my turn in the bathroom, a pair of skinny guys in skinny jeans pass by me. One of them looks at me with an arched brow. He looks upset.

"Oh, you're cute," he says all excited, which throws me because I thought he was mad. Then he goes on his way, heading toward the growing crowd. Probably to bounce and bob to bass.

A porta potty door opens. Finally. My turn.

I feel so much better after coming out of the bathroom. I've still got a tiny bit of a buzz going, and I'm ready to rejoin the party. I head back to the place where I left Rudy, but when I get there, he's not sitting on the curb waiting for me anymore. He's gone. I look around thinking maybe he decided to get up and stretch his legs or something. Maybe he went back to dancing. I don't know. All I know is that I don't see him.

The crowd has gotten bigger. More and more people keep coming and I'm starting to worry. Last I checked, Rudy was drunk. I don't know how drunk, but I know he drank more than I did, and I'm already hyper focusing to keep my wits about me. There's just too much going on to keep a clear head, and when you mix in the alcohol, it's hard to not feel like the world is spinning around you. I'm scanning every which way to see if I can spot him, but no luck. I don't see him here. I don't see him anywhere. How the hell am I supposed to find him in all this?

. . .

Duh! I'll message him. Hopefully he checks his phone. Hopefully he does it soon. People keep showing up here, and I expect that the more people that do, the more difficult it's gonna be for us to find each other.

"Where you at?" I message him through AphroDATEme. I let a moment or two pass, waiting to see if he responds. Nothing. Hmm. I suppose I'll just wait until he does. I decide to take one more look around before I sit down on the curb, spinning slowly in place to check all angles. Nothing to my left. Nothing behind. Nothing to the right. Then, as I turn to make a full circle, I notice a group of people in front of me moving forward but veering to the side as if to avoid something. I wait for a second for the crowd to clear, and when they do, everything stops.

I see that what everyone was swerving to avoid was Rudy. There he is, right in front of me, the leftover bottle of vodka he bought earlier dangling from his hand. And his mouth on some dude. I stare at them, taking in the sight of the guy I came here with making out with some rando. And not just any rando. A rando with a fucking manbun. Are you kidding me? Is that the same guy who was smirking at me when we first got here? Is this for real? What. The. Fuck? Seriously? Rudy is so tangled up in his mouth that he doesn't even notice I'm staring at them. I guess it doesn't matter. Clearly, he's not trying to hide anything anymore, what with him holding the bottle of vodka out in the open like that.

. . .

Why?

Why would he do this?

Why would he invite me out to Pride? Why would he flirt with me the way that he did? Why would he call me "babe" and practically claim me as his, if he was just gonna go and do that? He never even let *me* kiss him and yet here we are. There he is. Here I am. If this isn't the most sobering experience… I can't be here anymore. I can't be here right now. I need to leave. I just start walking, not thinking about anything other than getting away from this place and getting away from Rudy. I don't manage to get very far though.

"Andrew!" I hear him call out to me. I don't know why I stop. I have nothing to say to him and I don't care about what he might have to say to me. I should just leave, but something's stopping me. "There you are," Rudy smiles, jogging up to and then in front of me. Amazing. He's still wearing my letterman and he's not acting like anything's wrong. He must be really drunk off his ass. "I've been looking everywhere for you."

"Really?" I say. He's full of shit, but what am I gonna do? Start a fight? I can smell the vodka on his breath. How much more did he drink while I was in the bathroom? Good lord. "Can I get my jacket back?" I say, more as a demand than a question.

"Yeah." He slips off my letterman and hands it back to me like it was nothing, before immediately changing the subject. "I met a guy. He just told me his name. He's got, uh… LDS." Rudy bursts out laughing. "That's not right. You know, the drug."

"That's great." I'm not finding anything about this funny. I just put on my jacket. "I think I'm gonna go," I say.

"What? Why?" Rudy blinks, his drunken smile quickly fading.

"I'm not feeling very good anymore."

"Oh, okay. Well, here. Let me just give away this bottle and then we can leave."

"No, you don't have to come with me," I say. I really don't want him to come with me, for obvious reasons, but he waves as if dismissing it.

"I'm not gonna let you leave alone. I love you," Rudy slurs, then smiles casually. It's like he's twisting the knife, isn't it? He quickly stumbles over to Manbun, and hands him the nearly empty bottle of vodka. Then he comes back to me, takes my hand in his, and pulls me down the street back towards BART.

The whole walk back, I don't say anything. What would I say? "You won't kiss me, but you love me? But you kiss *him*, and yet you love *me*? Make it make sense. I can't make any sense of it." I want to say that. I do. But I don't. I don't, because in the several blocks that we walk to get back to the station, I start to wonder… How did I get put second to a stranger? A stranger with a manbun, no less. But then I remember the title that Rudy gave to me the night that we first met: *Silver Boy*. I know he meant it as a sort of compliment then, but maybe I should've taken it as a hint or a clue. Maybe for him, I was never meant to be gold.

chapter twenty-two

This BART ride feels forever long. And I think Rudy is way more drunk than I initially thought because, as soon as we sat down, he knocked out right onto my shoulder. As pissed as I am at him, I don't have the heart to shrug him off. He snores the way I imagine a baby koala might. I mean, he kinda looks like one, the way he's slumped against my arm with his little backpack on. To think, a guy this precious could play such messy games. Then again, I do hear koala's have STDs, so I guess you never know.

I'm still trying to make sense of what he did. I don't understand how he can make out with a complete and total stranger when he won't even let me give him a peck. Like, what is that? I mean, yeah, tonight's only the third time we've hung out, but we've been talking for weeks. You'd think that would count for something. It really makes me think that he doesn't like me at all. I mean, he says he does, but his actions just don't match. Who rejects a guy they like and then turns around and kisses some random dude in front of him? Is this what dating is like for adults? A bunch of mixed signals? Ugh, why can't it just be simple? Like, how in those old movies, they'd pass notes to each other that said, "Do you like me? Check box yes or no." Wait… Those movies are about teenagers, aren't they? Well, they're usually played by adults, so it kind of counts.

I just want to know what he's thinking. Like, do you like me, Rudy? Do you *actually* like me? Check box yes or no. I know he's sitting right here. I know I could just nudge him awake and ask, but I don't want to get a drunken answer. I've seen what he does when he's drunk.

Suddenly, a voice comes through over the intercom, "Now arriving at MacArthur Station." Shit. This is Rudy's stop, but he's still asleep on my shoulder. I know I should wake him up, but I'm debating whether or not it's a good idea for me to leave him here. I mean, the guy's literally knocked out drunk. Would it be terrible if I left him? Would that make me, like, a shit person? If I'm being honest, I want to. I want to leave him here. I want to be done with him. I want to get away from him. Can you blame me?

The train comes to a stop. Time to make a choice, Andrew. Are we waking Rudy up and ditching him or are we gonna be responsible and handle the situation like a grown person? Decisions, decisions. I stare at the open doors leading out to the covered platform of MacArthur Station. This is where I'll leave him, I think. All I gotta do is wake him up. But I'm hesitating. I think about the night we had before the Manbun situation. I think about how good I felt being with Rudy. I think about how freeing it was. Of all the possibility. Do I really want to let that go? Do I really want to let *him* go? I take too long to make a choice. The doors begin to slide close. I let out a heavy sigh. I guess I don't have to decide right now.

We're just a couple of stops from where I get off when I feel Rudy lift his head off my shoulder.

"Hmm… Where are we?" he says, rubbing his eyes, all groggy-like. His hair's a little flat from resting on my shoulder, but it sorta adds to the whole koala vibe I imagined for him. He blinks at me, trying to get his eyes to focus. God, he's cute even when he's waking up.

"We're on BART," I answer. I can't let myself fall for this. I turn my head to face forward and keep my eyes straight ahead.

"Did we pass MacArthur?" he asks.

"Yeah, a little while ago."

"Why didn't you wake me?" Good question. I wonder that myself.

"And do what? Just leave you there?" I say, letting my eyes shift toward him. "You're drunk."

"Huh. And they say chivalry is dead," he smiles. Ugh, I can feel myself softening up towards him. How is it that he has this effect on me? Maybe I like him more than I think I do... This is so stupid.

I keep my hands in my pockets as we exit the BART station and make our way across the parking lot. The lot is pretty big, and I parked towards the back, so it's a bit of a walk. I try to keep to myself — at least, I *want* to — but it's difficult because Rudy keeps skipping ahead, spinning around, and waving his hands in the air like he's dancing to some sort of hippie music playing only for him. God, how drunk is he?

"Are you okay?" I ask, doing my best not to sound frustrated.

"Dance with me," he says.

"I'm good."

"Come on."

"No, you're drunk."

"I'm not drunk anymore," he insists. "I slept most of it off. I'm just... feeling the vibe."

"And what vibe is that?" I ask. Rudy walks up to me and smiles with hooded eyes, looking all sorts of flirty. He grabs my arms and puts my hands around his waist before placing his hands on my shoulders. He then proceeds to sway us back and forth, humming under his breath beneath the gentle glow of the parking lot lamp posts. I have to admit, had it not been for earlier, this probably would've been pretty romantic. Too bad, I guess. Right? "We should get you home," I say. I turn him around and begin to guide him forward.

"You're no fun," he whines. "What happened to the guy that was like, 'Just chill?' You've got, like, no chill right now."

"Yeah, I wonder why." We get to my mom's car in the back of the parking lot, and I pull the passenger door open for him. "Here. Get in the car," I tell him. I'm probably coming off like a douchebag right now, but I know if I soften up to him, he's gonna find a way to make me not hate him. And I really want to hate him right now.

I climb into the driver's seat and hand Rudy my phone so he can map his address. When he hands it back, I see that he's plugged in the address to another BART station.

"What's this?" I ask.

"I gotta pick up my car," he replies with a shrug.

"Yeah, I don't want you driving tonight."

"Aww, does someone want to take care of me?"

"You're drunk," I insist. He scoffs, rolling his eyes like it's no big deal.

"I told you, I slept most of it off. I didn't even drink that much. I'll be fine," he says, smiling. He then reaches over and tousles my hair a bit. "You know, it's really cute that you think you get a say."

"I'm just trying to look out for you."

"Why?" That's actually a really good question. I'm wondering that myself. I look over and see that Rudy is staring at me expectantly, waiting for me to say more. I can only guess what he wants me to say. He probably thinks he's got me wrapped around his finger like a lock of my hair.

"Because I'm not a complete and total asshole," I mumble. Rudy looks at me curiously, if not a little deflated. I don't think he realizes he's already shown me his hand. Or the back of it anyway.

We get onto the freeway heading west along Highway 4. Rudy and I sit in silence for a while, listening to the sounds of the road moving beneath us. Eventually, the road takes us through this hilly and undeveloped area. There are no lights here and I can't see much more than a dozen or so feet in front of me. The road twists and turns so much, I have to slow down just to make sure we don't end up sliding against the roadside barrier. Is this really the road Rudy took to meet me for our first two dates? This is further than I've ever driven along Highway 4 and, glancing down at the map on my phone, it's looking like this is only about half-way to where we're going. This is a straight up journey. No wonder me and Rudy didn't meet up more often.

"You drove all this way to meet up with me?" I ask, suddenly breaking the silence.

"Twice," he says. "I must really like you." I can hear the smile in his voice when he says this, and it kills me. "Hey, how come you've been so quiet since we got in the car?"

"I was focusing on driving," I reply.

"Mmm... So serious."

"Well, you weren't talking either."

"True. I guess I just like being in the quiet with you." I can feel his eyes on me like he's watching my every move. It's starting to make me nervous. And in more ways than one. I feel like I'm gonna pass him the ball when I really should be keeping it from him. What is this weird power he's got over me? "What are you thinking about?" he asks. And I see no reason to lie.

"Us."

We drive for a little while longer. Finally, we get to a place where there are streetlights, and I can actually see more than just what's right in front of me. The scenery changes from seemingly undeveloped wilderness to "Welcome to Suburbia" real fast. According to my map, the highway ends, and I'm supposed to take an exit to merge onto the interstate, so I do just that. All the while Rudy doesn't offer me any guidance or directions. In fact, when I look over, he's texting. Yeah… I'm starting to understand why people think my generation's rude. I'm ready for this night to be over.

"Ah, shit," Rudy groans.

"What?" I immediately ask, not thinking.

"My friends need a ride home from Pride."

"Can't they just take BART?"

"Well, they're kind of drunk off their asses. And, uh, I don't know if they know how to get back to BART," Rudy explains. "What time is it? Do you know when the last train runs?" I glance down at the clock.

Sunday. June 29th.

"It's just past midnight," I say. "And no idea." Rudy lets out a huge sigh.

"Well, tonight's gonna be fun."

"You're not actually thinking of picking them up, are you?"

"I have to."

"Why?"

"For the same reason you didn't wake me up on BART earlier," Rudy says. "Do you want to come?" Well, shit. The whole reason I'm here right now is because I didn't want to leave him alone, much less have him drive. And yeah, I might be taking him to his car, but it's one thing for him to pick it up and drive home. It's another thing entirely for him to pick it up and drive all around the Bay Area. Like, seriously?

"Ugh, fine," I answer. "I'll come. But you're not driving."

Rudy reaches over and pats me on the head.

"It's really cute that you think you get a say," he teases. It's not funny. It wasn't funny to me the first time he said it, and it's really not funny now.

"Stop," I demand, brushing his hand aside. He just laughs. "I'm serious. You're not driving."

"Okay."

"You're not."

"Okay."

We pull into the BART station parking lot and Rudy directs me to his car. I park in the space beside it, and he immediately pushes my passenger door open and begins to climb out. You've got to be kidding me. Really? I climb out of the driver's seat of my mom's car and run to intercept him before he can get to his car.

"Dude, what is your problem?" I say. It's less of a question and more a demand. "I told you you're not driving. Give me your keys."

"Are you really gonna fight me on this, Andrew?" he replies, wearing a smug smile. I cross my arms. I'm not playing with him about this. We stare at each other for a moment, neither one of us backing down, until finally he rolls his eyes and groans. "Ugh, fine." He pulls his keys out of his pocket, unlocks his car, and pops open the trunk with the attached key fob before shoving the set of keys into my hand. "You know, the assertive side of you is far less endearing than the naïve side," he says, tossing his backpack into the trunk. He then walks over to his front passenger door and climbs in.

I pull out my keys and double click my fob to make sure my mom's car is fully locked, then walk over to the driver's side of Rudy's car. I stop when I see him sitting behind the wheel, smirking at me through the window. I fucking swear…

"Seriously?" I say, when I pull his door open.

"Looks like all sides of you are a little naïve," he smiles. "Did you really think I was gonna let you drive my car?"

"Rudy, come on. Quit playing."

"Babe, give me my keys."

"Get out of the driver's seat."

"No, Andrew. This is my car. You can either get in the passenger's seat or we can sit here all night. It's up to you," he says, sounding as playful as ever. It's almost a little cocky. "My seatbelt's already on." Yeah, I don't think he's budging. This whole thing is getting ridiculous. I have half a mind to just bail and go home, but... I don't know if I'd feel right letting him go alone. So, as much as I don't want to, I hand back his keys and climb into the passenger seat.

I have a feeling I'm gonna regret this.

"You realize how stupid this is, right?" I say.

"And yet you still got in the car," Rudy replies with a wink. He starts the engine, quickly backs out of his space without bothering to look over his shoulder, and then speeds out of the parking lot, running every stop sign on the way out.

Yup, already regretting this.

The whole time I'm in the car, I've got this really uneasy feeling in my stomach. Surprisingly, Rudy's driving isn't terrible. He's keeping both hands on the wheel and his eyes quietly focused on the road. We're going just a few miles over speed limit, but he's managing to keep his driving smooth enough for us to not get pulled over, probably. Still, seeing how drunk he was earlier, has me clutching my seatbelt for dear life. Lord, help us.

I start watching the scenery go by to distract myself and eventually start to relax. There's something about night that just forces you to chill out a little bit. Maybe it's because all the world's asleep. You just want to move about quietly without disturbing anyone, you know? It's a vibe.

It doesn't take long for us to get close to the city. We're currently on the Bay Bridge approaching the Treasure Island tunnel. I know that's not the actual name of the tunnel but, uh, I forgot the name because I've never heard anyone actually use it. Anyway, you know how there's that thing where if you hold your breath through a tunnel, you can make a wish? This is the only tunnel I've ever been able to hold my breath through because it's so short. I've made wishes on a bunch of things like a new bike, my family getting rich, a boyfriend. None of it has ever come true. Except for the bike — wait, no. That was actually Art. Never mind. Tonight though, I'm feeling… a lot of things. I just want these feelings to go away. I just want to be free from them. I just want to be free in general. So, as we enter the tunnel, I hold my breath.

The best part of the Treasure Island tunnel is the moment of exit. We're greeted by this incredible view of suspension cables and bridge support structures, or whatever, towering over us, which I know doesn't sound great, but hear me out. There's something about how the cables and the bridge stuff are arranged that makes you feel like you're passing through a gate. And because everything is so big and grand, you just know that you're gonna make a memory. It's overwhelming. And if you weren't holding your breath, it would take your breath away. And then you see San Francisco through the wires and it's like… that's cool. That's a feeling you just don't forget. You can forget about everything else, but you never forget how something makes you feel.

"It's pretty, huh?" Rudy says. I take a breath then turn to him. He smiles back at me, reaches for my hand, and laces our fingers together. I have to turn away because I feel a tear start to roll down my cheek.

What the fuck?

Once we're over the bridge, we drive around the city making random turns and going down long stretches, only to turn around and go the other way. Rudy swears he knows where he's going but, uh, he doesn't. I keep telling him to just stop and map where his friends are, but he won't do it. He's being so stubborn. He's like my dad. Oh, God. That means in this situation, I'm my mom. "Jeremy, just stop and look it up, my goodness!"

I can't.

Eventually, we find ourselves on this street that borders this big grassy park. Being in the city, I imagine it probably gets really crowded here during the day. Right now, it's empty. It's a little creepy too. Just a wide-open space with a handful of trees and few lights beyond the ones lighting up the street. It's really dark inside the park, so naturally, this is where Rudy's friends are hanging out. That's what he says anyway.

"Are you sure they're here?" I ask when Rudy slows the car to a crawl. "It's really sketch."

"That's what they said," he replies. "I swear, they better not be boning in the shadows."

"Is that something you and your friends do with each other?"

"You're adorable." We roll down the street at a snail's pace, just staring out into the darkness of the park. Nothing. There's no one here. No one that I can see. "Maybe we should drive around the whole park," Rudy suggests. I shrug. I'm starting to get annoyed with the whole situation. As if I weren't annoyed enough already.

"Just call them," I say, sounding harsher than I mean to. Thankfully, Rudy doesn't seem to think anything of it. He just pulls out his phone and places the call. A moment later, he hands his phone to me and starts driving. "What? They didn't answer?"

"Nope."

So, now we're driving in circles around the entire park. God, I'm so over this shit. I just want to go home.

We circle the park for another five minutes or so before Rudy decides to pull over at a corner and park in a red zone. He leans back and sighs, then turns to me.

"So…" he begins.

"So…" I begin.

"How's your night going?" Well, Rudy, where do I start? I could go off on him, rattle off all the ways tonight's got me fucked up. I *could* do that. And I want to. But I also know I have to sit in this car with him until he decides to take me back, and Lord knows when that will be. So, instead, I just bite my tongue and shrug. "Hmm… You're so silent and brooding," he comments. I turn to him and find him staring at me with a certain look in his eyes. He then reaches over and takes my hand into his. With his thumb, he draws circles in my palm. It's a nice feeling. Relaxing even. If it hadn't been for earlier, this would've been the perfect moment to kiss him. But now, I'm just wondering what the hell goes on in his head. How has he not once acknowledged what he did? Was he *that* drunk? Does he just not know what he did?

Suddenly, as I'm sorting through my thoughts trying to make Rudy make sense, something slams against the driver's side window. Rudy and I both jump. Then I see some random, pudgy Hispanic dude with some really arched eyebrows smiling at us, waving through the window. Rudy breathes out and starts laughing. I'm guessing this is one of the friends we're picking up. The next thing I know, Eyebrows is climbing into the backseat along with another Hispanic guy with a goatee but no mustache and a girl, who kinda looks like Becca, but thicker and also Hispanic.

"Oh, my God, Rudy, it smells like sex in here," Eyebrows says, getting settled into the seat behind me. "Are you pregnant now? Is he the father?"

"Shut up," Rudy replies, looking both amused and embarrassed. "Andrew, this is Hector." He gestures to Eyebrows. "And this is Gabe, and Gloria." I'll be honest, I'm probably not gonna remember their names. I will remember those eyebrows though. And that no 'stache goatee. And, of course, Hispanic Becca.

"Andrew? Wait, is this the guy?" Hispanic Becca says to Rudy. Rudy nods, so Hispanic Becca leans forward to look at me. "Oh, my God, Rudy, he's so cute. You're so cute."

"Uh, thank you," I reply, feeling myself tense up.

"Girl, sit down. You're gonna make the poor boy shrink below the waist," Eyebrows says, swatting playfully at Hispanic Becca. He then turns to me and leans forward himself. "So, Andrew. Are you cut or uncut?"

"Okay, we're not doing that. We're not gonna be talking about his penis," Rudy demands.

"Bitch, you're no fun," Eyebrows says. "Let the boy answer."

"You don't have to answer that," Rudy says.

"Okay, I won't," I reply.

"Gosh, Rudy, how are you always getting these cute ass white boys? It's not fair," Eyebrows whines. The comment catches my attention. Just how many guys like me has Rudy had? Am I just another number on his scorecard? But if that's the case, how come I didn't score? I don't get it. "How come I can't get a cute ass white boy?" Eyebrows whines again.

"Por gordo!" Goatee finally chimes in, and everyone in the car except for me and Eyebrows bursts out laughing. Eyebrows looks dramatically upset. I'm just confused. I feel like I don't belong here.

After we start driving, Rudy and his friends start having entire conversations in Spanish and I feel super out of place. They're talking, and laughing, and making the whole drive into some sort of party I wasn't invited to. I guess it's my own fault for showing up though. Ugh, why'd I have to care?

About half an hour into the drive — which by the way feels way longer when you're sitting quietly next to a bunch of people you don't understand — Eyebrows demands that we stop for some food. And some other things like cigarettes and lube.

"I'm trying to get pregnant tonight," he says.

"You already look it, babe," Goatee adds. Everyone laughs except Eyebrows. Even I get a good chuckle out of that one.

We pull into the parking lot of a 24-hour convenience store. Eyebrows and Goatee immediately climb out of the car.

"I'm gonna grab a soda. You boys want anything?" Hispanic Becca offers.

"Water. I need to sober up," Rudy says, and as soon as the words leave his mouth, Hispanic Becca reaches over and grabs him by the hair, yelling what I think are a whole bunch of Spanish swear words. "I'm joking! I'm joking! I'm sober!" Rudy cries.

"You better be! You better not have been driving drunk!" Hispanic Becca lets go of his hair then turns to me, probably expecting me to vouch for him, but like…

"I told him not to," I say. Hispanic Becca punches Rudy on the arm, then opens the back driver's side door.

"Pinche pendejo," I hear her whisper to herself as she climbs out of the car. And now, me and Rudy are alone. He's rubbing his arm and pouting at me.

"Thanks for that," he says, and I can't help but crack a smile. It doesn't last though. I can't stop thinking about earlier. I can't get the picture of him making out with another dude out of my head. Then I think of that off handed comment by Eyebrows, and it all starts to feel like too much. I need a distraction, so I pull out my phone, which is a bad idea. I see that I have a bunch of missed calls from my mom and a few text messages from Dad from a couple hours ago. Dad's messages read:

"Your mom wants to know where you are."

"Where are you?"

"Call your mom. She's worried."

"Have you called your mom?"

I look over at the clock on Rudy's dashboard. It's already past 2:00am. Shit. I'm definitely gonna be hearing about this when I get home.

"Everything okay?" Rudy asks.

"Yeah, it's just a missed call from my parents," I explain, slipping my phone back into my pocket.

"Aww, is it past somebody's bedtime?" Rudy pouts at me again. I get that it's supposed to be playful, but I can't help but be bothered by it. Like, he knows that I'm younger than him. I don't know. Maybe I'm just being overly sensitive because of what happened. Plus, I'm not exactly in my element here, you know?

Hispanic Becca returns, carrying a large bottle of water and a bottle of Coke. She climbs into the backseat and hands the water to me.

"I figured you guys could share," she says.

A minute later, Eyebrows and Goatee come strolling out of the convenience store holding hands. They come over to the front of the car, talking and laughing. Then suddenly, Eyebrows pulls Goatee towards him, and they start making out right there in the open.

I'm watching them through the windshield, fascinated by the whole thing. It's sloppy and kinda gross. Like, you can see their tongues slipping out from in between them. Still, I appreciate that they're not hiding from anything. I think I might be the only one though, because Rudy and Hispanic Becca don't sound too thrilled.

"Ay, Dios," Hispanic Becca groans.

"I take it they do this a lot?" I ask.

"All the time," Rudy answers.

"Huh, I never would've pictured the two of them dating."

"They're not," Hispanic Becca says. "They just hook up from time to time. Why they can't do it on their own time is beyond me." Interesting. Hooking up with my friends has always been nothing more than just a passing thought. I'd never actually do it. And yet here I am, watching two friends casually hook up. Doesn't that make things complicated? "Don't worry, Rudy's never hooked up with them," Hispanic Becca assures me.

"Oh, God, no. I could never," Rudy adds. "I could never hook up with my friends. It's too much drama." So, you just hook up with strangers instead then, huh? Definitely not saying that out loud. But I am thinking it. I mean, how could I not, what with Eyebrows and Goatee tongue wrestling right in front of me?

"After we drop them off, can you guys take me home?" Hispanic Becca asks. "I don't wanna be around when the clothes start coming off."

"Sure," Rudy replies, before slamming his car horn. Eyebrows and Goatee jump apart at the sound, and I swear I see a thread of spit swing down from between them. This is probably what the straights are so afraid of. And shoot, I don't blame them.

By the time we drop off Hispanic Becca, it's already well past three o'clock. We kept on getting lost because Rudy kept taking wrong turns, because no one wanted to give him directions. Eyebrows and Goatee were busy sucking face and Hispanic Becca was constantly yelling at them to stop groping each other under their clothes. A lot of Spanish curse words were yelled. At least, I assume they were curse words based on their tone. And when that wasn't happening, they were all chatting it up — again, in Spanish — so I had no idea what they were talking about. The whole time, I just sat staring out the window, twiddling my thumbs quietly. I just kept thinking, "Why am I here? Why did I bother?" I mean, Rudy's been fine driving the entire night. Whether I had come along or not wouldn't have made any difference.

We're driving down this long road that's lined on either side with what look to be office buildings and, like, industrial factory-looking places. There are a bunch of trees around, so you can tell it's well maintained here and not, like, scary. Still, I have no idea where we are, and Rudy hasn't said anything since we dropped off the last of his friends. We just drive and drive until eventually we come to a little roundabout. There's a parking lot on one side and a massive factory-looking building made up of mostly windows on the other, part of which is built on top of a dock that sits right on the bay.

"Where are we?" I ask as Rudy pulls us into the parking lot and finds a place to park.

"The harbor," he replies.

"Why?" Rudy just shrugs. He then opens his door and climbs out of the car. I sigh and do the same. I follow him out of the parking lot and, together, we cut across the roundabout, and head towards the mostly glass building. Once there, we round the corner and find ourselves on the dock. A light breeze hits my face and, after sitting in the car for God knows how long, it's the most refreshing thing.

Rudy slows his pace, and we wander along the dock, staring out at the bay. In the distance, I can see the lights of San Francisco floating above the water. It's been such a long night; it seems like forever ago that I was there. It's pretty but…

"Why are we here?" I ask, keeping my voice low. There's something about the night and the view of the city that just feels like I need to respect the quiet. You know, because the world's asleep. Or maybe I'm just worried of being found.

"Why not? The view's amazing, right?" Rudy says. "I had a friend who had an event here once. It was, like, her quinceañera. That was the first time I came here, and I always loved the view." He moves over to the railing of the dock and leans onto it. "Sometimes, when I can't sleep, or if I'm just up really late — like tonight — I'll come down here and stare at the city for a while, thinking about stuff. You know, 'just chill.'"

"You are an asshole," I say, smiling. Though, I actually kinda mean it. He laughs, and I go to join him at the railing. "So, what do you think about when you're down here?"

"All sorts of things," he begins. "Like, look at the city. Do you ever think about how dense it is? You know, there are so many people there. There are so many people around and yet everyone's just there, going about their business, ignoring each other. Like, one time I was there, and I asked this random lady for directions; she ignored me. But then, when I acted all offended, she had the nerve to yell at *me*. Crazy, right? It's like no one bothers to stop to give anyone the time of day, let alone connect with anyone — like, *really* connect with someone — and it's sad. It's so sad." Rudy pauses for a moment. A part of me thinks whatever he's on about might be getting to him, but all that goes away when he suddenly continues. "But then I think… Maybe they're onto something. Like, everything: life, friendships, relationships, love — it's all temporary, so what's the point? What's the point in letting yourself get invested in something, in someone, if one minute they're there, and then the next, they're just gone?"

We go silent.

I'm trying to absorb what Rudy's saying but my mind goes back to earlier in the night, and I start replaying the moment in my head. The moment that I caught him locking lips with some random dude. And I can't help myself anymore.

"Is that why you did it?" I say, finally letting it slip. "Is that why you kissed that guy at Pride? You just hook up with guys and don't try to connect with them?"

"Isn't that the expectation?" Rudy replies, seeming entirely unphased. It almost surprises me how quickly he answers, as if he's thought about this before. And who knows? Maybe he has. "Isn't that what we do?"

"I don't do that."

"We all do that. Think about it, Andrew. How many guys did you go out with between our dates? I mean, I figure that's why it took you so long to get back to me. How many guys did you hook up with?" Rudy's question throws me for a loop. Do I really do that? I start to recount the guys in my mind. I can remember them pretty clearly except I can't seem to remember their names. God, what were they? "It's okay," Rudy says, continuing. "Really. I get it. You know, we kiss boys, we fuck boys, and we hook up. That's how we are. We do it so we can get close to ourselves. So we can feel what everybody else feels. And we've been so repressed that we just keep kissing, and fucking, and hooking up —"

"So why not just kiss *me?*" The words slip out before I can stop them. I don't even think about it. "Why kiss a stranger?" Rudy goes silent. I'm staring at him, hoping that he'll help me make sense of everything, but he's not even looking at me. He's just staring out across the water. My heart is pounding a mile a minute. This silence between us, it's suffocating. Finally, after what feels like forever, he turns to me. My hope is that he'll put me out of my misery.

"I'm not afraid of strangers," he says softly. Then he turns back and stares blankly across the water. I'm still not sure I understand. But maybe that's exactly what he wants. Maybe this lack of clear explanation is his way of keeping me at arms-length. Because, like he said, what would be the point?

chapter twenty-three

"God, I'm so hungry," Rudy says, looking over the breakfast menu. We're sitting in a booth beside a window at a 24-hour diner. I'm not sure what time it is, but it's still dark outside, and this lack of sleep has me feeling a little delirious. I'm currently nursing a cup of coffee, but I doubt it'll be much help.

When our waiter comes, Rudy and I place our order — he gets pancakes, eggs, and bacon with a side of fruit, and I get a ham and cheese omelette with toast. Then our waiter collects our menus and leaves us alone with nothing to distract ourselves from each other. Rudy seems unaffected, but I haven't had much to say to him since the harbor. I've been stuck in my own head, racking my brain, trying to make sense of everything. I mean, okay, if he wants to kiss another guy, but why would he think that that's something I'd be okay with? Because that's the "expectation?" If that's the case, maybe he just doesn't know me very well. But then, thinking about my own history, maybe he knows me better than I know myself.

"You okay?" I hear Rudy ask.

"Huh?" I reply. It takes me a second to remember where I am.

"You've been really quiet. Actually, come to think of it, you've been really quiet all night. Do you want to talk about it?"

"No. It's nothing. Really, I'm just tired."

"You sure?" Rudy's staring at me in a way that makes me think he's pitying me, and I kinda hate it.

"It's been a long night," I insist. "You know, from Pride, and having to drive everywhere, to picking up your friends, it was all really exhausting."

"Yeah, I can see that. I wasn't expecting to pick my friends up tonight. I hope it wasn't too uncomfortable."

"No, they were cool. I just wish I could understand you." Rudy tilts his head curiously. "You know, I wish I could understand what you were saying," I explain.

"Ah, sorry," he says. "I didn't mean for you to feel left out." I shake my head.

"It's okay." To be honest, even if I did understand Spanish, I'm not sure how much of a difference it would've made. I just don't get Rudy. And maybe I never will. We're two different people with two different ways of looking at things, and those ways don't exactly complement each other. And that sucks. Because I like him. I like him a lot. I just don't know how this is gonna work between us. I'm not sure it can.

Rudy is staring at me, wearing a peaceful smile. I stare back at him, and in my mind, I hear the beginning notes of *Moonlight Sonata* start to play. I'm not sure if it's the song I would've chosen for this moment exactly, but it's the one I've become most familiar with. And after the first few measures, it starts to become its own thing, because I don't remember very much past that.

"You know, you have the most beautiful blue eyes I've ever seen," he says, practically at a whisper. "I could float away in them." Then, he places his hand, palm up, on the table. For a second, I hesitate, but then… Fuck it, I place my hand on top of his. His grip is surprisingly strong. It's stronger than mine right now. We sit here holding onto each other — me trying to not care if anyone sees — and I just listen to the music in my mind as it continues to play, eventually fading into silence.

It's just about dawn when we arrive at the BART station where I left my mom's car. After breakfast, I asked Rudy if he could take me back so I could go home. He agreed, though he seemed almost disappointed by it. Or maybe that's just wishful thinking.

He pulls into the open space on the passenger side of my car, and we sit for a moment. I'm looking out the window at the almost completely empty parking lot. Everything looks a little fuzzy with that sort of dark blueish tint of the early morning when the sun's still low. The open pavement makes for a really dull scene. Sad even. It's just as well though. It feels almost... appropriate.

I've been giving this a lot of thought — me and Rudy — and I think I've made a decision. But when I catch myself absentmindedly reaching for the door handle, I know I'm hesitating. I can feel myself shaking, I'm so tense.

"Everything okay?" Rudy asks. I pause to think about it again. Am I really sure about this?

. . .

"Actually, I've been thinking," I start to say after letting out a heavy sigh. My voice is wobbly. I'm super nervous, because even though I'm sure about what I'm gonna say, I'm not sure that I'm sure. If that makes any sense at all. "Um... I... I don't think... I don't think we should see each other... anymore." The car is suddenly filled with a ringing sort of silence. It's the loudest sound that can't be heard. And it feels like it lasts forever.

"Oh," Rudy begins. He seems to be caught off guard by this. And really, I don't blame him. It was just about an hour ago that we were sitting in the diner holding onto each other. "Okay."

"'Okay?' Is that all you have to say?" I feel stupid asking this. Rudy shrugs, which just pisses me off. I would've thought he'd have a reaction. Like, dude, give me something here.

"What do you want me to say, Andrew?"

"Anything." My voice comes out louder than I mean for it to. Rudy turns away from me and goes quiet. I sit here, waiting for him to say something. I need for him to show me that I wasn't nothing to him. That I wasn't just another guy he could *not* connect with. I need to know that I was more valuable to him than that.

But then again… Who am I kidding?

He passed me up for a stranger. Why? Because he's not afraid of them? What does that mean? That he's afraid of me? Why would he be afraid of me?

"You know, Andrew, from the first night that I met you, I got this feeling," Rudy finally says. "Quisiera enamorarme, pero no ahorita."

"What does that mean?" I ask to which Rudy replies with a soft smile and a light shrug.

"I guess we'll never know," he says. And with that, I pull on the door handle and let myself out of the car. God, if I could only understand what he was saying, maybe it would all make sense. Maybe I wouldn't be walking out of this like such a fucking loser.

As I'm heading over to my mom's car, I feel my heart drop into my stomach. I'm overwhelmed by the whole thing; I'm angry, I'm confused, I'm frustrated. I want to cry, which I know is stupid, but sometimes that's the only thing you can do when you're all filled up with emotions. I have to clench my jaw and bite my back teeth to keep myself together. The few steps to my driver's side door might as well be a thousand miles.

"Andrew, wait," I hear Rudy say as I'm walking along beside my back bumper. I stop and turn to see him standing there. As soon as we make eye contact, he immediately starts walking towards me. The next thing I know, he's got both his hands on my cheeks and he's pulling me towards him. I feel his lips press against mine, his tongue slipping into my mouth, and I can taste his every single shallow breath. If I had to describe it, he tastes like maple syrup with a touch of cinnamon. That could also just be from breakfast. Either way, it's a taste I know I'll crave, so I kiss him back, pushing my weight forward, and wrapping my arms around his tiny waist to hold him against me. I let my eyes shut to lose myself in the moment, and I take mental notes to remember how everything feels: his lips, his tongue, his breath. I wish I could have this moment forever.

When our lips part, I see a beam of morning light come across Rudy's face. It strikes me how beautiful he is. His eyes are the color that his breath tastes: maple with a touch of cinnamon. There's a comfort I'm finding in him staring at me. At least, until he smiles and starts to pull away.

"Bye, Babe," he whispers. As much as I don't want to, I remove my hands from Rudy's waist and watch as he takes a step away from me and begins walking back to his car.

"Babe?" I say, stopping him as he reaches his driver's side door, which he'd left slightly open. He turns to me and smiles once more — Rudy's always smiling.

"You *are* a babe," he says. And with that, he climbs back into his car, pulls out of the parking space, and drives off. Now, I could stand here and list all the reasons why me ending this makes sense. I could stand here and reassure myself that I made a good decision. But Rudy… He's like the Bay Bridge. Being with him, you just know you're gonna make a memory. It's overwhelming. And even if you're holding your breath, he'll manage to take your breath away. That's a feeling you just don't forget. You can forget about everything else, but you never forget how something makes you feel.

And in this moment, right now… I feel like I'm making a mistake.

It takes me, like, an hour or so to get home. The whole hilly undeveloped drive over, I kept thinking about Rudy and all that he left me with. That kiss was the first time I felt a kiss held any sort of meaning. You know, other than "Do you wanna go somewhere and bone?" That kiss was tender. It was sweet. Hell, it tasted like maple syrup and cinnamon. That kiss… That kiss was everything. And when it happened, I couldn't help but feel like I was making a mistake. Part of me still feels like I'm making a mistake. I thought about a lot of things during the drive. I even thought about turning the car around and going after him, but where would I have gone? I don't know where he lives. And I couldn't call him, I don't have his number. We only ever talked through AphroDATEme. Why didn't I get his freakin' phone number? Why am I so stupid?

I'm pulling into my driveway now. It's just about 7:00am. I'm hoping my parents aren't up yet. I'm not ready to have the conversation about why I didn't come home last night, or why I didn't bother to call. Luckily, the house is quiet when I get inside. I head quickly and quietly to my room, making sure to take extra light steps as I pass my parents' door. Their bedroom just so happens to be the first door in the hall, so there's no getting around it. Convenient, huh? Whoever designed our house, I'd like a word. I just wanna talk…

I manage to get to my room safely. As soon as I get my door shut, I let out the breath I've been holding since I stepped inside the house. I then kick off my shoes and plop myself onto my bed, where I immediately open up AphroDATEme. I can't shake the feeling that I'm fucking up. I need to talk to Rudy. I need to take back what I said about not seeing each other again so we can figure out this thing between us. I navigate to my inbox and start scrolling through all my messages, but I can't find our chat log. I scroll up and down multiple times, hoping I'm just missing it 'cause I haven't slept, but nothing. It's not here. I figure I'll just search up his profile, but when I find it, my heart drops.

RudeFern69 has blocked you.

At first, I don't believe it, so I reload his profile.

RudeFern69 has blocked you.

I reload it again.

RudeFern69 has blocked you.

And again.

RudeFern69 has blocked you.

Is this really happening? Is this for real? You've gotta be kidding me. Still not believing it, I reload the profile again, and again, and again, hoping it'll change and say something different. But it doesn't. It doesn't change. It just keeps repeating:

RudeFern69 has blocked you.

RudeFern69 has blocked you.

RudeFern69 has blocked you.

Fucking Rudy. You know what? Maybe I'm not making a mistake. In fact, maybe I dodged a bullet. I mean, how mature is this? I suggest that we don't see each other anymore, for totally valid reasons, and suddenly we can't be friends? We can't even talk anymore? Really?

Whatever.

I'm done.

Have you ever been so exhausted that you're too tired to sleep? That's the point where I'm at right now. I've been tossing and turning for God knows how long.

No matter how hard I try, I just can't relax. And can you blame me after the night I've had?

I'm lying on my bed, listening to the silent performance of *Moonlight Sonata* swell in my mind when, suddenly, there's a knocking on my chamber door.

"Nevermore," I say. Well, actually I don't say that, but it'd be clever if I did, right? What I really say is, "Go away." Of course, they don't. And then I hear my door open.

"Hey, Andrew, you up?" Art's voice fills my room, totally killing the vibe. He's like the broken Middle G on my mom's keyboard.

"Nope," I mumble.

"Well, Mom and Dad want to talk to you," he replies. Ugh, great. I knew it was coming. I knew they'd want to talk about it. I was just hoping that they wouldn't.

"Right now?" I ask with the tiniest hope that maybe, just maybe, I can get out of this. Art just shrugs.

"I mean, if you want to live," he says. Well, alright then. I guess I'm not catching a break today. I pull myself out of bed and follow Art out of my room, through the hall, across the living room, and into the kitchen. Dad's at the fridge, while Mom is sitting at the table with a coffee cup. Art goes to grab a bowl and a spoon, then joins Mom at the table after grabbing the cereal from the cabinet.

"Look who decided to show up," Dad says when he notices me. He pulls out the eggs and bacon from the fridge and sets them on the counter by the stove. "When did you get home?"

"Uh, late," I say. I figure if I keep my answers short and to the point, this won't turn into something bigger than it needs to be. I don't have the energy for it to.

"How come you didn't answer your phone last night? Or any of your messages?" Dad asks.

"Um, I didn't notice them until late."

"Sorry, sorry," Art whispers, cutting in between me and Dad as he crosses to the fridge and back. "Just needed the milk." Fuckin' Art.

"Where were you?" Mom chimes in from the table. Crap, what did I tell her? Where did I say I was gonna be last night?

"I… Um… I went to a movie," I say, hoping it's not obvious that I'm not sure of my answer.

"With Riley and Jacob?" Mom continues.

"Yup."

"And then where'd you go?"

"Does it matter? I mean, I'm home now." I notice Mom's eyes start to narrow and so does Dad's. Meanwhile, Art's watching everything happen with a dumbfounded look on his face while he's munching on his cereal. It's so uncomfortably quiet, you can hear him chew.

Crunch…

Crunch…

"I'm just trying to figure out why I was sitting here last night, past midnight, with my son missing, my car missing, and not a single word of communication shared," Mom explains, her tone coming out much sharper this time. "Now, do you want to try this again, or do you want to skip straight to the grounding?"

"Grounding?!" Is she serious right now? "Mom, I'm a fucking adult!"

"Hey, don't talk to your mother like that," Dad yells.

Crunch…

Crunch…

"I'm sorry, Dad. But don't you think this is a little overkill? All I did was stay out all night. It's not like I killed anyone."

"All night?!" Mom jumps back in. "What do you mean 'all night?'"

Crunch…

Crunch…

"I was hanging out with a friend. We drove around all night. Things didn't go well with them, and now we're not friends anymore. Is that what you want to hear?" At this point, I don't even know what I'm saying.

The words are just flying out of my mouth without me giving them a single thought. I think the lack of sleep is finally getting to me. That, mixed with the pressure my parents are laying on, coupled with Art's loud ass chewing is enough to make anyone a little cranky. Or in my case, really cranky.

Crunch…

Crunch…

"WILL YOU SHUT THE FUCK UP?!" I hear myself yell. Art's face drops and his eyes get so big, they look like they might fall right out of his face.

"HEY!" Dad screams.

"I'm just eating my cereal," Art mumbles with his mouth full.

"I don't know who you think you're talking to, Andrew," Dad begins, stepping up to me. "But this is *my* house, and you better show some FUCKING RESPECT before I knock —"

"Jeremy," I hear Mom cry. "That's enough!"

"Dad, chill out," Art says, jumping in front of me. It happens so fast I don't even see it happen. Art's trying to get Dad to break his focus from me, but it doesn't seem to be working. Now, I may be delirious, but I haven't completely lost my mind. My dad can be an ass, but he's not one to lose his temper very often. Not seriously. So, when he does, you know he's mad. And if I wasn't so tired, I'd probably be pissing myself right now.

Did I mention that my dad was almost a pro football player? He's a *big* dude. He looks like what Art would look like if Art ate me. I know my only hope of not dying this morning is to get out of the situation, so I quickly start to back away until I get far enough that I feel like it's safe to turn around, then make a beeline straight for my room.

Today is not going well at all. I'm tired, I've been blocked by a dude whose kisses taste like breakfast — whatever, I'm over it — my mom's trying to ground me like a child, and my dad's trying to square off with me like I'm a grown man. It's a lot, okay? And the worst part is I don't even have a lock on my door, so I can't just shut everything out. Do you know what happens when you can't just shut everything out? Things come to bother you.

"Andrew?" Art's muffled voice comes through my door. You see? I don't even answer before he lets himself in. "Dude, are you okay?" he asks, poking his head into my room before stepping inside. "What was all that about?"

"Go away," I say, my voice coming out all sad and one-note.

"Okay, well, you know you can talk to me about anything, right?"

"Go away."

"I mean, you're my kid brother. I care about you."

"Art, you got into a good college, right?" I ask. "What part of 'go away' haven't you learned by now?"

"Right," Art says, looking all defeated. Not that I care. He's being so nosey. "Well, I'm here, if you ever want to talk —"

"I really don't," I say. And with that, he steps out of my room and slowly shuts the door. Thank freakin' God.

Monday. June 30th.

I wake up around 10:00am to a notification on my phone. It's a text message from Mackenzie.

"We still hanging out today?" her message reads. Shoot, I totally forgot. It's been so long though I don't want to cancel on her. That being said, I'm not feeling particularly well rested. I didn't get very good sleep.

After managing to get about a four-hour nap in yesterday, I randomly woke up before sunset. Since I wasn't about to go out and deal with my dad again, I just holed — or is it held? Helded? I holded myself up in my room the rest of the night. Much of my time was spent scrolling through social media, watching animal fails and videos of shirtless guys working out.

I actually watch for the workouts…

. . .

Anyway, I eventually found myself back on AphroDATEme. I figured since I'm not seeing anyone anymore and it's been so long since I last scrolled, it couldn't hurt to see if there was anyone new. There were a few. But sadly, they were all uggos, oldies, and torsos. Though, if I'm being completely honest, the torsos were pretty tempting. They could be, like, a fun little gamble. Like, "Please don't be ugly. *Please* don't be ugly." But I decided it was better not to go down that road. As far as I'm concerned, at this point, men are better from afar. Especially ones without heads.

I ended up scrolling until around four o'clock in the morning. I couldn't get back to sleep before then. But now, I am up, and I am starving. I guess I can't stay in my room forever. Time to brave the parentals. At least I know for sure Dad's not around. Thank God for Mondays.

I slip out of my room and quietly make my way down the hall. But, as luck would have it, Mom's sitting on the couch, knitting while watching a TV show about some Japanese lady who organizes people's homes. I feel like my mom *wants* to be the kind of person who keeps an organized house, but she's really more like one of those people who just buys stuff to organize things — like bins and whatever — and never uses them. Either way, I'm hoping right now her mind is too busy working out how to organize her shoe and purse collection to notice me. Maybe if I just walk by real fast, I can avoid having to talk to her. Here goes nothing.

"Oh, Andrew," I hear Mom say as I'm making my way across the living room. Damn whoever designed our house. They made it impossible to avoid anyone. "Honey, sit down. I want to talk to you." Ugh, here we go. I'm bracing myself for the worst as I go to take a seat on the opposite side of the couch from her. "How are you feeling?" she asks, setting aside her knitting and pausing her show. I just shrug, not really sure what I'm supposed to say. "Okay. Well, first off, I just want to say I'm sorry about yesterday. That conversation should not have happened like that. I was just worried about you."

"You knew I was going out," I say, trying to be extra careful with my tone. I'm not looking to start another argument. "I don't see why it was such a big deal."

"It's a big deal because you didn't tell me. I didn't know how late you were gonna be out. You weren't answering your phone. I didn't know where you were, and that's scary for me. I want to know that you're okay." Mom pauses for a second to let the words settle. She's looking at me like she wants me to say something, but when I don't, she asks, "*Are* you okay?" I want to answer her and tell her that I am. But I don't know if I am. I mean, I'm not *not* okay. But I don't feel great. There's just too much that I'm holding on to that I'm not ready to share.

"I'm fine," I say simply.

"You know, I get it," Mom continues. "You're growing up. You're an adult now. You're gonna want to go out there and experience things and stay out all night. But you still live in my house. You're still my kid. And there has to be some mutual understanding if things are gonna work out here. So, I will agree to try to let go a little more, so long as you agree to communicate. Keep me in the loop. Deal?"

"Okay," I agree, and we sit here silently for a moment. I'm not sure if the conversation is over. It feels like it is, but it also feels like Mom is waiting for me to say more, and really there's so much more that could be said, but… you know… Then I remember I'm supposed to be meeting up with Mackenzie, which gives me the perfect subject change. "So, am I grounded?"

"You're an adult. What do you think?" Mom says.

"Okay, well, I totally forgot I promised to meet up with my friend today," I explain.

"Is this the same friend you stayed out all night with?"

"No. It's a friend from school. Actually, it's the girl from Antonini's, remember? You met her."

"Oh, you're hanging out with a girl?" Mom gives me this almost confused look.

"Uh, yeah. Why?"

"Nothing."

Weird, but whatever.

"Anyway, is it cool if I borrow the car again?"

"As long as you're back by three. I have to work," Mom says, reaching for her knitting and picking up the TV remote.

"Will do. Thanks, Mom," I reply, getting up.

"Oh, and, Andrew, if you tell your father I loaned you the car, you will actually be grounded."

"Got it."

Mackenzie and I agree to meet around 12:30pm. We decided to meet for lunch at the local mall. You know, the one that's like a ghost town. It's just on the other side of the freeway from Antonini's and since Mackenzie has to be at work at 3:00pm, I figured this would be a good enough place to go. At the very least, we can wander around and gawk at all the shops — that is, if there are any still open.

I pull into the parking lot and quickly head inside through the glass front entrance. Being inside this mall is, uh, sad. I remember coming here as a child and having my favorite spots: the fountain, the toy store, the video game shop. I even loved Riga-Tony's, the cheap pizza and pasta place that everyone said tasted like cardboard and wet paper. I mean, it wasn't, like, the fanciest place — not like Antonini's — but Riga-Tony's was where I first tried baked ziti. And that was amazing. But now, even Riga-Tony's is gone and been replaced with some shop called PasTa-da! Yeah, the name sucks. But that's where I find Mackenzie.

"Hey," I say as I approach. Mackenzie is sitting at a table in the back corner of the shop with a large slice of pepperoni pizza and a fountain drink in front of her. The pizza's only got a single bite taken out of it.

"Why'd you bring me here?" Mackenzie asks when I sit down across from her. "This tastes like cardboard."

"Cardboard's not the worst thing to taste like."

"Mmm, you're really selling it there, aren't you?" She pushes the pizza slice towards me. I help myself and rip off a piece. No regrets.

. . .

Nope. Just kidding. Only regrets. This pizza's nasty. How do you mess up pizza? Good lord. I gesture to Mackenzie for a drink. She hands me hers and I take a sip as she leans in.

"So, tell me about your weekend," she says, looking all excited. "Are we expecting?" Ah, classic Mackenzie. Jumping straight to the point. I wasn't really looking forward to rehashing everything but what else were we gonna talk about?

"Uh… me and Rudy… we aren't gonna see each other anymore," I explain, feeling the hesitation in my words. I don't know why it's hard for me to say. I mean,

I know I'm not gonna see him anymore. I guess it's just weird saying it out loud. Like, it makes it official.

"What? Why?" Mackenzie asks.

"Well, basically, he got drunk and made out with some random dude at Pride," I say, ripping off another piece of her cardboard pizza. "The guy had a manbun."

"A manbun? Ew."

"That's what I thought! And then he drove us around the whole Bay Area to pick up his drunken friends in the middle of the night."

"Wait. He drove drunk?" Mackenzie gives me a look like *I'm* the one who did something bad.

"Don't look at me, I tried to stop him! And then, when I finally got to confront him about the whole kiss thing, all he said was, 'Isn't that the expectation? Isn't that what we do?' talking about how we just hook up with guys without making connections. Like he fuckin' knows me." I'm feeling myself getting riled up, and I don't know why I keep eating this pizza, but it's not stopping me from talking. I kinda wish it would though, because I don't need to be causing a scene out here at the mall, no matter how deserted it might be.

"Doesn't he though?" Mackenzie says while I pause to chew the cardboard crust in my mouth.

"What?" I manage to say.

"*Know you.* I mean, isn't that what you've been doing this entire time?"

"No. I was looking for a relationship."

"Why?"

"What do you mean, 'why?'" I don't really know what Mackenzie's getting at, but this whole topic is starting to piss me off. I rip off another piece of pizza and pop it into my mouth, hoping to chew off some of this frustration. "Doesn't everyone want a relationship?" I suggest. Mackenzie shrugs.

"Sure," she says. "But what do *you* want?" What do I want? Hmm. I stop to think for a second, swallowing the pizza in my mouth.

"I want…" I begin, letting the words linger. I'm not really sure what I'm about to say, so I just let whatever's gonna come out come out. "I want to feel special. I want to feel like somebody picked me. Like I'm not just an afterthought. I want somebody to look at me and think, 'That's the one.' Like I'm somebody's first choice. I want to be worth something to someone. I want to be worth something." Mackenzie stares at me silently, wearing a concerned look.

"Do you not think you're worth something?" she asks. I shrug. That's not an easy question to answer.

"I mean, I do," I say. "It's just… It seems like other people don't." Mackenzie pauses for a moment, seeming to consider what she might say next. She then lets out a heavy sigh.

"Andrew, I don't understand," she says. "Look at you. You are exactly the type of guy that every guy wants to be — you're tall, in shape, attractive. You're a little dumb, but it's okay because you're blonde. But you can be charismatic. And you're fun to be around. You have so much going for you, yet you're sitting here talking about how you're not worth anything because why? Because other people decided for you? Why do you want to let someone else determine your worth? Why can't you see how great you are?"

"If I'm so great, why am I still single?"

"Maybe you need to be. I mean, let's face it, Andrew, based on everything you've been doing, you're not exactly boyfriend material."

"Wow… Is that supposed to make me feel better?" I say, feeling my blood starting to boil. I almost don't believe what she's saying. Like, who says that to a person? Here I am opening up to her and she's throwing it in my face. I knew Mackenzie could be cold-blooded, but I thought even she'd have a little more sympathy.

"I'm not trying to make you feel better," she explains. "I'm trying to be honest with you."

"Yeah? Well, there's a difference between being honest and being a bitch."

"Excuse me?" It seems I've struck the Middle G.

It's funny. You know, I actually thought of Mackenzie as a safe space. I thought she was my friend. I should've known better. I mean, she offered me this cardboard ass pizza. What kind of a friend would do that? I could've choked and died right here in this ghost town of a mall. You know what? I don't even care.

"Are we done here?" I say abruptly. This seems to catch her by surprise, even more so than me calling her out of her name.

"I guess we are," Mackenzie says. And I pull out my wallet, toss a five on the table for eating her cardboard pizza, then head off. It's so tempting to tell the PasTa-da! cashier that their pizza could kill someone as I pass by. Mackenzie would've called me a Karen for that. But Mackenzie's also a bitch.

It's only about 1:30pm when I get home from the mall. It's amazing how much time you save when you don't waste it on people who don't lift you up.

"Oh, you're home already?" Mom says, when I step inside the kitchen. She's in the middle of putting together a casserole, I think. Easy dinner for tonight. "How's your friend? Everything good?"

"Yeah. I think I just ate something gross," I explain. I'm trying to take what Mom and I talked about earlier to heart, so I don't want to lie — which I technically don't — but I also don't want her asking any questions. I've had enough concerned judgement and lecturing for the day, so I head into my room to scroll through more animal fails and shirtless guy workouts.

I swear, I really do watch for the workouts.

Mostly.

Partially.

Anyway, I get to my room, plop on my bed, and pull out my phone which greets me with a notification. It's from AphroDATEme. Interesting. I tap on it and am taken to my inbox, where I find a message from a user named MrIvoryPlay. I notice their profile picture is just a close-up of piano keys. It looks like a stock photo too. I don't even have to enlarge it. What gets me is the actual message.

"*write," it says, followed by another message which reads, "Or are you just clever? [Winky face with tongue emoji]"

Huh. This has a really familiar energy. Or maybe I just have a soft spot for guys correcting my typos. Either way, I'm intrigued. But do I dare? I did have a nice conversation with a guy who had a white square for a photo once. But he was hideous, so…

"What do you look like?" I write back.

"Bit forward, aren't you?" their response comes in a moment later.

"I like to know what I'm dealing with." Another moment or so passes, and then I receive a photo. It's a picture of an older guy. He's got dark hair and beady eyes, with a full beard and mustache. He's dressed in a plaid button up and a casual gray blazer. From what I can tell, he's a bit thick, but in pretty good shape. I'm not sure if I find him attractive, but he's not ugly. He just looks like he could be one of my teachers. I could hang.

> **GoldenBoy513:** Well, you're not hideous.
> **MrIvoryPlay:** Haha. I will take that as a win.
> **GoldenBoy513:** How come you don't have your picture up?
> **MrIvoryPlay:** Protecting myself.
> **MrIvoryPlay:** I'm a teacher.

Ha! Totally called it.

> **GoldenBoy513:** Oh? What subject?
> **MrIvoryPlay:** Music.
> **GoldenBoy513:** Huh. Do you teach piano at all?
> **MrIvoryPlay:** What gave you that idea?
> **MrIvoryPlay:** [Winky face with tongue emoji]
> **MrIvoryPlay:** Do you play?
> **GoldenBoy513:** I dabble.
> **GoldenBoy513:** I had a teacher who suggested I take lessons.
> **MrIvoryPlay:** I could give you lessons.
> **GoldenBoy513:** For how much?
> **MrIvoryPlay:** We can work something out.

GoldenBoy513: What? Like sex?
MrIvoryPlay: I mean…
MrIvoryPlay: [Winky face with tongue emoji]
MrIvoryPlay: I'm kidding, btw.

I suddenly get to thinking. Rudy talked about how this is what we do. "We kiss boys, we fuck boys, and we hook up. That's how we are." And even though I tried to deny it, he still thought that that was exactly what I was doing. Even Mackenzie thought that that was exactly what I was doing.

I quickly think back on every romantic interaction I had with a guy. There was the shoe man, then the chubby guy with the furrow-y brow, then the ghosting dick flasher. Why did none of those dates work out? What did all those guys have in common? I guess it was just me. I guess it was just how I was dealing with them. Come to think of it, I was dealing with guys this way since even before I got on AphroDATEme. I mean, look at Erik Park.

Maybe Mackenzie was right. Maybe I don't want a relationship. And if people want to paint me a certain way, maybe that's exactly how I should be.

GoldenBoy513: Do you want to fuck me?
MrIvoryPlay: I wouldn't say no.
GoldenBoy513: Good.

GoldenBoy513: I think it's time I lose my virginity.

MrIvoryPlay: You're a virgin?

GoldenBoy513: Yeah. You excited?

MrIvoryPlay: If you're sure you want to do this, then yeah, I'm excited.

MrIvoryPlay: But are you sure?

GoldenBoy513: It's just sex.

MrIvoryPlay: It doesn't have to be.

GoldenBoy513: No, it's just sex.

MrIvoryPlay: Okay then.

GoldenBoy513: When's a good time for you?

MrIvoryPlay: I'm mean, I'm free tonight.

GoldenBoy513: Perfect.

GoldenBoy513: I'll see you tonight.

GoldenBoy513: What was your name, btw?

chapter twenty-five

It's official.

I am planning a sexcapade.

I will be losing my virginity to a thirty-five-year-old named Robert, who lives in another city that requires me to cross a toll bridge to get to. I think I have about seven dollars left in my wallet. That should be enough to pay for sex, right? What am I talking about? He's doing me for free. I'm just paying for the bridge.

Now, since I impulsively agreed to meeting him tonight, I've got a couple things I need to figure out, and fast. Number one.) how does sex between two men work? Does it just slide in easily? Do I have to do anything special beforehand? It's kind of a scary thought, isn't it? Going against the flow of traffic. And two.) how am I supposed to get there? I can't ask my mom to borrow her car. She's about to leave for work. And me and my dad haven't spoken since he blew up on me, so that's not even an option. What to do? What to do?

I'm tempted to message Robert back and let him know the situation when I glance out my window and notice a fancy white car pulling up to the curb in front of our house. Looks like Art's home. Huh. I wonder… Would Art ever let me borrow his car? It might be worth a shot. I mean, it couldn't hurt to ask, right? I wait for a second, listening for the sound of Art's door. His bedroom is right next to mine, so I'm always hearing him come and go. I figure it'd be best to catch him in his room than somewhere where Mom might be lurking. As soon as I hear his door open, I make my move.

"Hey, Art," I say, casually stepping into his room and leaning against his doorframe. He turns to me, still dressed in his work uniform of a black polo and khaki shorts. He seems surprised.

"Hey, Andrew, what's up?" he asks.

"I was actually wondering if we could talk."

"You want to talk? To me?" He doesn't seem to believe it. In fact, he looks downright suspicious of me. I just nod and he takes a seat on his bed. "Um, sure. What do you want to talk about?"

"Actually, I wanted to ask a favor," I begin, then reach for his door and slowly shut it behind me. "I was wondering if, maybe, you'd let me borrow your car tonight?" I give him a hopeful, if a little awkward, smile. He stares at me silently for a second before suddenly bursting out laughing.

"You're kidding, right?" he says. "I'm not gonna loan you my car."

"Art, come on. Please? I can't ask Mom 'cause she's leaving for work, and Dad's probably still mad at me. You're the only person I can ask. You said I could come to you about anything."

"I said you could *talk* to me about anything."

"We're talking now."

"Well, where are you going? I can just drop you off," he suggests. Why is he coming up with alternative solutions? Ugh, this is so annoying.

"You can't just drop me off," I say.

"Why not?"

"Because!" My voice comes out louder than I mean for it to. Stupid Art. Why'd he have to be so sensible? I guess I'll just have to tell him. "I have a date, okay? And I was planning on spending the night with them. How's it gonna look if I get dropped off there?"

"Like you took a rideshare," he replies. God, he is just the worst.

"Are you gonna loan me money for that?" I say. "You know what, never mind. I'll just cancel." I don't want to deal with him anymore. I'm over it. I turn to leave, but as soon as I reach his door, I hear him say…

"Wait. I'll make you a deal." I'm not sure I even want to hear it at this point. I just imagine it'll be something underhanded so that he can come out better than me. He's always coming out better than me. "I'll loan you my car, but you have to promise that you'll talk to me. And none of that 'go away' bullshit you pulled yesterday. You gotta let me in. Deal?"

Is that all he wants? Really? What a nerd.

"Easy," I say, still not sure I believe him. I mean, there's gotta be some sorta catch to this, right?

"Alright then." Art gets up and crosses to his dresser, which is positioned next to the door, where his keys had been sitting this entire time. Had I noticed them earlier, I probably could've swiped them without him even noticing. "Be back before three tomorrow. I have to work," he says, handing me his keys. He then places a firm hand on my shoulder. "And, Andrew, if you get even a scratch on my car, I will murder you."

"Got it."

"Good. Now leave me alone. I'm gonna take a nap." And just like that my second issue is solved. Now, let's circle back to my first issue. How exactly does butt sex work? You know what? I've watched a lot of porn. I'm just gonna wing it. How *hard* could it be?

I'm very mature.

It's getting close to midnight. I'm sitting in Art's car, parked in a lot outside of a big-box bookstore. I ended up leaving around 11:00pm because I had to wait for Dad to go into his room for the night. At dinner, he barely said two words to me, so it's safe to assume he wouldn't have been cool with me leaving the house. It took forever for me to get here too. I had to cross a toll bridge and everything. I'm really hoping Art's not gonna want gas money. Not that he needs it. His fuel gauge hasn't moved since I left home, and I drove, like, forty miles.

I'm starting to wonder if this was a good idea. The bookstore is already closed, the parking lot is pretty dark, and my genius self thought it would be smart to park towards the back of the lot next to a bush and a cluster of trees. If someone wanted to rob me, this would be the perfect time to. But the joke would be on them. I've only got two dollars in my wallet.

While I'm waiting for MrIvoryPlay to show up, I find myself on AphroDATEme staring at his profile picture. I still can't decide if I think he's cute or not. He's just older than I expected to date, and he looks it. Which is weird because I'm excited. I don't usually get excited about guys who… well, don't excite me. Maybe it's the idea of finally turning in my V card that's got me feeling this way. Maybe I'm just ready to finally feel what everybody else feels. To hit that milestone that so many people my age have hit, and probably hit multiple times. Even people like Erik-Potato-Park have hit that milestone, I'm sure of it. You don't date a guy like Nick Santiago and not let him tap it. Meanwhile, I've just been playing catch up.

Suddenly, I hear a light tapping sound on my driver's side window. I quickly turn to look and see MrIvoryPlay waving at me.

"Hi, Robert?" I greet him, after rolling down the window.

"Yeah. Andrew, right?" he replies. I look him up and down. He's different than in his picture. Like, he's the same guy, but he seems more relaxed. Casual, even. It might just be the clothes though. He's dressed in a gray pullover and loose-fitting jeans. And to think I almost dressed up for this. Good thing I didn't. I just threw on a plain white tee, some jeans, my red hoodie and called it a day. "Bookstore's closed," he says with a smirk.

"Yeah… I was trying to be safe about this meetup. But nothing's open this late," I explain. "Do you wanna just get in?" Robert nods, then circles around the car to climb into the passenger seat. When he does, my heart starts to race. I don't know if it's the lack of lighting or the blood rushing to certain places, but he's immediately becoming way more attractive to me. "You're cuter in person," I whisper. And the next thing I know, me and Robert are making out in the backseat of my brother's hybrid. I don't know how we got to the backseat. My seatbelt was on when he got in the car.

Kissing Robert is like trying to tongue wrestle out the jelly from a rye bread sandwich. Like, the rye bread is questionable because only old people enjoy it — Mom brings it home from work every now and then, ugh — but the jelly is just sweet enough to keep you licking. So, that's what I do. I lick and I lick until I'm breathless and my mouth is dripping with spit. I can feel my forehead starting to sweat. Man, it's hot in here. And in more ways than one.

"Wanna go back to my place?" Robert breathes. I nod and pull him in for another round of licking the jelly out of the rye. I feel his weight on top of me, and I relax into him. It's comfortable, like wrapping yourself in the covers on a cold night. I've never known the loving of a man, but tonight, I will.

Yeah, tonight, I will.

Tuesday. July 1st.

Robert lives in a relatively small two-story house. From the looks of it, it's smaller than mine, and the front yard could use some attention, but it's cute, nonetheless.

I pull up to the curb right in front as Robert's climbing out of his car on the gravel driveway. When he gets to his door, he turns to wave me in. I breathe a heavy sigh before letting myself out of the car. Tonight's really happening.

"Excuse the mess," Robert says, when we step inside. "We're in the middle of renovations." And he's not kidding. This first room is packed with a bunch of boxes laying around and there are stacks of books everywhere. I slowly make my way around them, careful not to knock anything over and find myself in a short hallway that connects to the kitchen and possibly another room around the corner. There are no floorboards here. This seems like a lot of work if they're doing this themselves. That's when it hits me.

"We're?" I ask.

"Oh, me and my boyfriend," Robert says. I immediately tense up. Excuse me? What does he mean boyfriend? Is my first time gonna be a tag team event? I don't know if I'm ready for that. The worry must be painted all over my face because Robert starts to chuckle. "Sorry. I meant *ex*-boyfriend."

"You live with your ex-boyfriend?" The idea seems ridiculous to me. I can't imagine why anyone would do that, unless there was, like, a family involved that he's not telling me about. But what do I know?

"It's complicated," he says. "Besides, I couldn't afford a place like this on my own. Some days, I'm not sure I'd want to."

"How come?" I ask.

"I like the company." Robert smiles, but there's something about it that just seems sad. Like he's putting up a front. I guess I don't blame him. "Don't worry. He's out of town for work. You won't run into him."

"Shame. This could've been a party."

"Yeah, I don't know if you're ready for that." Robert and I laugh. We make our way through the hall, around the corner, and into the next room. It's the biggest room in the house — probably the main living area — and there are boxes and books piled around here too. There's a narrow set of stairs on one side, a couch in the center, and a TV against the wall opposite the stairs. Aside from the mess, I'd probably describe this place as cozy. I look around, taking all of it in. I don't know if I'll ever see this place again. But if tonight goes the way that I hope it does, this place will likely be etched into my memory for the rest of my life. I think I'm okay with that. And then I see it, something sitting in the corner near the bottom of the stairs.

"Oh, cool, a piano," I say, excitedly approaching it, as if it's a surprise to see a piano in a Music teacher's house. It's one of those fancy upright wood ones, the kind that look more suited to a museum or an antique shop than someone's living room.

"You in the mood to tickle some ivory?" Robert asks, wearing a suggestive smirk.

"Is that, like, a sex thing?" I reply.

"No, uh, ivories are the piano keys. It's an old saying. It means 'to play the piano.'"

"And that is why that's your username, isn't it?" Well, this is embarrassing. I feel incredibly stupid. It's not like it was obviously a piano reference. It's not like he had a stock photo of a piano keys as his profile picture or anything. Whatever. He's laughing. At least one of us is amused by this.

"You're very cute," he says, smiling. Robert is somehow looking more and more attractive to me. It's either the soft warm lighting of the living room or I just can't wait anymore.

"Should we go to your room?" I ask. He nods and then turns to go up the stairs. I follow him because, yeah, tonight's happening.

Robert's room is one of two rooms on the second floor. I'm not sure if it's the master bedroom or what, but it's about the size of mine and Art's rooms combined, and it's got its own bathroom. Nice. His closet doors are those sliding mirror kind, and his bed is positioned right across the room from them. We're likely to see everything. Kinky.

We're sitting on his bed making out. Robert's got his hand resting on the back of my neck as if to pull me closer, and he's kissing me with such care and gentle passion, I feel... *precious*. Like a little boy that plays with dolls.

That's a weird image. Never mind.

I don't know a better way to describe it though. I mean, I am a little distracted. His tongue is dancing with mine to the sound of a silent soundtrack only the two of us can hear. The jelly in the rye is tasting really sweet now. So much so, I think I can smell it. I get the scent of maple syrup. And cinnamon. Huh. Strange.

I let myself get caught up in the moment and gently place my hand on his thigh. It almost surprises me that he doesn't try to stop me or remove it. This is usually the point when things like this stop for me. I give his thigh a squeeze, my heart pounding like crazy.

"Are you sure you want to do this?" he whispers into my mouth. His breath smells like breakfast. I can almost taste it. Weird. But I nod. "We can stop this at any time, you know?" he adds.

"Do you not want to?" I reply.

"I just want to avoid giving you any regrets." What a gentleman, he is. I appreciate the thoughtfulness, but I didn't come here for his thoughts. So, I kiss him again and then peel off his shirt, revealing a surprisingly firm and broad chest, covered in a thin layer of hair. It's not usually what I go for, but I'm not about to stop myself. Robert then begins to push his weight forward. I lean back to accept him, spreading my legs so he can rest in between them. I feel his body shift back and forth over and over, moving like a dog in heat. I'm hard as a bone now. I can feel he is too. Then, suddenly, he stops.

"Are you sure this is what you want?" he asks, breathing heavy now. God, why is he being so weird about this? We're already basically doing it. All that's stopping us is the fact that our pants are still on. You know what, let's fix that. I reach down, undo the button of his jeans, then slip my hand just past the waistband of his underwear. I watch as his jaw drops, and his eyes roll back momentarily. Must've been a long time for him too. His eyes then meet mine. And with as much authority that I can put into a whisper, I tell him…

"I want you to fuck me."

And so, he does.

When the whole losing my virginity thing is said and done, I find myself lying in Robert's bed alone. Robert's already in the shower. He invited me to wash up with him, but I haven't wanted to move since we finished. I have to admit, sex feels much more like practice than an actual game. At least for the first time. You don't just go in and play. First, you gotta suit up, then it's a whole lot of trial and error before things actually get going. And when it does get going, there's no telling how long it'll be before it starts to get uncomfortable.

Robert was playing with, uh, adequate equipment. I always thought that bigger was better, but I'm sorta glad he wasn't bigger because that first poke was hell… fire. It burned. I think it was my body being in such shock that something was happening down there. It wanted to nope right out of the whole thing, but… I wanted it. I wanted to feel it. It had to get good at some point, right?

Once he was inside, which took a long time — again, a lot of trial and error — it started to feel okay. I don't know if I'd say it felt good. But it didn't feel bad. I guess I would say it was like getting a massage, but on a spot where you had a really tight knot. Like, it's satisfying, but it hurts a little bit, and you're still kind of uncomfortable after. Every now and then, Robert would hit a spot or go at an angle that had me clenching my jaw and questioning how guys could like this. But then he'd hit another spot and move in a way where I just wanted him to keep going. It was all so hot and cold. Good and bad. I wasn't expecting that. I don't know. I guess I was expecting it to be the best feeling in the world, you know? I blame porn for that.

Anyway, the whole time Robert was having sex on me, I just felt really numb. Not physically, but mentally and emotionally. For some reason, I couldn't get the smell or the taste of maple syrup and cinnamon out of my mind. I tried to focus on the ceiling while Robert was pushing himself into me, but the scent and the flavor just kept getting stronger. Then I thought I could ignore it by focusing on what was happening inside my body. I mean, there was *a lot* going on in there. That's when I closed my eyes and saw the worst thing I could've possibly seen in that moment...

I saw Rudy.

I saw his dumb face, his stupid changing hair, his wannabe hipster emo lip ring thing. I saw him dancing in the parking lot. I saw him silently sitting in my passenger seat texting. I saw him driving after a night of drinking...

I saw him smiling at me while holding my hand. I saw him standing on the dock with the backdrop of the city. I saw him looking into my eyes like they were the most beautiful thing in the world. I saw him kissing me...

And then I saw him getting in his car and driving away. I saw what I let go of just a day ago. I saw all the possibilities I denied myself of. I saw all the memories I'd made. And all the memories I'd never get to make... with him.

I didn't want to, but I started to cry. I bit my lip so I wouldn't let out a whimper. And if Robert heard any, I'm guessing he just assumed it was because I was enjoying myself. *He* certainly was. I caught sight of us in the mirror and I watched. I watched myself lying lifelessly while this man, who's little more than a body to me, just went to town. Aside from whatever was happening physically, I felt nothing.

Now, I'm not opposed to the idea of casual sex or hooking up, clearly. I think what bothers me about the situation is that I feel like I had a chance to have something special. And I traded it in. For what? I held my breath in the tunnel on the Bay Bridge just to turn around. I can see now why Robert would keep living with his ex. Company is better when you care.

"You okay?" I hear Robert ask.

"I'm fine," I answer, rubbing my eyes dry in case of any more tears. I sit up in his bed and see him standing in his bathroom doorway, toweling himself off. Apparently, I'm not very good at hiding my emotions because he gives me a look of pity. Normally, I'd hate that, but I don't have the energy to be mad about it. I'm already upset.

"Do you want to talk about it?" Robert offers, coming over to sit down next to me.

"I was just thinking… about a guy."

"Someone special?" The question hits me like a knife to the heart. And no matter how much I don't want to, I start crying again, my eyes bursting into tears and my face scrunching into full-on ugly mode.

"I don't know," I sob. I don't remember the last time I sobbed. I don't remember the last time I cried this hard. What did Rudy do to me? "It should've been him," I cry. "It should've been with him." Robert puts his arms around me and pulls me close. I cry into his bare chest so much that he could use another shower. The crying is painful. It's the kind of crying where every breath feels like I'm choking on it. Like I'm suffocating under the weight of myself. But I can't stop. I just cry and I cry until I can't cry anymore. And then Robert tells me to take a shower while he goes downstairs to throw a pizza in the oven. That's probably a good idea. I should probably eat.

You know how in the movies, there's always, like, a scene where it's raining after something sad happens? I feel like the main character in my own movie, sitting in Robert's tub, cold water beating against my skin to really drive the point home: *this is sad.* What makes it even sadder is that it's not even raining. This is just shower water. And I made it cold so I wouldn't get tempted for round two with Robert, which I'd almost be down for if it wasn't for all these *feelings,* ugh.

When I get out of the shower, I'm faced with the fact that I didn't think to bring a change of clothes to this sexcapade. That means I gotta put on the same clothes I came in with, including underwear. This *is* sad. Maybe I can just skip the underwear… No, no. I wore jeans tonight. That's not a good idea. I'm already uncomfortable enough as it is down there.

I get myself dressed, underwear and all, then head out of Robert's room to join him downstairs. When I get to the stairs though, I'm stopped by the soft sound of a familiar melody playing. Looks like someone decided to "tickle the ivories," as he'd put it. I stand at the top of the stairs and listen to Robert's playing for a moment. Each note rings out in a haunting fashion, slowly floating through the air as they find their way to me. Eventually the music changes into something totally unfamiliar. I'd never gotten this far into the song. Even if I had taken the time to practice, how could I? The Piano book from school only had the first page.

"Is that *Moonlight Sonata?*" I ask, approaching Robert at the piano after finally coming down the stairs. I see he's got a printout of the sheet music — five whole pages — set up in front of him.

"You know it?" he replies, stopping his playing to turn and look at me.

"Not really. I was trying to learn it when I was taking a Piano class, but…"

"But…?"

"I dunno," I shrug. I hadn't thought of what to say after. I mean, I guess I have valid excuses: the class is over, I don't have the sheet music, the piano I have has a broken Middle G. All of that's true. But none of it explains why I didn't try more. Maybe it just wasn't important to me. Or maybe I just didn't give it a chance.

"Well, here. Why don't you show me what you know, and I can teach you a little bit," Robert offers. Aside from Mrs. Dolittle, I've never really played for anyone before. It's a little nerve racking being put on the spot like this, but regardless, I take a seat on the piano bench next to him. I lift up my right hand, place my fingers on the keys, and start to play the familiar notes.

G hashtag, C hashtag, E normal.

G hashtag, C hashtag, E normal.

The sound of my playing comes out slower, lingering with a fearful sort of… uncertainty. I feel my hand shaking the whole time. I really don't know what I'm doing. As much as I'd like to pretend that I do.

Robert then places his left hand on the piano and begins to play the portions of the song I haven't learned yet. I play my notes over, and over again, until he stops me to show me which keys come next. There's so much to this song I haven't figured out and I start to realize just how much I'd been missing by avoiding it. By refusing to confront it.

"Here. Why don't you take it?" Robert asks, gathering up the sheet music and offering it to me. "That way you can finally learn it."

"You sure?" I reply.

"Yeah, it's just a photocopy. I'm sure I got the actual sheet music somewhere around here." Suddenly, a beeping sound comes from the other room. "And that would be the pizza. You hungry?" I'm not really, but I nod anyway. He's being so nice, it's a shame I feel nothing for him. But I already decided that before. I did tell him this was just about sex, but still… I can't help but wonder if I'm just a shit person.

Robert and I hang out in his kitchen for a little while. We munch on pizza while chatting about this and that — music, sports, whatever — just chillin'. At around 5:00am, I decide I should probably leave. Robert offers to let me stay and get some sleep before heading out, but I don't like the idea of sleeping here. I don't know him like that. As a "Thank you for everything," I let him use my mouth one more time before I go, so it's closer to 6:00am when I'm actually stepping out of his house.

"Hey, I know this was just about sex," Robert says to me when I get out on to his front porch, "but don't be a stranger." I nod and he gives me a gentle smile before shutting his door. I then cut across his yard to Art's car parked at the curb and climb in, setting the sheet music Robert gave me on the passenger seat. I'm not really in a rush to leave, so I just sit here for a second, thinking. I thought I could make myself feel better by having sex. You know, finally satisfy that urge. After all, that's what I was trying to do this entire time, right? But instead, I just feel like I wasted an opportunity.

When it comes to losing my virginity, I don't know if I ever thought it needed to be something special. It didn't really. At least, not until I realized that it could've been. But now that I know it could've been… Now that I know it could've been with someone who I can't seem to get my fucking mind off of… I just want it back. I want my first time back. I want that opportunity back. I want another chance to get something right. I just want another chance to make something worth remembering. To make something gold.

But who am I kidding?

chapter twenty-six

RudeFern69 has blocked you.

I'm sitting on my bed, back pressed against the wall, staring at Rudy's AphroDATEme page, or what would've been his page anyway. It's about 8:00am in the morning. Despite the night I've come back from, I'm not sleepy. Tired, but not sleepy. I've got the lights off in my room, but the sun's creeping in through the blinds of my window. All I want to do is sit in the dark and let myself feel all of my feelings. Maybe even throw a pity party or some shit. It's a party, right? Party for one. Or it would be if there wasn't someone knocking on my door.

"Go away," I yell lazily. Of course, whoever's knocking doesn't. Nope, instead they open my door and poke their head in. And of course, it's Art. It's always Art, the constant figure lurking in the background, reminding me of everything I'm not. Is there a word that describes a long and exasperated internal sigh? We'll just go with *ugh!* That'll do.

"Morning," Art greets me happily, stepping into my room. He's in a plain white tee and pajama bottoms. Like, dude, just go back to bed like a normal person during summer break and don't get up till noon. "I wasn't expecting you to be home this early," he says. "Can I get my keys?"

"On my desk," I reply. He goes over to grab his keys from my desk where I set up Mom's keyboard. I'm watching him, counting the seconds it takes him to leave, but he doesn't seem to be going anywhere. Instead, he lingers at my desk, hovering over the keyboard. I stare at him through the tops of my eyes, imagining I have laser vision and his stupid face melting in my gaze. If only looks could kill.

"You actually learning to play this thing?" he asks smiling, all amused, as if he wasn't the one responsible for ruining the Middle G. It's partially his fault — actually, let's just say it's all his fault — that I don't play. Let's just blame everything on Art because he's dumb and he won't leave. Just leave, bro!

"Art, go away."

"What?"

"I said, 'go away.'"

"Dude, what's up with you?"

"What part of 'go away' don't you understand, huh? Did no one teach you that before they let you into college?" I can hear how harsh my voice is sounding, but I don't care. All I want right now is to be alone so I can wallow in peace, and he won't freakin' go away. How am I supposed to throw a pity party for one when I have company over? I didn't send out invitations!

Art stands there looking at me all dumbfounded. At first, he doesn't say anything, which is annoying because if he has nothing to say, he should just leave. I keep telling him to. Suddenly, he takes a breath.

"You know what?" Art says. "You're not doing this." He quickly moves to my door and shuts it, before turning back to me with his arms crossed. Is this, like, his "Now we mean business" pose? God, he's so corny. "Alright, what's going on with you?"

"Will you just go away? My God!" I say, getting more and more frustrated by the second. Why is he dragging this out? Why can't he just leave me alone?

"No. You're gonna talk to me, Andrew. We had a deal."

"What deal?!"

"Last night! I loaned you my car; you have to talk to me. No more bullshit. No more of this 'go away' nonsense. You yelled at Mom. You're fighting with Dad.

You're staying out all night. And I try to do something nice for you and you're still a dick to me, but what else is new? Something's going on, man. Now, what's up?" The whole time he's talking, I'm clenching my jaw. I want to fight him. I want to yell, scream, and knock him in his big ol' face. I can feel my whole body starting to shake. The frustration and anger of it all is starting to boil over. The pressure of him trying to get me to come out with it… it's too much.

"You really want to know?" I say, more like a threat than a question.

"Yeah," he nods.

"I'm fucking gay!" The words leave my mouth like an angry *Blaaang!* from the broken Middle G on my mom's keyboard. Everything falls silent for me. It's like the world has suddenly stopped in a moment of anticipation. My stomach is twisting, tied up in knots. I feel like I'm waiting for a referee to call it. Like I've just been tackled in the middle of a football game while running the ball to the end zone, and I'm not sure where I landed.

I don't know how much time actually passes once the words come out, but I see the almost confused look on Art's face and my heart starts to sink. But then… he smiles.

"Yeah? And?" he says. I'm a little confused now. What does he mean by that? "Dude, we know."

. . .

Um, what?

"What do you mean, 'We know?'" I ask.

"I mean, *we know,*" Art replies. I'm still not understanding. How in the world would they have known? I never said anything. I never did anything, not until recently. I never brought guys around, at least not anyone I was, like, interested in. And my family never gave me any indication that being gay was a thing that they'd acknowledge, much less accept. How would they have known? "I mean, we didn't know for sure," Art starts to explain, "but we all had our suspicions." He comes over and takes a seat on my bed. "Growing up, you were always hugging on me, laying your head on my shoulder, clinging to my arm. I didn't mind it, and I think people thought it was cute… until I got to junior high."

"That's when we stopped hanging out," I mumble, remembering back on it.

"Yeah… My friends started noticing you doing that stuff. They didn't want to be around you. They kept saying you were gay. It also didn't help that you played with dolls. Eventually, I started to believe them, so I asked Mom and Dad about it. They started noticing more stuff as you got older, like how you never had any girlfriends, and how uncomfortable you'd get the few times you took a girl to a school dance. I think they even caught you checking out a waiter at Antonini's once."

"So I was that obvious?" I ask, the heavy feeling of disappointment filling my gut. Art shrugs.

"You have really expressive eyes," he adds casually. "Actually, for a while, Dad thought you were dating your friend, Jacob. He said if you had to date one of your guy friends, he rather it'd be Riley. He thought Jacob was a brat."

"Yeah? Well, I'm not really friends with Jacob or Riley anymore," I say, to which Art offers a sympathetic smile. "Riley did try to text me about a week or so ago though."

"Well, you should get back to him. At least he's trying," Art replies. We both go silent for a moment. I don't really know what to say. I'm still in shock that, apparently, the entire time I've been in the closet, the door's been wide open. I don't know what to do with that information. I guess it's a relief, but it doesn't feel like one. Like, I don't feel any better or more free. If anything, I just feel kind of pathetic. Why can't I just own up to it? Why can't I just be like, "Look at me! I'm here and I'm queer?!" Why is it so hard for me? "So, was that it?" Art asks. "Was the gay thing eating you up? Is that why you were acting out?"

"Actually, there's more. Like, a lot more," I say.

"Well, I don't have to get ready for work till two, so…" he replies. It's weird for me talking to my brother like this. I feel like I'm naked and he's fully clothed, which now that I'm saying it out loud, sounds really gross 'cause he's my brother. But I've always felt sorta at a disadvantage when it comes to Art, so the idea of telling him about my love life — or lack thereof — is uncomfortable. If only we were on an even playing field, but the last time I can recall feeling like we were was before he went to junior high.

"Yeah? Then let's make a blanket fort. Make a whole thing out of it," I suggest sarcastically. Art doesn't seem to take it that way though, as he practically lights up with excitement.

"Dude, we should! That would be so fun."

"Art, I was joking."

"Too bad. We're doing it. I'll grab the snacks and you can start on the fort." And before I can say any more about how dumb or pointless the whole fort thing is, Art's running out of my room on a mission. It surprises me how fast he moves; he must be really excited. I'd call him a nerd, but if I'm honest, I think I might be excited about it too. Let's hope he brings the Oreos.

Now, I'm not sure how this fort thing is gonna work, seeing as Art and I are both at least twice the size we were since we last built one, but I start building it anyway. I drape my comforter over my desk, keeping it in place using Mom's keyboard. I throw my bedsheet over my desk chair to create an additional wall. I figure we'll need the extra space. It's a strange experience building this fort. I feel like I'm just making a mess, and for what? I will admit though, it is kind of fun.

While I'm arranging my pillows into floorboards and my sweaters into carpets, I notice the stuffed cow Art gave me for my birthday lying tipped over under my bed. I have to pause for a moment because the sight of it… I don't know. It's making me sad. I mean, here I am building a fort for a guy whose gift I'd thrown under my bed and forgotten about, all out of spite. I'm starting to realize that this blanket fort thing, it's just me getting ready to play pretend. And I don't want to play pretend anymore. So, when Art gets back to my room with the snacks, I say bluntly…

"I hate you." I don't know what his reaction is. My back is to the door. I'm staring at the cow under my bed. If Art has words, he's not gonna get one in edgewise, because I can sense mine are gonna get away from me like the single teardrop rolling down my cheek. "I hate that everything you do is perfect. I hate that Dad's so proud of you. I hate that no matter what I do… I'm never gonna be like you."

"Why do you want to be?" I hear him ask.

"You're the golden boy."

"Eh, it's not all it's cracked up to be. It's a lot of expectation," Art explains. I hear him walk towards me. He takes a seat beside me on the floor, dropping the snacks he brought into a nice little pile. I feel the tiniest spark of joy seeing he brought the Oreos.

"Expectations you prove right," I say snidely.

"That's not exactly a good thing. I don't want to be defined by what other people expect of me. That's pressure. I get enough of that from Dad. Besides *this*," he replies, gesturing to the fort, "this isn't about me." He then takes the pack of Oreos, opens it, and offers me a cookie. I stare at him, reluctant to take it. He simply smiles. I know what he wants. He wants me to talk. He wants me to tell him everything that's been bothering me, everything that I've been going through. So, I do. What can I say? I already agreed to it when he loaned me his car. Plus, I want the cookie.

I tell Art everything. I start with Erik Park and my feelings about him landing Nick Santiago. Then I go into the stuff with the shoe man, followed by the fat guy with the furrowing brow. I tell Art every detail I can remember, he insists on it whenever I hesitate. I even tell him about the ghosting dick flasher.

"He just whipped it out in Mom's backseat?" Art asks with a sort of amused disbelief. I nod, and he bursts out laughing.

Eventually, I tell him about Rudy. Having to relive Pride, Rudy kissing a stranger, driving all around the Bay Area, the harbor, the breaking up, all of it… It's hard. It hurts. It still hurts. I hear my voice shaking the whole time I'm talking about it. And Art, he just listens. He eats some jalapeno kettle potato chips and Oreos, complains about how he forgot to grab drinks, and he listens.

Finally, I tell him about last night.

"Wait. You didn't have sex in *my* car, did you?" he interrupts as soon as I mention losing my virginity. I should say that I did just to get his reaction, but I don't. Wasted opportunities, I'm full of 'em, aren't I?

"And now I'm here," I say, once I've finished telling him all there is to tell.

"Wow... That's a lot," Art replies.

"Yeah. I kinda feel like I'm messing up my life. I just keep making all these terrible choices, you know?" I feel awkward, and not just because Art and I are laying under my blanket covered desk, with our lower halves poking out of this rickety, half-assed excuse for a "fort." I've got so much tension built up from this talk, I can feel it in my hands. I need to do something. So, I grab an Oreo and absentmindedly start twisting the two sides of the cookie apart. Getting the cookie to separate while keeping the cream totally intact was always the holy grail of pulling apart an Oreo. Whenever I managed to do it, I'd always get really happy. It's too bad I don't manage to do it now. "I'm a disaster," I mumble to myself.

"Yeah, you are," Art says. It throws me, but before I have a chance to get offended, he goes on. "But so am I. And so is the next person. It's part of growing up. We make bad choices. We do stupid shit because why not? We're all just trying to find ourselves. You just happened to be looking for yourself in other people. I think you just need to stop for a minute. Forget about dating for a while and just spend some time with *you*. Get to know yourself, you know? You can take your mistakes and all the bad choices you made and build yourself a better person."

I don't respond. I just sit here silently, letting everything Art's saying sink in. And as it does, my mind goes back to the last conversation I had with Mackenzie. She said, "You're not exactly boyfriend material." When she said it, it really pissed me off. But now, I wonder if this is what she was trying to say the whole time. And the more that I think about it, the more I feel like an idiot.

"You know, I think my friend, Mackenzie, was trying to say something like that," I mumble.

"Oh?"

"Well, sort of. Actually, she said I wasn't boyfriend material."

"You should listen to her. She sounds smart," Art replies.

"Fuck you," I say. Art laughs. And as much as I might not want to, so do I. Then, when our laughter fades, Art pauses for a moment and a certain sort of thoughtful sadness seems to wash over him.

"You know, Andrew, if there's one thing I regret, it's that I let other people decide what you were worth to me. I left you behind when we were growing up and I hate that. And I'm sorry." Art offers me the saddest smile and I don't know if it's the sugar or the lack of sleep, but it's making me want to cry. I don't want to cry about this. I need a subject change. Time to pivot.

"Stop making this about you," I say playfully, in a fake angry voice. We burst out laughing all over again. It's a nice release of the tension. Suddenly, this rinky-dink fort has turned into something almost comfortable. Or maybe it's just us. Either way, I offer Art half of my Oreo — the half with less cream — as a peace offering of sorts. "You don't think I'm hopeless?" I ask, taking a bite of my half of the cookie.

"Nah, I think you're pretty cool. Half the stuff you did, I didn't experience until college," Art explains, popping his half of the cookie into his mouth. "Dad was always up my butt about carrying on the family legacy. Which don't get me wrong, I'm happy to. I just wish he wasn't so *proud* of everything. It's like I'm not allowed to mess up."

"Mmm… Must be hard being you."

"Shut up." Art chuckles and I can't help but smile. It's strange. He was always there, whether in real life or on the mantelpiece. He's always been a part of my life in some way, but today, it feels like we're meeting each other for the first time. And in a way, I think we are. I spent so many years hating him because I could never be him. Thinking about that and sitting here in this fort takes me back to this time when we were really young. Art and I built a fort, just like the one we're lying in now, and we were talking about how he overheard Mom and Dad saying I was gonna get held back in kindergarten. Rather than focusing on the thing that was gonna hold me back, Art decided to look ahead and talk about what we wanted to be when we grew up. I wonder what he'd say now.

"Art, what do you want to be when you grow up? I ask. "Like, after college and stuff."

"I want to be… the greatest person ever," he laughs. Some things never change.

"You're an idiot," I say. Art shrugs.

"Well, what about you, Andrew? What do you want to be when you grow up?" I stop to think about it. If I'm remembering right, back then, I said I wanted to be just like my big brother. But now…

"I think I just want to be me," I say. "Whatever that means. Is that stupid?"

"No," Art responds, smiling. "Corny, but not stupid. I think you're pretty great." Art and I chill in our fort a little while longer, chatting about everything and nothing. We chat until all the bad stuff that filled my head is replaced with stupid dad jokes Art learned from his college friends and his crazy experience trying acid where he was convinced he was a tree. I guess drugs and bad puns are popular among those who pursue higher learning.

Eventually, I hear my phone go off. When I check it, I see it's a text from Riley of all people. That's surprising. I also see it's around one o'clock. Art and I decide it's time to take down the fort. He helps me clean up by gathering all the pillows from the floor, while I pull my comforter and sheets off the furniture. If I'm being honest, it makes me a little sad having to take it all down, considering the quality of the time we spent in it, but blanket forts are temporary. They're things you make memories in and then simply fold away. And I think that's what makes them so special. The fact that they're not permanent means that you have to enjoy them while you can. That's the whole point.

"Alright, well, it's been real, brother," Art says once we've put my bed back together. "Don't be a stranger." I give Art a slight smile and nod, then watch as he heads for the door.

"Hey, Art," I say, stopping him just as he's about to leave. "Would you mind telling Mom and Dad?" He cocks his head to the side, looking all sorts of confused. "You know, about the whole…" My voice trails off. I'm hesitating, which I know is weird because I just told Art *everything.* Still, for some reason, I'm struggling to bring myself to say it. Luckily, it seems to click for Art.

"Are you sure you want that coming from me?" he asks.

"Well, I want them to know for sure. It's just... I don't know. There's something about saying it out loud that just feels like everything's gonna change. I don't know if I ever want to say it out loud. And I hate that I feel like I have to." It takes Art no time to respond.

"Okay," he says. "So don't. I mean, you're not with anyone. You don't owe anybody an explanation."

"So you'll tell them?"

"Yeah, sure."

"Thank you," I say. He shrugs.

"Eh, it's no big deal. And really, it doesn't have to be, so, yeah."

"I love you." The words leave my mouth long before I even register that that's what I was gonna say. But I actually don't regret it.

"Gross, you're my brother," Art says with a playful grin. Never mind. I totally regret it. And with that, he exits my room. I take in a deep breath and let it out slowly. Having told my brother everything, it feels like a weight's been lifted. I smile to myself, soaking in the feeling. It's nice, this honesty thing. I don't know if Art and I will ever be, like, super close, but it's nice knowing that he's there and not just on a pedestal. Then, I suddenly remember the cow tipped over under my bed. I get on my knees and reach for it, brushing off the dust it's collected after so many weeks of being forgotten. He could use a wash. I think I'll name him Artie.

What?

Art's the one who gave me the cow, saying it reminded him of me. It's not like I'm just being an ass for no reason. But, seriously, how funny would it be if his school mascot was a donkey?

Anyway, I go over to the window and pull the blinds open before grabbing my phone and plopping myself onto my bed with Artie. You know, the cow…

On second thought, this is weird. Never mind. Let's call the cow Betsy. So, Betsy and I unlock my phone and my eyes immediately go to the red notification bubble hovering over my text app. That's right, Riley texted me. My stomach ties itself in knots again. I glance down at Betsy, who I've got wrapped in one arm, looking at her like she'll have an opinion. I know what that opinion would be, and I sigh.

I decide to bite the bullet, which I still think is the weirdest saying. I imagine if you did bite a bullet, it would just hurt your jaw? And why would you put a bullet in your mouth anyway? Eh, whatever. At this point, I've had worse things in my mouth. I go ahead and open Riley's message.

"Hey, can we talk?" it reads.

"Yeah," I type. "I'm dead tired now. You free tomorrow?" And send. Just about a minute later, Riley's response comes in.

"Yeah," is all it says. One word. At the very least, he's reaching out. I suppose this is him trying. And if he's willing to try, I should be too.

But tomorrow.

Today's been trying enough.

Wednesday. July 2nd.

It's a little past noon.

Riley just texted.

"Hey, wanna meet up around 2?" he asks.

"Sure," I type and hit send. I'm not totally awake yet. When you figure in the last couple of days, my sleep cycle is totally fucked. Like, yesterday, I fell asleep after my talk with Art and woke up around eight o' clock. I couldn't get back to sleep and I was super horny, so I took care of myself. Then, I stayed up watching videos of shirtless guys dancing in gray sweatpants, which made me need to take care of myself again. You'd think that after losing my virginity, I would've calmed down a bit, but now I'm just, like, craving it. I wonder if that will ever go away? Whatever. I roll over, hoping to catch another hour or so. And, of course, just as I'm starting to doze off, there's a knock on my door.

"Go away," I yell lazily, my voice muffled in my pillow. I hear the door open. I'm assuming it's Art, and what do you know? It is.

"Oh, good you're awake," he says, poking his head into my room.

"No, I'm not. Go away."

"Are you still saying that? 'Go away?'"

"Because you haven't learned it yet," I reply, sitting up, rubbing my eyes awake.

"It's lunch time. Mom wants you to come and eat," Art explains. I yawn, raising my arms to stretch. "Also, heads up. I told her about… you know…" That news is enough to wake me.

"What'd she say?" I ask.

"She just said for you to come and eat." And with that, Art pulls his head out of my room and shuts the door. I take a moment to gather myself. Breathe in and out, Andrew. In and out. After a couple of breaths, I get myself out of bed and head for the kitchen. I have to admit, I'm feeling a little uneasy. The one thing I don't want is to have to go through a weird adjustment period where it feels like my parents are tiptoeing around me, just waiting to talk about it so they can assure me that everything's okay. Like, I don't want coming out to my family to be this big thing that forces them to come out about whether or not they're okay with me being gay. At this point, I'm pretty sure they are. I mean, according to Art, they kinda already knew, so I don't see the point in rehashing it. Here's to hoping Mom's reaction to the news will be nothing. Here's to hoping that me being gay is just an accepted truth, like water being wet or the sky being blue, and no one makes a fuss about it.

When I get to the kitchen, Mom's at the counter chopping up some lettuce and Art's setting the table. Mom glances over at me as I enter, and I immediately freeze up.

"Oh, honey, are you just now getting up?" she asks, focused on chopping, not even looking at me anymore. "Do me a favor and grab the chicken from the oven, will you?" It takes me a second to register what she asked, but when I do, I go over to the oven, grab a kitchen towel from the handle, and pull out the baking dish of roasted chicken.

"Where do you want it?" I ask.

"Just on the table."

I take the chicken over and set it down before taking the seat across from where Art's now sitting. I watch as he sits there typing something into his phone.

"Who you texting?" I ask.

"Coworker," Art replies. "They made plans for Friday. They want me to cover. You didn't want to do anything, did you? It's the Fourth of July."

"No. Take the shift. I didn't plan on anything."

"I'm so glad you boys are actually hanging out together now," Mom says from the counter. She seems genuinely excited by just the idea of it. I guess I can't really blame her.

"Yeah, but Art's still a loser," I joke.

"Says the guy who begged me to build a fort with him yesterday," Art fires back.

"I didn't beg you. I was joking."

"Oh, stop, both of you," Mom says, raising her voice slightly. Though I can tell she's finding this amusing. I mean, when I look over at her, she's smiling so… "Andrew, Art tells me that you started dating." And there it is. The start of Mom's coming out to tell me everything's okay. I tense up. I don't know why. I know she's not gonna scold me or anything since, according to Art, she already knew. But I guess I just don't like the idea of it being made into a thing. Because if it is, it's like a reminder that I'm different. And I'm not. Not any more than anyone else is. "Did you meet anyone nice?" Mom asks. I pause for a moment, feeling my heart sink into the twisted mess of my stomach. This is exactly what I didn't want to have to talk about with my mom. I really don't want to continue with this line of questioning, but… what am I gonna do?

"Uh, I thought I did," I say. "It didn't work out."

"Oh, that's too bad," she replies, tossing her now chopped lettuce into a bowl, along with some tomatoes, croutons, and salad dressing. She dries her hands on a paper towel then brings the bowl over to join us at the table. I'm expecting her to keep questioning me about my dating life and what not. I'm already coming up with responses in my head that are short and to the point, but still family friendly. To my surprise though, I don't need them because when Mom sits down, she says, "So I'm thinking we should have a garage sale. I've been watching a lot of this home organization show with this Japanese lady, and she says that you should get rid of things that no longer spark happiness. I was hoping you boys would help me go through all the boxes."

"Come on, Mom," Art says. "You know you're never gonna get rid of that stuff. You won't even get rid of your old shoes."

"Yes, I will. If I don't wear them, I will."

"But you don't wear any of them," I add. Mom's jaw drops as she looks from me to Art and back again.

"You know what doesn't spark happiness? Both of your attitudes. Why don't we start there?" she says, sounding genuinely offended. The three of us talk, and joke, and laugh, digging into the chicken and salad. Art complains that the meal is missing biscuits and Mom tells him he's ungrateful and to make some himself. No one brings up my love life, or me being gay, or anything like that. We just have lunch and enjoy each other's company. And the gay thing, it just is. It is what it is and nothing more. And, really, that's what I hoped for it to be.

It's about half past two when Riley shows up at my house. He texts me that he's outside and it's kind of weird because he's never been one to avoid coming to my door. I mean, he's been to my house. He knows my family. I guess, considering how we left off, I don't really blame him. It's just sad to think about how far we've drifted. I hate it. I'm still the same. Everything could be the same if only people would let it. But that's why he's here, right? To get back to that sameness. At least, I'm assuming. I throw on some jeans, slip into a pair of my dad's flipflops, and go out to meet Riley.

"Hey," I greet him when I open the front door. Riley's standing there on the doorstep, his hands shoved into his pockets, and he's looking all sorts of uncomfortable. Admittedly, I'm not totally comfortable either, but we're both here, so that's something.

"Hey," Riley replies.

"So…" I begin, letting my voice trail off.

"So…" He does the same. Neither one of us says anything else for a moment, and the silence is so uncomfortable, I don't think anything could break the tension. I'm waiting for him to start talking, but he's just standing there, awkwardly avoiding eye contact.

"Okay, bro, this is stupid," I say. I figure if I don't get the ball rolling, we'll be standing here all day so... "Say whatever you're gonna say." Riley still doesn't say anything. Instead, he responds by nervously biting his bottom lip. He looks even more uncomfortable now, I swear I can see his shoulders tense. And while I don't want to be an asshole about this, the longer we stand here not talking, the more I don't want to be here. "Dude, come on. You texted me saying you wanted to talk, so talk."

"I don't know, dude," Riley sighs. He bends down and takes a seat on the doorstep with his back to me. "I don't really know what to say other than I'm sorry," he continues. "I feel like a dick." It doesn't feel right listening to him while staring at his back, so I step out of the house and take a seat next to him. "It wasn't even the gay thing that bothered me," Riley goes on. "I mean, yeah, it's new but... I think I was more butthurt about the fact that you didn't tell me."

"I didn't tell anyone really."

"Yeah, I get that. But it was hard to not be mad at you when people were telling me I should be. You know how Jacob —"

"How is Jacob?" I ask, cutting him off.

"Fuck Jacob," he says, which is surprising.

"You guys fell out?"

"Yeah. We hung out a couple times after school ended. I thought me and him were mad at you for the same reason but, like, it turns out he's just a bigot," Riley explains. "He kept talking all this shit about you, and it made me realize I picked the wrong side. That kid has issues. Or, I don't know, maybe he's in love with you. You *are* the hot one of the group." His last comment catches me off guard and I can't help but chuckle. Riley chuckles too, but nervously.

"You're stupid," I say. A moment passes as we let the little bit of laugher between us fade.

"I missed you, bro," Riley suddenly says. I get this nice, warm feeling in my chest, like his words somehow grew arms and hugged my little heart. I always imagined Riley being really huggable. I mean, he's built like a giant teddy bear, so he's gotta be.

"I missed you too," I reply, wearing a soft smile.

"You're not gonna kiss me now, are you?" And of course, Riley has to go and ruin the moment. Then again, what do you expect from a guy who steals a Rubik's cube from his teacher all for some chicken nuggets?

"Shut up," I tell him, laughing. He laughs too. And it's almost like no time has passed between us and very little, if anything, has changed. Now, I might be speaking too soon, but I'm hopeful, because we're here and we don't have to be. We both are. And I kinda just wanna see how normal me and Riley can be together. "Hey, what are you doing for the next couple hours?" I ask. He shrugs. "You wanna just chill? We can probably sneak a few of my dad's beers past my mom. Shoot the breeze."

"What is that? Like farting?" he says. I can't tell if he's being serious or not. In his defense, it is kind of a weird saying. Like I said, English is weird. Either way, I invite him inside where we immediately head into the kitchen and grab ourselves a couple of beers from my dad's stash. Mom's holed up in her room — probably getting ready for work — so we don't have to be sneaky about it or anything.

When me and Riley get to my room, I turn the TV onto a rerun of that home buying show that my parents like before taking a seat on my bed. Then I notice Riley standing over the keyboard at my desk.

"Wow, so you're actually learning to play piano?" he asks, taking a sip of his beer.

"Eh, not really," I reply. "One of the keys is busted. It's, like, one of the main ones too."

"Ah." Riley takes another sip of beer then plops himself down on the floor beside my bed. The two of us watch the show for a little while, laughing at the ridiculous demands the potential home buyers have. Like, the couple in this episode are looking for a vacation home on the beach, and they want something small that has eighteen bedrooms, a horse stable, and a place to dock their boat, because horses and boats are just things people casually have. There must also be a dedicated room for entertaining. I guess that's what the horse is for. As if the boat wasn't enough…

I hate people.

I couldn't even get a bike growing up.

"Hey, can I ask you something?" Riley says at the start of a commercial break. "Like, don't take this the wrong way, but how do you *know* that you're gay? You've never been with a girl, right?"

"I mean, I've kissed girls. My first kiss was in a game of Truth or Dare," I explain. "It didn't really do anything for me though."

"Maybe you just didn't like the girl," Riley suggests.

"I didn't like it because it was *with* a girl," I insist. "What about you? How do you know you're straight? You've never even kissed a guy before, have you?" Riley stares at me with wide eyes, like his mind was just blown. I suppose it's not something people consider when they fall into the default.

"Shit, you're right," he says, his eyes looking like they're searching inside his head rather than where they're pointed. "Should we just, like, make out then, so I can be sure?" Um, what? I narrow my eyes at him, my brow all scrunched up, not sure how to take his suggestion.

"Uh… I mean, if you want, I wouldn't say no," I reply. Riley cracks an uncomfortable smile and starts laughing.

"Careful, bro. One day I might be desperate enough to take you up on that offer," he says.

"You'd be so lucky," I reply. "You know, you're really only threatening me with a good time."

"Gay!" Riley yells. I burst out laughing. It's not a good joke, but his timing is just too perfect. I get the feeling that he and I have found ourselves in a good place. It's comfortable, almost like it used to be. Better even because I'm not afraid of him finding out about me anymore. It really sucks about Jacob though.

But Jacob sucks, so whatever.

It's like my dad once said, "Not everyone's gonna be a good fit for your team."

I should probably talk to my dad…

Friday. July 4th.

Happy Independence Day!

So, today, me and Riles have plans to watch fireworks at the marina. Yes, our town has a marina and no, it is not as fancy as it sounds. Other than this one locally famous Mexican restaurant in that area, there's not usually any reason to be there unless you have a boat, and mine's currently docked in my dreams alongside the horse I use for entertaining. Anyway, I've got a bit of time before Riles is supposed to pick me up, and since today is a holiday — even though, apparently, no one gets the day off — I figure I'd pre-game. Celebrate a little, you know?

It's around 5:00pm. I'm heading into my kitchen. I've got my phone in hand, casually scrolling through animal fail videos — no shirtless guys in sweatpants for me today — when I get to the fridge and notice something that makes me stop. On the refrigerator door, there's a newly posted sheet of paper, a report card, which at first, I think is really weird because, like, how many grades does Art get per semester? But then I remember that Art doesn't get his grades in a report card and these grades are, like, not good — holy shit, they're mine. What is this? Is this some weird sort of joke? These grades are not refrigerator door worthy. There's a C- in there, which is basically a D. And I've seen my fair share of D's lately and this one is not impressive. I don't really know what to make of this, so I just open the refrigerator door and reach for a beer. That's when my dad comes in through the garage, having just come home from work.

"You drinking my beers again?" he greets me, seeming entirely unconcerned.

"You keep buying them, I'll keep drinking them," I shrug. He doesn't respond to this. He just goes to the sink to empty his lunch bag. There's still a bit of tension between us. He hasn't mentioned the fight and I don't really want to bring it up because I don't want to rehash everything. So, instead of us talking about it, we've just been slowly letting the ice melt. I'm sure eventually we'll get to a place where things aren't awkward, but right now, I don't know where he stands on everything. Plus, I don't even know if he's been told yet... about, well, everything. I guess I could make the effort and talk to him — even just small talk. I mean, I am curious about my report card on the fridge.

"Hey, Dad?" I begin as he starts to wash out his Tupperware. "Why is my report card on the fridge?" He turns to take a quick glance at me from over his shoulder before immediately going right back to his business.

"Why wouldn't it be?" he replies. I pause for a moment, letting his answer sink in. I could just be reading too far into things, but somehow those four words that he says manage to say everything that I ever wanted or needed to hear from him. And I can't help but get a little choked up over it.

"Thanks, Dad," I say, then head back to my room.

I'm gulping down the last bit of my beer and scrolling through more animal fails when I get a notification on my phone. It's a text message from Riles.

"Hey, gonna head over now," it says. I tap open my text app to respond and as soon as the window opens, right under Riles' name, I see Mackenzie's. She's the last person I texted before Riles and the last time I talked to her was Monday. God, that feels like so long ago. I don't like how things ended with her and, up until now, it didn't occur to me that maybe *I* should be the one to apologize. I was just so blindsided by her take on everything that I put myself on the offensive, despite the fact that she's on my team. I don't know if she's gonna wanna hear from me, but… You know what? Fuck it. I send Riles a thumbs up emoji, then immediately call Mackenzie. I don't expect that she'll pick up, but I let it ring all the same.

She's not gonna pick up.

It rings again.

Yeah, she's probably not gonna pick up, so I start planning out what I want to say to her voicemail. It's gotta be short, sweet, and to the point because they never give you enough time to say everything —

"Hello?" Mackenzie's voice comes through after the third or so ring. Well, what do you know? It actually catches me off guard, I really thought she wasn't gonna answer.

"Hey," I say, my voice coming out sudden and sharp, sorta like a hiccup, which by the way get more painful as you get older. "Uh… What's up?"

"What do you want, Andrew?" Ah, classic Mackenzie. No beating around the bush with her. I know what I want to say, but I'm not sure how to say it. I guess I could just say what I would've said into her voicemail, but I didn't really have time to plan it because she actually answered. I guess we're winging it.

"Um, well… I would, uh… like to say… I'm sorry." Nailed it.

"For what?" Fuck. She's gonna make me explain it, isn't she? Okay, then. Here goes…

"Look, Mackenzie. I wasn't in a good place when we last talked. I was sad, I was frustrated, I was overly sensitive, I was —"

"— being a bitch?"

"I deserve that." I do deserve that. "I just wanted to say that I'm sorry because none of it had anything to do with you, and I get you were just trying to be a good friend. I shouldn't have taken it out on you. And if you're cool, I'm cool." I hear her sigh over the phone. I imagine she's rolling her eyes at me. That's sorta the picture I get whenever I think of her.

"Okay," she says, after a moment.

"'Okay,' as in we're cool?"

"Yeah, we're cool."

"Cool," I say. I'm feeling pretty great about everything right now. Seems like things are finally starting to fall into place, and it's making me really excited about tonight. I'm looking forward to celebrating. You know, I should invite Mackenzie. I'm sure Riles wouldn't mind. In fact, he might like having a girl around. She's way better than Jacob. "Hey, so, um, I'm going over to the marina to watch the fireworks with my friend tonight. You wanna come? It's been a minute. I figure we can catch up."

"I would, but I'm actually about to head into work," Mackenzie replies. See? No one gets the Fourth of July off. Like, where's the fun in a holiday if everyone has to work? Oh well.

"Next time then," I say.

"Sure." I smile to myself and in my mind, I imagine Mackenzie's smiling too. We share a moment of silence and I linger on the phone for a bit. I feel like it'd be rude to hang up right now, so I wait for her to say something else. And finally, she does. "Hey, Andrew?"

"What's up?"

"Thank you."

"For what?"

"For thinking of me."

"Well, I'm still single so…" I say, and I hear Mackenzie chuckle.

"I gotta go," she replies. "Have fun tonight though. We'll hang out soon."

"Definitely." And with that, we end the call. It sucks that she can't come out with us tonight, but I'm just happy that we're on good terms. She's basically been my quarterback, and I would've hated having to lose her. That's a funny thought though, isn't it? Mackenzie playing football. Now that's a game I'd pay to see. I don't even think she knows what a football is.

Riles comes to get me in his dad's old pick-up and we get to the marina around 6:30pm. The sun's still out, but it's already pretty crowded. I guess everyone had the same idea we did about getting here early. There are a couple of different parking lots around the marina but Riles doesn't want to risk getting trapped in one of them after the fireworks end, so he parks us on the street not far from the locally famous Mexican restaurant.

"You up for a burrito?" Riles suggests.

"I'll pass. I've got, like, two dollars in my wallet," I answer.

"It's all good. I'll spot you. You can get me next time." So, we end up walking to the restaurant and getting a couple burritos to go. It takes a little while, and by the time we get our food and leave the restaurant, the marina has gotten way more crowded and the sky's gotten all yellow and dusky. Sunset's not too far off now.

Riles and I head out to find a spot to watch the fireworks. It's a little tricky wandering around the area, what with all the cars arriving and circling to find parking. We cut through a lot where Riles flips off a guy who honks at us for crossing in front of his car — but, like, where is he going anyway? — and we end up on this paved walkway that overlooks the docks. There are a few boats moored — moored-ded? Moor-*red*-ded? Are these even words? Whatever. There are a few boats here and I get to thinking about what kind of people own boats. Like, do regular people just casually own boats? Fuck, is my family just *that* poor?

"It's funny to me that people in this town actually have boats," I comment, "It's so bougie. It's like those people on those home buying shows."

"Eh, I don't know how bougie you can be living in this town," Riles says. "We don't even have a Cheesecake Palace. All we've got is an Antonini's."

"Hey, watch it. Antonini's is fancy as fuck."

"Ha! And *you're* the gay one? Dude, they don't even have tablecloths."

"Tablecloths are a waste."

"Come on, Drewster, have some class."

"Shut up."

Riles and I come across a stone bench, and we decide this is as good a spot as any. We plop ourselves down and dig into our food, talking, laughing, and joking all the while in between bites, as we wait for the sun to set. I take in the moment — the water, the boats on the dock, the sound of the cars in the parking lot, honking as if they have somewhere to be. I watch as the sky slowly changes from yellow to orange, then orange to pink. Then finally, once the sky has darkened, I hear a whistling sound. And in the distance, the first of the fireworks bursts into color. I take in a breath and hold it with anticipation, knowing that soon, the sky will be lit up again. I expect dozens, if not hundreds, of temporary lights, each one a different color, each one an experience all their own. It's corny, I know, and this would be so much better high. But still, these fireworks are something I'm looking forward to. Tonight is a memory to be made. Because after everything I've been through in these last couple of weeks, and especially in the last couple of days, I'm finally looking up.

Like, literally.

epilogue

So, school starts next week, which is crazy. It feels like it just ended and already it's time to go back. I swear, every year, summer break gets shorter and shorter. I don't actually know if that's true but it sure as hell feels like it. That being said, this school year is gonna be different for me. I've given it a lot of thought and I decided that I'm not gonna be continuing football. Don't get me wrong, I'm not quitting because I don't like it. I love it. It's just… going into my senior year, I want to give myself the chance to try new things. To find something that's entirely mine, that I didn't inherit from someone else, you know? And with piano, I think I might have. I've been practicing a lot lately — trying to, anyway. It's been rough goings with the broken Middle G. Despite that, I think I'm getting better and I'm really enjoying it so, I decided to enroll myself in a piano class at the local community college. The scheduling wouldn't have worked with football so, sadly, I had to choose.

Aside from that tough decision, things have been pretty great since the Fourth of July. Well, *most* things have been pretty great. I introduced Riles to Mackenzie. It did not go well. She told me that she thinks he's obnoxious and he told me that he's in love with her, so there's that. We all only hung out once. They might've hung out together without me when I wasn't looking, in which case, rude. But honestly, I don't really know. They can do what they want. I don't keep tabs on them, so...

My home life is good. Me and Dad are back to normal, though he has taken up the habit of teasing me whenever I get together and hang out with Riles. He's always reminding me to bring protection which is, uh... fun. But aside from that, he's been cool.

Mom and I started on that garage sale project she mentioned way back when. We went into it with the plan to keep only the things that "spark happiness" and two hours later, we had done absolutely nothing because everything she touched sent her on a massive nostalgia trip. I did end up sorting through some of *my* old stuff though. Like, I dug up my old rag doll, Daisy, and gave her a wash. She now has a permanent place on my bed, right there next to Betsy. Whenever I look at the two of them together, I think about me and my brother. He's the cow.

Speaking of my brother, Art had to go back to school in mid-July for training. Football preseason just started, so I think he's aiming for the draft. I don't know how good his odds are, but I hope he gets drafted into the NFL someday. I made him promise that if he ever did, he'd buy me a boat so that I could be one of *those* people and use the marina for what it's built for. I wanna be fancy. Tablecloth fancy. I probably won't use them though since tablecloths are a waste, but you know.

Now, I wouldn't say that Art and I are, like, super close, but we're getting there. We hung out a few times before he left, and he texts me from time to time to complain about his roommate. The thing I'm most happy about though is now I can walk by the mantlepiece without feeling insignificant, because the guy that I thought was so annoyingly perfect thinks that I'm pretty cool. Plus, knowing that he feels pressure from Dad's high expectations of him makes me thankful that Dad doesn't expect anything from me. I know that sounds like a self-own, but it actually works to my advantage. Just hear me out.

So, I've been working on *Moonlight Sonata*. I've gotten a fairly solid grasp on the first two pages of it. That five-page sheet music printout I got from Robert has been a total game changer. I hope that guy's doing well. Anyway, Dad overheard me practicing one day and he freaked out.

"Well, what do you know? My son's a musician!" he said, practically yelling. It was such a total shock to him that it was all he could talk about for a while. He's *still* talking about it. In fact, he's got me on the hunt for a new affordable piano — emphasis on *affordable* — because the Middle G was just ruining everything. And I think I actually found a lead. We're gonna check it out later tonight. Right now, I've got some business to attend to.

With all the extra time I'll have not doing football, I thought I'd take a page from Art's handbook and get myself a job. I, too, would like to buy an environmentally friendly fuel-efficient vehicle. I'm tired of always having to borrow or ask for a ride, okay? I sent out a bunch of applications over the last few weeks and I managed to land a job at the local big box electronics store, TechnoLobby. Is it pronounced Techno-Lobby or Tech-nol-oh-bee, like technology? I don't know. I'll ask at orientation. Right now, I'm just going in to fill out some paperwork.

I step inside TechnoLobby. The cool air gives me a shiver. It's hot as balls today, so the AC is nice. It's just the sudden switch that's a little shocking. I head over to the customer service counter. There's no one manning it at the moment, so I pull out my phone and start scrolling through AphroDATEme while I wait. I haven't actually messaged anyone on the app since I hooked up with Robert. For a while, I couldn't even get on it without finding myself lingering on what would've been Rudy's page. I'm not totally over him yet. I wanna be, but it still hurts to think about what could've been if I hadn't walked away. We probably would've been a disaster, but... oh well. I've just been trying to take this whole focusing on myself thing seriously, you know? Plus, everyone who's messaged me has either been an oldie, an uggo, or a torso, but what else is new? Either way, it's still fun to look.

Uggo.

Uggo.

Old.

Uggo.

Torso.

Another torso.

Oh, he's cute.

"Can I help you with anything?" I hear a somewhat familiar voice say. I look up and, oh... he's *really* cute. Of course he's cute. The guy standing in front of me, it's fuckin' Nick Santiago. Are you telling me that

Nick Santiago works here? At TechnoLobby? My eyes quickly dart up and down. No way he works here. Except he's wearing a TechnoLobby polo that's hugging him as tight as a tank top. And he's got a nametag. What are the odds? I guess it's not that crazy that he works here. I mean, we live in the same town. We go to the same school. I once tried to sleep with his boyfriend out of sheer desperation, but that was a long time ago. It's a very small world apparently. Shoot, I've been standing here too long without saying anything, haven't I? And I know this because Nick Santiago's looking at me all sorts of confused.

"Uh, yeah, sorry. Brain… fart," I say, practically falling over my words. What the hell is wrong with me? Ugh, great, now he's raising one of his perfect eyebrows at me like he wants to back away slowly. Just tell him what you're here for, Andrew. It's not hard. I mean, it is, but not like that. Oh, God. "Um, wow… I think the heat might be getting to me. Sorry, I'm a new hire. The manager asked me to come in and fill out paperwork."

"Oh, okay. Give me a second," he says. He then reaches for a phone behind the counter, pushes a few buttons and talks into the receiver. "Call for a manager. We've got a new hire at customer service to fill out paperwork." He hangs up the phone and offers me the cutest, if slightly uncomfortable, half-smile. "The

manager will be out in a minute. You need anything else?"
he asks.

"Um, nope," I reply. I shove my phone into my pocket and stand here quietly. I'm super uncomfortable right now, but Nick Santiago pays me no mind. He just goes over to a computer behind the counter and starts doing whatever people do on computers when they're working the customer service desk. I feel like I should say something, make small talk. Is that weird? That's probably weird. I don't know. I just don't want things to be so uncomfortable between us since we're gonna be working together and all that. I'm, like, super attracted to him, yeah, and I know he's taken, but I still wanna be cool with him. Maybe even be his friend. I feel like it'd be nice to have someone in my life who's like me in *that way*, you know?

. . .

You know what? I'm gonna go for it. Why not?

"Hey, Nick?" I begin nervously. I'm hoping my voice doesn't sound as shaky to him as it does to me. "Um, look, I know you and I didn't really get off to a good start, what with the whole me bullying your boyfriend thing, but I just wanted to say that I'm sorry about that. It was dumb, and childish, and I wish I'd never done it. And I really hope that, um, we could maybe start over. Maybe we could even be friends someday?" He stares at me blankly for what feels like forever. I feel my heart pounding in my chest and all the air stopping in my lungs. The moment seems to last forever. And then…

"Okay," he says. "Sure, why not?" I suddenly feel like I can breathe again. I catch myself smiling and I don't even try to hide it. It's nice, you know, knowing that me and Nick Santiago could be friends. Though I should probably stop referring to his boyfriend as a potato. I don't think he'd appreciate it.

In the evening, after dinner, I have Riles come over with his dad's pick-up and he, my dad, and I go to follow up with my lead on the affordable piano. The other day, I came across an ad on one of those used marketplace websites. It said that they, the owner, were looking for someone to take their old piano. They didn't want anything other than for it to go to a good home and to be played. To be honest, I thought it was too good to be true, but what could it hurt to check?

The owner of the piano lives in the next city over, just past the old ghost town mall. Their city is actually so close to our town that no one really knows where the border is, but that's beside the point. We drive down a long road that cuts through a wide-open field until we get to a collection of newer neighborhoods where all the houses look the same. Riles slows down the pick-up and I double check the address on my phone.

"I think this is it," I say as we pull up to a big, fancy two-story home.

"Wow," Dad mutters in awe. "Nice houses. You sure they don't want anything for the piano?"

"That's what the ad said." I shrug.

Me, Riles, and Dad hop out of the pick-up and head up the short driveway to the house. I ring the doorbell and we wait. Moments later, the door opens and the owner, an older bald man dressed in an oversized t-shirt and worn-out sweat shorts, appears in front of us.

"Ah, you must be here for the piano," he says. I nod with a smile. "Come in, come in." The man turns and we follow him into the house. I hear my dad let out a "whoa," probably over the needlessly high ceilings. It's nice, I'll admit, but it's one of those houses that are big for the sake of being big. Like, we pass by a couch that looks like it's never been sat on and there's a mini chandelier in the corner for why? I bet this guy has a boat. And a horse for entertaining. Shoot, I would not be surprised if he bought this house on a home buying show.

The man leads us into a smaller room — I assume it's the main living space since there's a big ol' TV in here — and then shows me to the piano, which is tucked away in a little nook beside an electric fireplace. The piano itself is an upright wooden one with a certain dullness to it. It's clearly old but looks to be in good condition. It sorta reminds me of the one in Robert's house but not as antique-y.

"Do you mind?" I ask the owner, gesturing to the piano.

"By all means," he replies. I go ahead and approach it, then slowly slide the cover open. The keys are dusty, but not worn out at all. It's almost like seeing a sad person smile for the first time. Considering the ad mentioned wanting it to be played, it's obvious now that this thing was rarely ever touched. I wonder why.

"So, you're just giving this piano away?" Dad asks. "You don't want anything for it?"

"Nope. Nothing," the man says. "We bought it years ago as a sort of show piece. I figured that at some point, someone would learn to play, but no one ever did. Seems like a shame for it to just sit here collecting dust with all that music it never made." That does seem like a shame. I can't help but think about it in terms of me. I was so resistant that it took me this long to discover this part of myself, so much so that I almost didn't. I let my fingers brush against the keys and start at the low end, slowly working my way up. "Now, it might be a bit out of tune, but you can have someone come out and tune it for you," the owner explains. I hear him, but I'm not listening. Instead, I focus on the sound of each note, letting every one of them sing out as I climb the scale. Eventually, I hit the Middle G and I stop.

"Huh, that's funny," I mumble to myself.

"What is?" Riles asks.

"This is the same key on my keyboard at home that would just scream at me every time I'd hit it."

"And?"

"Nothing. I just find it funny. It's a little out of tune." It *is* a little out of tune. It's just a *little* bit off. But the thing that I'm learning about music is that even if a note is off, it's still in tune with *something*. It may not be in tune with the song you're playing, or even with any of the other keys, but it's in tune with itself. And this time, it's not screaming at me anymore.

"So, kiddo," I hear Dad say. "Did you find what you're looking for?"

I take a breath and hold it, letting it come out ever so slowly.

"Yeah," I answer. "I think I did."

acknowledgements

While I was in the process of publishing my first novel *drown*, I put a lot of pressure on myself to come up with a follow up. The process of writing and putting out a novel is a lot, and I have number of people who helped me along the way. With that, I want to give particular thanks to…

… my husband, Richard. This wasn't a story that I initially intended to tell. Andrew was meant to be little more than a one-dimensional plot device in *drown* and, as that story evolved, a sort of antagonist. I really didn't think too much on what his story would be until you brought it to my attention how intriguing of a character he was. Your investment in him and in me, really, allowed this story to bloom and flourish into what it is now. Thank you for always supporting me in every way that a person can support someone. Without you, this story probably never would have been written.

… Carla De Leon Zeitoune, you've been with me throughout the entire writing process, giving me thoughts, critiques, and feedback as I went along. Having someone to discuss things with as I was writing was invaluable.

… my beta readers: Edith P., Anthony C., Victor L. Mark M., Mark N., Veronica V. Thank you all for taking the time and for all your feedback. Whether I took your suggestions or not, you gave me a lot to think about as I went into the editing process and, because of you, I believe the story was made better. I'd also like to give particular thanks to Veronica V. who took the time to look at and correct all of the Spanish.

… you, the reader. Since putting out my first novel *drown,* I've received such a great amount of support and interest in my work — more than I've ever experienced before — and I'm incredibly humbled that my stories are resonating with people. Especially considering how much of myself and my experiences have gone into these stories. Thank you so much for being a part of that. It really means a lot, because without you, what are books but just a bunch of words? It's because of you that they mean something.

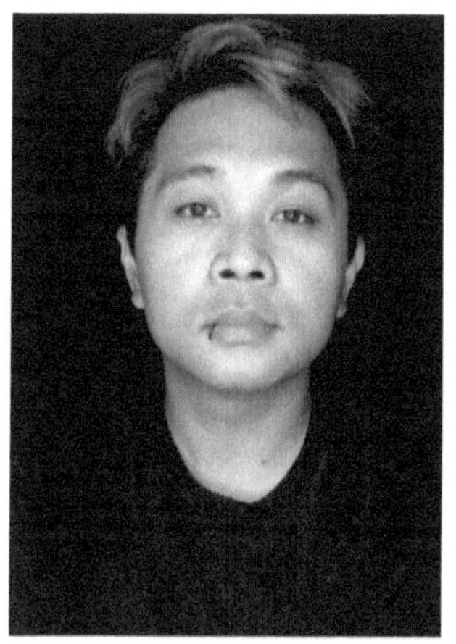

about the author

Daryl Leonardo is an independent writer. Born in the Philippines and raised in the San Francisco Bay Area, he spent years pursuing a career as an actor, prior to taking up writing as a way to create roles for himself. He currently resides in Los Angeles, California with his husband and two dogs, where he continues to take roles in independent projects and local theatre.